To Michele:

DESERT ENIGMA

Plague in Chaco Canyon

With warm wishes
Condolences ...

FREDERICK ROSS M.D.

FriesenPress

Suite 300 - 990 Fort St
Victoria, BC, V8V 3K2
Canada

www.friesenpress.com

ISBN
978-1-5255-7705-5 (Hardcover)
978-1-5255-7706-2 (Paperback)
978-1-5255-7707-9 (eBook)

1. Fiction, Historical

Distributed to the trade by The Ingram Book Company

For Trixie,
wife, friend,
and fellow explorer.

Who can find a virtuous woman?
for her price is far above rubies.

~ Proverbs 31:10

Preface

This book is a historical fiction that attempts to offer an explanation as to why the great civilization of the Anasazi people in Northwestern New Mexico abandoned Chaco Canyon around the end of the twelfth century. Several theories over the past century have been offered by academic archaeologists and cultural anthropologists yet the true reason for their disappearance still remains unknown.

Archaeologist Stephen Lekson in his book *A Study of Southwestern Archaeology* throws out a challenge to his graduate students and anyone else with a curiosity regarding the demise of the Chacoan culture:

"And that, graduate students, is what I want you to do: Reinvent a North American pre-history that is fundamentally historical. As it should have been, from the beginning. You don't have to stop doing Anthropology or Science. But to do good science, first you must get the story right. Understand the baggage, recognize and control the bias, and see what wonderful new possibilities open up for the ancient Southwest."

Taking up Lekson's challenge, I developed my own theory to explain the migration of this remarkable people from their elaborate ancestral city at Chaco Canyon. As a medical doctor I have been intrigued by the upheavals in history which pandemics and plagues have caused. The Black Death in the fourteenth century in Europe for example, almost completely transformed medieval European society. The feudal system and the institution of serfdom, a form of enslavement for the poor, could no longer be maintained. Because so many people had died from the plague, it resulted in greater autonomy and better wages for those who survived, creating an entirely new labour force.

We have seen how plagues continued to destabilize and reduce populations even during this modern era. Consider the current COVID-19 pandemic that has caused a huge and dramatic global upheaval. The societal and economic ramifications are still yet to be seen. So could a plague not be a valid explanation for the dissolution of the Chaco civilization?

My attempt is to create a fictional narrative with a mixture of both true and imagined historical contents. Using alternate chapters, *Desert Enigma* presents two stories with two different timelines. We first meet Shadow Dancer, a teenage apprentice to the medicine man of his tribe in Chaco Canyon in the twelfth century. His life with his family and his new love, Spotted Deer, is turned upside down when a mysterious illness consumes the local population. Eight hundred years later, archaeologist Rachel Thompson and her husband Rolly Boudreau find themselves in the Chaco Canyon region where Shadow Dancer's people were wiped from the face of the earth. With a new job in New Mexico, Rachel uses her skills as a forensic archaeologist to solve the mystery of the disappearance of the Chaco civilization.

Driving to Arizona and back from Winnipeg on an annual basis has allowed my wife and I the luxury of exploring much of America's past. The numerous battlefield sites, early Pre-Columbian Native habitations, and the thousands of antiquities in museums and interpretive centres scattered across the West is a goldmine for history nerds.

Fortunately, my wife has found much of this fascinating as well. We have enjoyed exploring Ancestral Puebloan sites such as Mesa Verde in Colorado, Chaco Canyon in New Mexico, Acoma Mesa, and Canyon de Chelly in Arizona. Along the way we have visited Wounded Knee in South Dakota, the Little Big Horn Battle site in Montana, and the amazing Pecos National Monument near Santa Fe, New Mexico. America takes its history seriously with strings of museums, cairns, and monuments along whatever route one takes to reach the warm winters of the Southwest. Of course, after a few years of sleuthing these places one is left with more questions than answers.

Of all the places we visited, none impressed us more than Chaco Canyon, a conglomeration of great houses rising four and five stories tall, holding over eight hundred rooms apiece, built in the middle of nowhere. Blending in with the sandstone rocks and cliffs, the great houses appear as if the same geologic forces that created the surrounding buttes and mesas has also thrust up the numerous great houses in the canyon. Such an amazing series of buildings constructed over a nine-mile stretch in Chaco Canyon begs the question of who built these architectural wonders in the first place? Why did these clever builders leave their homeland and where did they go? Where are their descendants today?

This is a story about the Ancestral Puebloans — the Anasazi as they are still commonly known, who have morphed over the centuries into the various Pueblo Indians of New Mexico and the Hopi of Arizona. One of the places to which they migrated is a mesa in New Mexico known as Acoma. The story follows the migration of the Anasazi to their new home at Acoma and their tragic encounters with enemies over the centuries.

A list of acknowledgements at the back of the book may help to expand the reader's knowledge base on the history of the American Southwest and the Spanish Conquest. Footnotes have been used in an attempt to clarify and enhance the narrative.

Desert Enigma also describes the narrative of Southwest American native pottery—its creation, its collection, and its pillaging. The search for ancient pottery features as one the driving forces behind the story and the characters involved. This novel is a sequel to my first book *A Deadly Thaw: The York Factory Connection* (Friesen Press, 2018) and features the two main protagonists from that book.

"For generations, the ruins of Chaco Canyon have intrigued explorers and archaeologists. Yet, as they try to refine their explanations through better technology, additional data, native perspectives and creative theories, definitive answers often slip through their fingers. In the end, there have been few definitive answers to the most intriguing questions. For the present, the mystery of Chaco Canyon remains just that—a mystery."

(Vivian and Halpert 2011:43)

Desert Enigma:
Plague in Chaco Canyon

Introduction

We, in the ages lying
In the buried past of the earth,
Built Nineveh with our sighing,
And Babel itself with our mirth;
And o'erthrew them with prophesying
To the old of the new world's worth;
For each age is a dream that is dying,
Or one that is coming to birth.

~ Arthur O'Shaughnessy, 1874

One of history's great ironies is that over eight hundred years ago, the largest city in Europe – Constantinople and the largest city in North America – the Chaco Canyon complex both began their decline following a series of tragic events in approximately the same year. The capital of the Byzantine Empire and Christendom's most beautiful city lay in ruins at the hands of marauding Christians from the Western church in 1204 AD as the Crusader rabble made its way to Jerusalem. Constantinople never recovered its former glory. Ironically, the largest metropolitan establishment in North America,

Chaco Canyon likewise suffered a catastrophic event around the year 1200 AD from which it also has never recovered.

Between the years 850 and 1250 AD, Chaco Canyon was a major centre of Ancestral Puebloan culture in the arid desert of the Four Corners region of the American Southwest. These industrious people quarried sandstone rocks and hauled massive timbers over vast distances in order to build fifteen major complexes known as *great houses* – multi-storied masonry pueblos of several hundred rooms each. Painstakingly constructed from desert materials, these canyon cathedrals were the largest buildings in North America until the nineteenth century. For example, Pueblo Bonito at Chaco, occupied four acres in area and rose five stories high. With more than eight hundred rooms it was home to about one thousand people and until 1882 it was the largest apartment building anywhere in the world.

The Chaco complexes were erected in such a way as to orient them to lunar, solar, and cardinal directions. Most of these remarkable buildings are still standing in the canyon and have become a major tourist attraction. Recognized as a UNESCO World Heritage Site, Chaco Canyon has become a showcase of Anasazi antiquity featuring an interpretive centre with guided tours and campsites nearby. Yet these same areas are now regarded as the sacred ancestral homelands to Pueblo people of today–the Hopi, Acoma, and Zuni people to name a few, as well as the Navajo who arrived from the north around the year 1500. Through oral tradition, they acknowledge the historical migration of the Chaco people to their pueblos of today. Simply put, the Chaco Canyon complex was the greatest architectural achievement of any of the North American Indian groups.

The Chacoans traded with Central Americans from 1200 miles to the south who brought macaw feathers, cacao beans, sea shells, and even copper bells to the area. DNA analysis of the residue of eight hundred year-old cylinder jars from the arid neighbourhood has even identified the remains of chocolate. The pre-Columbian

Chacoan cylinder jars were not much different from mugs used today by Starbucks customers. The Chacoans practiced dry farming supplemented by water control management with check dams and irrigation. Corn was heaped in stone storage bins to be ground into meal. Squash, beans, nuts, and meat supplemented this dietary staple allowing them to flourish for centuries in their water-less landscape.

The Chacoans were a complex society with deeply rooted belief systems, building dozens of underground kivas where they practised their religious rituals and held community meetings. One such kiva was the massive Great Kiva, over three hundred square metres in size, capable of holding hundreds of people. Six such Great Kivas were constructed at the Chaco settlement, all of them built before the year 1100. One Great Kiva aligned within one-quarter degree of true north; indeed, we are dealing with an advanced culture here that was deeply religious and astronomically adept.

Eight hundred years later, archaeologists studying the remains of Chaco Canyon estimated that upwards of thirty thousand people lived, hunted, and grew maize, beans, and squash within the thirty-mile stretch of this dry and desolate region. It is a mystery how so many inhabitants could thrive in this unforgiving place for centuries, creating the huge great houses that enclosed hundreds of people just as a modern apartment block does today. They planted crops in the river valley below, where they became experts at irrigating the fields. To store the abundance of food they produced, they built copious granaries from quarried sandstone blocks. This sophisticated community also studied astronomical phenomena, made elaborate pottery and baskets, and built a four hundred-mile network of roads. But it all ended abruptly and mysteriously around the year 1200. What happened?

The cause of the swift disappearance of the Chacoans has puzzled anthropologists and archaeologists ever since. For some reason the thriving society of Chaco Canyon began to disintegrate around the year 1200. Just at the pinnacle of the Chaco civilization, the wheels suddenly fell off.

This book proposes a novel archaeological theory regarding the cause of this catastrophe. Archaeologist Rachel Thompson and her husband, Rolly Boudreau begin working for the University of New Mexico, engaged in a project with the Office of Contract Archaeology in Chaco Canyon. What they discover in the process is frightening and unthinkable to many of their contemporaries. Could an infectious disease have played a major role in the eradication of this once thriving society? Was it a prolonged drought or something more sinister that finally brought this progressive culture to its dramatic denouement?

"The high level of community social organization, and its far reaching commerce, created a cultural vision unlike any other seen before or since in the country. However, all of this suddenly collapsed in the thirteenth century when the centres were mysteriously abandoned and were never revived."

-April Holloway, *Ancient Origins*

"The single greatest upheaval in Southwestern prehistory–as well as, arguably the most celebrated mystery in American archaeology–is the sudden, complete, and irrevocable abandonment of the Four Corners area in the last two or three decades of the thirteenth century. By A.D. 1300, in a huge, once fertile tract of land stretching from Moab, Utah, to the north of the Hopi mesas, from Pagosa Springs, Colorado, to Gallup, New Mexico, not a single person dwelt in a region that had once teemed with Anasazi."

~ David Roberts, *The Pueblo Revolt*

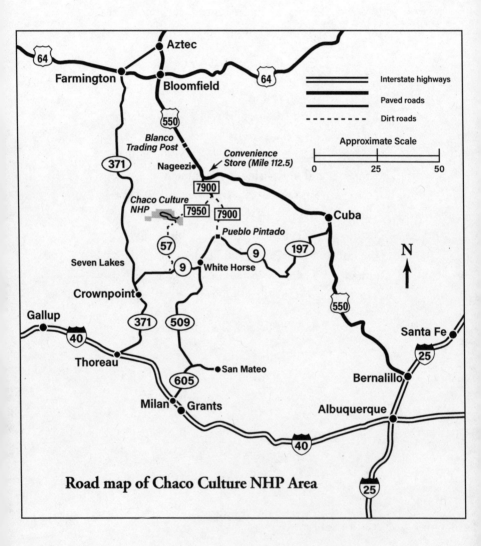

Road map of Chaco Culture NHP Area

Aztec
64
Farmington
Bloomfield
64
Interstate highways
Paved roads
Dirt roads
550
Blanco Trading Post
Convenience Store (Mile 112.5)
371
Nageezi
7900
Approximate Scale
0   25   50
Chaco Culture NHP
7950   7900
Cuba
57
Pueblo Pintado
Seven Lakes
9
9
197
N
White Horse
Crownpoint
371   509
550
Gallup
40
Santa Fe
25
Thoreau
San Mateo
Bernalillo
605
Milan   Grants
Albuquerque
40
25

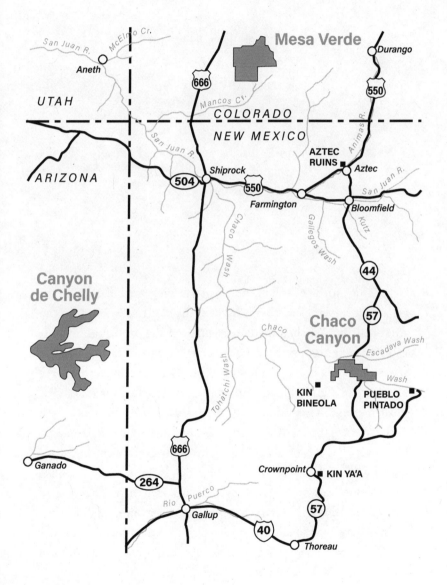

Mesa Verde

Durango

San Juan R.

McElmo Cr.

Aneth

666

550

UTAH

Mancos Cr.

COLORADO

NEW MEXICO

San Juan R.

ARIZONA

504

Shiprock

550

Farmington

Animas R.

AZTEC
RUINS

Aztec

San Juan R.

Bloomfield

Chaco Wash

Gallegos Wash

Kutz

44

Canyon
de Chelly

57

Chaco
Canyon

Chaco

Escadava Wash

Wash

Tohatchi Wash

KIN
BINEOLA

PUEBLO
PINTADO

666

Ganado

Crownpoint

KIN YA'A

264

Rio Puerco

57

Gallup

40

Thoreau

Chapter 1

Finding Peyote—
Chaco Canyon 1198 AD

We either make ourselves miserable or we make ourselves strong.
The amount of work is the same.
~ Carlos Castaneda

He was not used to walking in this stultifying heat. Earlier in the morning heavy bruised clouds hung in the eastern sky, but now the afternoon sun scorched the entire length of the canyon as Shadow Dancer walked along the wash looking for peyote cacti. The land was a desolate place, the only break in its harsh monotony being brittle scrub and wind-sculpted stone that stretched for miles. The medicine man, Grey Elk sent him on this mission on one of the hottest days of the year and Shadow Dancer was beginning to despise him for it. The part of the peyote cactus above ground contained the crown with disc-shaped buttons which he placed in a leather pouch slung around his neck by a strap. Shadow Dancer had never tried peyote himself but he had witnessed the effects on Grey Elk when the medicine man sought the spirits. He recalled both the trance-like state that the shaman entered after ingesting a few of the buttons and his inability to feel pain.

Wiping the sweat from his brow, he wondered whether this medicine might make walking in this desert heat more tolerable.

One of these days, I'm going to try some peyote myself.

As the afternoon wore on, the empty summer sky poured more heat into the blistering cauldron of the canyon. Dust devils lofted sand and dried leaves high into the air with the desiccating winds. Shadow Dancer knew he had to soon return to the great house where it was cool. But first, he had to find a few more peyote buttons before returning or Grey Elk would be displeased. Most of the vegetation in the canyon grew within a few hundred feet from the wash, which in the dry summer months had contracted to a trickle. A few feet from the shore a thin curtain of dried reeds crumbled readily underfoot, falling to dust. Finding peyote cacti required the young apprentice to stay within the confines of the wash.

Shadow Dancer's people, whom he simply called *the Nation*, survived only because the wash contained this thin ribbon of a creek coursing through their dry desert region, providing barely enough water much of the time. The creek's source was several miles east in the higher elevations of the Colorado Plateau. Shadow Dancer thought he had heard the faint rumbling of thunder earlier in the east yet he had dismissed nature's warning as he trod the dry creek bed in the enervating heat. He thought about his future as he walked and wondered whether he was cut out for being a medicine man. His parents had bequeathed him to the tribal medicine man as an apprentice only a few months earlier and he wanted to please them but so far, he had experienced only hardship and loneliness. Somehow he hadn't seen the massive thunderheads in the distance behind him. He just kept plodding along in the wash, grumbling, kicking up dust, and searching for peyote buttons as the eastern sky turned dark.

Chapter 2

Rachel's Rant

*He who would do great things
should not attempt them all alone.*
~ Seneca

"Those bastards! I don't believe it!" Rachel threw the envelope on the floor and stomped on it.

"Whoa! What's all this about?" Boudreau asked his wife.

The letter was from Rachel's employer at the Arctic Institute stating that due to a funding shortage her position was being terminated. She was devastated.

"This is just nuts Rolly. I've busted my butt for those people for the past five years and I almost died from smallpox in the process. I've written four papers on the archaeological project at York Factory. Oh, and that Bay blanket we found? It happens to be an invaluable artifact from the fur trade on Hudson's Bay. And this is the thanks I get! Now what are we going to do?"

Boudreau listened quietly to his wife's rant, picked up the letter from the floor, and read it slowly. Opening his laptop, he began whistling softly as he browsed the internet.

"I have to wonder if they're letting me go because of that damned Hudson's Bay blanket. It was a wonderful discovery but some of them think I should have left it in the ground. Yes, it could have caused an epidemic but how was I to know it was a fomite for a deadly virus?" Rachel exclaimed.

"Hmm. Maybe you're jumping to conclusions, sweetheart. It could just boil down to limited funding as they say. I suspect they're shifting a lot of their resources to the Franklin expedition ever since the two ships, the *Erebus* and the *Terror* were discovered a few years ago in Arctic waters.[1] I mean, wouldn't that make sense to an archaeologist like you?"

"Somehow I think there's more to it than that." Rachel bristled at the suggestion that the Institute felt she was dispensable. She poured herself a gin and tonic.

"Maybe, but there must be other job opportunities for a talented archaeologist like you. There's no point getting angry about it and I wouldn't send them any nasty letters. You don't want to burn any bridges with your former employer. You will need references you know?"

"References! References for what? If there really is a funding shortage where will I find a job in Canada?"

Roland Boudreau and Rachel Thompson had been happily married living in Winnipeg; both had recovered from the effects of smallpox the previous year. This illness had laid them low after they inadvertently resurrected the lethal virus from an archaeological project at York Factory on the shores of Hudson's Bay. Boudreau continued to fly to northern communities as a bush pilot and eventually sold his home in Gillam, Manitoba. Rachel commuted to Calgary

---

1. The *Erebus* and the *Terror* were the lost ships of the infamous Franklin Expedition of 1845 that went missing while searching for the Northwest Passage.

where she continued to work at the Canadian Arctic Institute as an archaeologist doing research on northern projects.

This arrangement seemed to work well and they enjoyed their condominium in Winnipeg, not far from the beautiful Assiniboine Park where they walked almost daily. A visit to the Leo Mol Gardens with its dozens of sculptures by the famous artist was always a highlight for both of them. Boudreau was fascinated by a life-sized sculpture of Tom Lamb, the bush pilot who established Lamb Air in 1935. The bronze piece of art was ingenious in its design with a hooded Tom Lamb grasping a large vertical propeller blade as if to start an invisible airplane engine with a mighty spin.[2] Boudreau always smiled at this creative piece of art at the entrance to the English Gardens as it so clearly depicted the challenges facing northern Canadian bush pilots. Both he and his father had served for decades as pilots flying to the remote outposts and communities in Manitoba's vast north ferrying scientists, historians, and archaeologists to various northern sites.

It was during these trips that Boudreau had acquired much of his knowledge of the north and its compelling history, while listening to the conversations and observations of his erudite passengers. After twenty years he could carry on a conversation with any one of the Parks Canada staff about the history behind places like York Factory or Churchill, Manitoba. In fact, he was frequently consulted by several of the employees regarding these places and the significance they held for First Nations people. The fact that he had relatives who had once lived at York Factory raised his status in the eyes of the docents there.

The newlyweds also visited the polar bear display at the Assiniboine Park Zoo. Seeing these regal Arctic creatures still gave

2. An exact replica of the Tom Lamb bush pilot sculpture sits in the Canadian embassy in Washington, D.C.

Rachel anxiety, having come face to face with one the year before when she encountered a mother and her cub at York Factory while she waited on the dock for the transport boat. Her therapist had advised her to visit this display as often as she could to desensitize her from the symptoms of PTSD from her frightening experience. After dozens of trips to the park, it seemed to be helping and her nightmares were diminishing. However, she still suffered occasionally from bouts of anxiety and depression for another reason.

Rachel had become self conscious about her smallpox scars. She developed the habit of examining them in the mirror every day as if they might somehow disappear by her own intense scrutiny. Like sunken nail heads they seemed deeper in certain lighting. Her husband escaped his own bout of smallpox with minor facial scarring which was no worse than a bad case of teenage acne but Rachel frequently referred to the "lunar landscape" on her own forehead and cheeks. Several faint pockmarks were hidden by her hair. She began to search the literature on how she might best treat them. Since smallpox had been eradicated over forty years ago there weren't any recent studies to help her. Dermabrasion and chemical peels had yielded disappointing results but a South Korean study on laser resurfacing intrigued her. After researching this treatment she found a dermatologist who treated her scars with laser. She was ecstatic with the results. Her self confidence improved and her depression quickly lifted.

Rachel kept busy writing papers about the York Factory project including one on the Hudson's Bay point blanket that was unearthed during the project. This blanket proved to be the oldest known Bay trading blanket in history and it likely arrived in North America around 1780. Unfortunately, it was a fomite for smallpox, carrying the virus in its frozen state, inert for 235 years in the permafrost of the York Factory cemetery. Scientists had always feared this possibility and two specialists in infectious diseases from the University of

Manitoba had actually visited the cemetery as early as the 1970s to see if river erosion might bring any frozen smallpox-infected bodies to the surface. These fears were dispelled when no evidence of disturbances was found in the cemetery back then.

Other scientists seriously questioned the possibility of smallpox surviving in the ground for that long. They postulated that the DNA would not withstand the rigours of time and temperature. Yet it was the freezing temperatures of the permafrost that enabled the virus to remain preserved and viable. For over forty years in the freezers of the CDC in Atlanta and the Vektor Laboratories in Novosibirsk, Russia, the smallpox virus was still being kept alive. No one stopped to consider that permafrost of the northern tundra provided a freezer that also kept smallpox alive.[3] No one that is, until Rachel and her fellow archaeologists unintentionally unearthed a smallpox-infested blanket during the exhumation of a Hudson's Bay employee by the name of Joseph Charles. Still, the question as to how long viruses and other pathogens can stay viable in permafrost remained an ongoing concern.

Rachel and Rolly had received a substantial financial award for their service to the Russian government during the great smallpox epidemic that took place the year before. They were able to buy their condominium with this unexpected good fortune. Life for the newlyweds in Winnipeg was good. At least until this letter from the Arctic Institute arrived.

Rachel continued her angry monologue berating the insensitivity and dismissiveness of her employers.

"Rachel. I think you need to look at this differently. You know what the Chinese say: 'In every crisis there is an opportunity.' In fact,

---

3. In recent years, researchers have pulled samples of smallpox, Spanish flu, bubonic plague, and even anthrax from thawing permafrost.

I've already found something on the internet that might work for you. Let me read the job description to you just for fun."

"Really? Whatever. What have I got to lose now?" Rachel poured herself another gin and tonic and began pacing as her husband read from his computer.

"Okay, number one: 'Excavates archaeological sites using shovels, buckets, and other digging tools; records relevant features by list, drawing, camera, and other appropriate means; packs and transports artifacts such as rocks, bones and soil samples; completes field data forms – .'"

"I'm okay with that. I mean that's all I did at the York Factory project. Hauling shovels and buckets and picks is right up my alley. What else?"

"Two: 'Identifies, records, and maps archaeological sites, and conducts field analysis of artifacts.'"

"Yup, I'm good with that."

"Three: 'Participates in archaeological laboratory activities such as record keeping and soil sample processing; cleans, counts, and catalogues artifacts.' You're good with that, too, right?"

"No problems there either. Keep going," Rachel said as she slowly swirled her drink.

"Now this next one is kind of interesting: Number four: 'Participates in activities to reconstruct and preserve artifacts such as ceramic pottery shards.'"

"Pottery shards! Just where is this job anyways?" Rachel was becoming intrigued and sat down beside her husband to look at the computer herself.

"Where did you find this job Rolly? I've always wanted to work with pottery but most of the really good stuff is in the southwestern

United States. Boy, now you have my attention. Just where is this position anyways?" Rachel leaned over Boudreau to read more about the job requirements.

"Look here. You'll need a valid New Mexico driver's licence and you will be operating out of the University of New Mexico in Albuquerque."

"Albuquerque? Omigosh, I was hoping you had found something here in Canada. How would we manage to get a visa and live in New Mexico? And what about your work as a pilot Rolly? Um, I don't know. This is such a change for both of us. But at least the weather would be warmer."

"Right, but you may want to start working on your résumé. As I understand it, the life of an archaeologist is one of travelling from one location to another. This job is just a little farther away from what you've been used to with the Arctic Institute. Actually, I think it's kind of neat. At least you won't be finding frozen blankets there," Boudreau quipped.

"Okay, but what else do they need in their job requirements besides a driver's licence from New Mexico?" Rachel asked impatiently.

"Well, it says you need to be able to communicate effectively, both orally and in writing. You need to be knowledgeable in mapping principles and techniques and be able to read topographic maps and aerial photographs."

"Uh oh. I don't know about topographic maps and aerial photographs. I studied that stuff in the past, although I've never had to use it. Aerial photographs? Gosh, I don't know, Rolly. They'll want someone with more experience I'm sure."

Boudreau cleared his throat. Putting his hand on his wife's arm he said, "Rachel, have you forgotten what I do for a living? I know all this stuff from years of flying to remote locations with geologists and engineers. Topographic maps and aerial photographs are right up my alley. I can help you with it. We'll work as a team."

"Yes, of course, you would know about maps and stuff being a pilot. Forgot about that. That's great, Rolly. What else are they looking for?" Rachel leaned in closer to read from the laptop.

"They're looking for people with the ability to utilize geographic survey instruments."

"No problem there. Gordon Dowling taught me a lot about those gadgets."

"And you must have a knowledge of 'general excavation, techniques, tools, and equipment.'" Boudreau read from the website.

"I can handle that, too. As I told you I did much of that work at the York Factory project," Rachel interrupted. "What else?"

"You need to have a knowledge of 'archaeological field and/or laboratory procedures and techniques.' See, most of this stuff you already know, Rachel. You should have no problem," Boudreau assured.

"Yes, but New Mexico? I've read about it, but to practise archaeology in the desert would be a challenge for someone like me who has been trained in Arctic exploration. I'm not sure about this job, Rolly."

"Well, I think you would find it interesting. Remember when we discussed the Chipewyan people from Canada's far north? I told you that many of their ancestors migrated to the southern United States where their descendants now live as Navajo or Apache Indians. When they arrived around the year 1500, they discovered several abandoned native dwelling places in the deserts of New Mexico and Arizona. Their owners just strangely disappeared in the twelfth century."

"Who were the people that lived there and what made them disappear?" Rachel asked.

"So the Navajos explored their ruins but they got spooked by them and stayed away after that. They called the missing inhabitants *Anasazi* even though they never met any of them. These people had disappeared from places like Chaco Canyon and Mesa Verde three or four hundred years before the Navajo arrived on the scene."

"Hmm. I've heard of the Anasazi. What does it mean again?"

"It means *ancient enemies,* a term which the Hopi and Zuni people despise."

"Why is that such a bad thing?"

"Well, the main reason is that the Hopi, Zuni, and other Pueblo groups see themselves as descendants of the missing tribes, which go back to 1200 BC. They don't like being referred to as *enemies'* Instead, they prefer to call the Chaco people *Ancestral Puebloans* or *Ancient Pueblo people.* It's the politically correct term to use nowadays and you would probably be well advised to avoid the expression *Anasazi* around Pueblo people, even though it's mentioned in many older history books written about them. Still, many anthropologists and historians still use the term '*Anasazi*' today. Modern day Pueblo tribes aren't too fond of the Navajo and consider them foreigners which they are, of course, having arrived in the Southwest only five hundred years ago. That's why they especially don't like the term *Anasazi.* It's considered to be politically incorrect."

"Okay, smarty pants. And why is it that you know all these things?"

"Rachel, don't you remember that I flew down there years ago and met many of the Pueblo Indians. Plus I happen to have a degree in native studies."

"Fair enough. So why is calling them Anasazi politically incorrect yet you refer to them as Indians?"

"Because they want to be called Indians. The term *First Nations* is only recognized in Canada. Down there they don't know what you're talking about if you refer to them as *First Nations.*"

"Okay, but you haven't explained why the Anasazi disappeared from Chaco Canyon."

"So, as far as the Anasazi are concerned, no one seems to know why they left their ancestral homes at Chaco Canyon and Mesa Verde. Most historians think a prolonged drought that lasted for thirty years drove them away. Others are of the opinion that internecine warfare and infighting between various clans drove them away. If you ask a modern-day Puebloan like a Hopi or a Zuni, they will quickly correct you if you say that the ancient ones just disappeared."

"Why is that? Do they know what happened to them?"

"Not really. You might recall that I once met an Indian guy named Victor Lewis from Acoma who believes that his people are direct descendants of the Anasazi from Chaco Canyon. He said that the Anasazi never disappeared in the first place. They just split up and moved away. Over centuries they became known as the modern Pueblo Indians which nowadays consists of about eighteen different groups scattered across southeastern New Mexico and Arizona."

"Really? How would your friend know all this?" Rachel was intrigued by the history of the Anasazi people.

"He knew because of oral tradition. Although they never wrote anything down on paper, they were great storytellers much like our own native traditions here in Canada. And much information comes from pottery drawings and rock art that date back hundreds of years. As an archaeologist you know all about this stuff, Rachel."

"Yes, I do, but I must admit that I'm unfamiliar with the story of the Anasazi. The story of Chaco Canyon certainly is haunting don't you think?"

"For sure. Most people haven't heard about them either, yet they constitute an important aspect of the history of the Southwest. So why not submit your résumé and if you're accepted, we can fly down and check it out. I mean, what have you got to lose? I think a new adventure like this would also help you to get over the experiences of the past year. I would personally find it very interesting to meet native people of the Southwest again. My friend Victor Lewis from Acoma could be a big help too."

"Okay. Since you put it like that, I'll do it. But you have to start teaching me about aerial photographs and topological mapping. I wonder what archaeological site the University of New Mexico is researching. Wouldn't it be exciting if it was in Chaco Canyon?"

Three weeks after submitting her résumé to the University of New Mexico, Rachel received an email requesting an interview for the position advertised. In the meantime, she had been researching pre-Columbian native history in the Southwest to prepare herself in the event she was offered an interview. In the process, she became fascinated with the beautiful pottery made by the ancient people of that era and their mysterious disappearance in the twelfth century. She also amassed a small library on the history of the Southwest.

She was excited to know that she was being considered for a position as an archaeologist in the United States. Yet she wondered how she would get around the work restrictions placed on foreigners. Fortunately, the Office of International Students and Scholars at the university had offered to arrange a work visa for her if she was accepted. It would also submit the necessary documents to the government and provide information that would explain why a Canadian was necessary for this position over an American citizen.

"Rolly, they want me to have an interview in Albuquerque as early as next week. Instead of flying why don't we drive down and stay for a few extra days and get familiar with New Mexico. Sort of make it a holiday, you know? We could visit some of the ancient ruins and enjoy Mexican food while we're down there. Maybe we could even visit a few museums and see some of the beautiful pre-Columbian pottery I've been reading about."

"Yeah. I'm good with that. I'll need to make a few phone calls to get some time off work which shouldn't be a problem. I think we could both use a vacation about now. I'll start planning a route. It should take about three days to get there from here." Boudreau was already scouring Google maps on his computer.

"You know, Rolly, you might be right about your Chinese proverb," Rachel said putting her arms around him.

"What do you mean?"

"Well as you said, this may not be a crisis as much as it is an opportunity. As the Chinese also say, 'May you live in interesting times.'"

Chapter 3

Flash Flood

We are all one child spinning through Mother Sky.
~ Shawnee

Caught up in contemplation under the anvil of the unyielding desert sun, Shadow Dancer never heard the rush of water surging through the wash behind him. He had forgotten that sudden and monstrous floods frequently occurred where everything living and dead was channelled into the narrow wash. He felt only a sudden cool breeze striking his back a few seconds before the water hit him violently from behind. Arising from the higher elevations in the eastern part of the canyon, the flash flood swept him off his feet, cold water swirling around him, instantly taking his breath away. Within seconds, the wash had swelled into a churning rust-coloured river, rumbling and hissing with sand and mud, heaving with the flotsam and jetsam picked up from the wide canyon floor.

Slicing through the valley it swallowed everything in its pathway; tree stumps, logs, the carcasses of various animals, and anything else caught unexpectedly by its overwhelming turbulence.

Submerged for an instant, Shadow Dancer just as quickly bobbed to the surface again. Struggling to keep his head above the desert maelstrom, he reached out clinging to anything that might stabilize him in the flow. His hand soon found a broken branch from a cottonwood tree that had snagged several juniper twigs which whipped his face from the force of the current. Rising to the surface, the branch revealed part of a tree trunk which he quickly grasped. Thundering past boulders and scrub, the flood scoured the bottom of the wash, uprooting small plants and cacti which scraped against his legs. Rough grasping fingers, the roots of brushes and trees point upwards to the burning sky.

Thousands of tons of sand, grit, gravel, and mud engulfed him in a swirling foul smelling broth. Shadow Dancer could barely keep his face above water with the powerful undercurrents dragging him down each time he tried to pull himself over the tree trunk. The roar of the flood was deafening as it resonated within the canyon walls, magnified like the rumbling of a thunderstorm. Completely overwhelmed by the turbulence of the river, Shadow Dancer sputtered and coughed, terror-stricken in his efforts to stay afloat in the rhythm of the undulating flow.

A coyote floated past him, paddling furiously to stay above the surface. A dead rabbit snagged in a willow bush surged on the crest along with other material from the canyon. Shadow Dancer tried to steer the trunk closer to the edge of the flow but its dead weight resisted his efforts and it continued to plough through the murky waters, bobbing and rolling as if it had a mind of its own. He finally gave up and allowed himself to be carried along with the momentum of the log in the middle of the current.

Afraid to let go, he continued his terrifying ride in the wash, which was now several feet deep. He could feel his feet touching the bottom at intervals. Digging in his heels, he was finally able to pull himself over towards the north side of the stream a few feet at a time. Looking up he could see the passing structures of the Nation; the great house with the enormous kivas, the granaries and the hundreds of gardens, many inundated as the water embraced the maize and squash plants, uprooted by the sheer force of the flood's bestial flow. Within minutes a third of the Nation's gardens were swept away.

Dozens of farmers stood by helplessly as the river ripped past them. No one ever learned to swim in this culture and if they did, the raging flood would be formidable without anything to cling to. Seeing the farmers, Shadow Dancer cried out as he struggled towards the shore. Several young men ran alongside the edge of the flood and one of them threw a long cottonwood branch towards him. He looked at it longingly knowing he likely couldn't reach it. The branch was only a few feet away, its leaves already sinking into the brackish stream. With a heave that took all of his remaining strength, he managed to grasp a handful of leaves attached to the end of the branch.

Pulling himself along the branch, he edged closer to the northern bank of the river. Both his feet were now scraping along the bottom of the riverbed and he awkwardly pushed himself further to safety. Suddenly a log struck him in the back of his head knocking him unconscious. He loosened his grasp on the branch and began to sink just as he got near the shore. A strong hand quickly grabbed him by his braided hair, pulling him to the safety of the water's edge and several more hands dragged him onto the sand. Shadow Dancer lay on the ground, spitting, coughing, and blowing, wearing only a tattered breech cloth covered in mud. Slowly regaining consciousness, he lay gasping for several minutes. The warm sand felt good after being immersed in the cold water for several terrifying minutes.

A family working nearby in their garden plot quickly attended him and an older woman, covered him with a small grass mat on which she had been kneeling. Her teenage daughter knelt beside the young apprentice whose body was bruised and scraped from his horrendous ride in the flood. Somehow, his sandals had stayed on his feet but he had lost the leather pouch around his neck containing the peyote buttons. Shadow Dancer was unable to open his eyes against the brightness of the sun. He felt the soft hand of the young woman who wiped the caked mud from his rawboned frame while others ran for help.

The young woman covered his eyes with a moist woven cloth and held his hand, singing softly to him while she picked debris from his hair. He lay there exhausted from his struggle against the current, which now burbled and twined itself westward into the Great San Juan Basin, carrying with it all the detritus of the desert, a conglomeration of its flora and fauna with rocks and boulders, colossal tangles of branches with innumerable twigs, and leaves, and animal bones. The river would soon return to a trickle within a few days, only the mounds of rubble and diluvium remaining as a stark reminder of its devastating power. Ebbing and sighing with mud and sand in the blistering heat of the sun, the flood formed twisted strands across the plain as it dissipated into the vastness of the desert basin.

Shadow Dancer was carried on a hide strapped to two long poles while he remained in a semi-conscious state. He was dragged by several perspiring young men towards the cooling shadows of the great house. The young woman stayed by his side holding his hand while he fell into a deep sleep on the travois, moaning softly whenever one of the poles hit a rock. She could not help but notice his perfect physique, his dry cracked lips, and his six toes on each foot. As with all Anasazi, the back of Shadow Dancer's head was flat from being carried on a cradle board as an infant.

Unknown to him at the time, Shadow Dancer had floated downstream over a mile and a half by the time he was finally rescued by the farmers. He didn't know the young woman who sang to him on the way back to the great house. All he remembered was her soothing and gentle voice. When he came to, he was too weak to lift his head and his face remained covered with the wet cloth. He remembered only a wonderful sense of comfort from her presence that horrible day when the flood passed through the canyon. His wounds would heal but the terrifying memories of near drowning would remain with him. Fragments of the experience visited him in dreams each night; he frequently awoke, kicking vigorously as if he were drowning in his sleep.

Chapter 4

Bandelier

It takes a thousand voices to tell a single story.
~ Tribe Unknown

After driving south for two days Rolly and Rachel stayed in a quaint motel in Taos, New Mexico called Hotel La Fonda de Taos, an adobe-styled building on the town's central plaza. Surrounded by boutiques, native pottery, and leather stores, and several Mexican restaurants, the 190-year-old hotel displayed Southwestern art and furniture that delighted Rachel. They explored the small city centre and visited numerous art galleries as well as the Taos Pueblo for which the town is famous. Tired after a long day of driving and sightseeing, they dined at a place called the Gorge, a Southwest restaurant on the corner near their hotel. They each enjoyed a nacho salad washed down with Dos Equis pale lager.

"This is one beautiful little town, Rolly. I just love the shops and galleries. And the Mexican food is a bonus. Boy, I could stay here for a week," Rachel exclaimed, quaffing her beer.

"So could I, but it's not cheap with the American dollar. Besides, we need to make it to Albuquerque for your interview on Monday morning."

"I know, but we still have an extra day. It's Friday and we can make it there in a matter of hours so why not stay until tomorrow and then drive to Albuquerque on Sunday?"

"I have a better idea. Since your interview may require some knowledge of pre-Columbian Indian habitations in New Mexico, why don't we stop at the Bandelier National Monument on our way south? I've read it's a beautiful Pueblo ruin dating back to the fifteenth century. After our visit there, we could see more art galleries in Santa Fe if we have time. We would then arrive in Albuquerque for a late Sunday afternoon check-in at our hotel," Boudreau said.

"Okay, I guess, but what's Bandelier National Monument and where exactly is it? You keep surprising me with all this stuff Rolly. I thought I was the archaeologist in this family," she quipped.

"Well, I guess it's my own personal interest in the history of the Southwest and its people. I told you I have an old friend at the Acoma Pueblo who taught me much about his ancestors. They believe they descended from the ancient Pueblo people from Chaco Canyon."

"Okay, I get that. So again, what's at Bandelier, Rolly?"

"I have a brochure I picked up in Taos at the hotel. Why don't you read it? I heard it's a beautiful valley that breathes history. It's only about ten miles from Los Alamos where they built the atomic bomb during the war," Boudreau explained.

"All right. I'm sold. When do we go?" Rachel grabbed the brochure from her husband.

"First thing in the morning, right after breakfast. It's only two hours from here off Highway 4."

After a hearty breakfast of Mexican eggs in Taos, New Mexico, the couple set out towards Los Alamos where the top-secret Manhattan Project had designed the atomic bomb in the 1940s. As they turned towards the science town nestled in the Jemez Mountains they found the scenery to be breathtaking.

"So why is this place called Bandelier National Monument?" Rolly asked.

"Well, according to the brochure, Adolph Bandelier was a Swiss historian and archaeologist who discovered the hidden Frijoles Canyon in the 1870s. He encountered the remains of an elaborate civilization which had lived there for a few hundred years before it, too, mysteriously disappeared."

"Really, where would all those people go?" Rolly was becoming increasingly more interested in this pre-Columbian civilization.

"Beats me. We'll have to take a tour when we get there to find out."

Turning towards the Bandelier National Monument down Highway 4 towards White Rock, New Mexico, they arrived at their destination on a sunny morning. Rachel grabbed her camera and her water bottle for the hike through this historic canyon. After spending half an hour in the interpretive centre watching a short film on the history of the Frijoles Canyon, the couple joined several other tourists and followed a park guide who began a narrative of the canyon's history.

"A thriving group of pre-Columbian Indians had dwelt in numerous caves for centuries in this canyon as far back as the 1100s. These people have been referred to as the *Anasazi* or *Ancient Pueblo* people." Following a brief lecture on the pre-Columbian Indians, the docent suggested that they set off on their own to find the cliff dwelling known as *Alcove House*.

Hundreds of the ancient caves stretched out over several miles in the canyon, pock-marking the cliff walls. Above each cave entrance, sooty licks stretched upwards from ancient fires used in cooking. Walking hand in hand along a mountain stream that murmured softly through the forest, they stopped to read interpretive signs. One read that the brook had once supplied the canyon population with water. Towering sweet-scented ponderosa pine and cottonwoods provided shade and numerous Gambel oaks shed their leaves, which Rolly and Rachel crunched under their feet as they walked on the trail. Thousands of yellow-leafed quaking aspens flickered with the bright overhead sun, providing a rich canopy of ochre over the leaf-strewn path. After walking for a mile, they arrived at the location of the Alcove House which was a typical Anasazi cliff dwelling hidden below a massive dome of overhanging rock. It was difficult to see from the canyon trail and they had to climb 140 feet using several sets of wooden ladders to reach the alcove. By the time they reached the top they were both panting from the climb and the altitude to which they were unaccustomed.

"Boy, I can sure see how any enemies attempting to attack the cliff house would be at a disadvantage with rocks being hurled at them from here. They wouldn't stand a chance," Rolly exclaimed as he looked over the edge.

"No kidding. According to the brochure this Alcove was previously known as the *Ceremonial Cave* where here some twenty-five Anasazi people once lived. The people who lived here seem to have mysteriously disappeared around the year 1500."

"Does it say what happened to them?"

"No, but by analyzing the rings of trees used in the construction of several of their buildings in the area, archaeologists are able to tell when the Anasazi first built many of the structures. After several hundred years of communal dwelling, hunting, and making pottery, they mysteriously left the area, as did many ancient Pueblo people throughout New Mexico and Arizona." Rachel folded the brochure and placed it in her backpack.

Looking down from the Alcove kiva, she said, "This must be the only approach to Alcove House. And what a great view. All they had to do was to retract the wooden ladders and no one could scale these heights. They would be perfectly safe here and they probably stored enough food and water to withstand a prolonged siege. After being pummelled with hundreds of rocks their enemies would eventually just give up and go home."

"I would love to learn more about this interesting place. It's so neat to actually be inside a cliff dweller's home," Rolly said.

"Let's find the park guide and get more information," Rachel suggested.

After climbing down the sets of ladders to the bottom, they walked back to the interpretive centre where they caught the tail-end of a guided tour. The park guide was a middle-aged woman wearing drab olive green slacks with sharp creases, a grey shirt, and the distinctive *Smokey the Bear* hat with the National Parks logo. Her matching jacket was adorned with a variety of pins and badges. A name tag said "Cheryl" and she introduced herself as an anthropologist doing part-time research at the Bandelier site. She was explaining to a small group of tourists the conditions of the canyon dwellings when they were first discovered by Anglo -Americans.

"Some six hundred years later in the late nineteenth century, treasure hunters discovered pottery with corn maize still in them at many of these sites. Clothing, weapons, cooking utensils, and jewellery also remained as if their owners had just 'stepped out' for a while. It took archaeologists from the Smithsonian Institution in the 1890s to begin an organized collection, cataloguing these priceless artifacts. Meanwhile, much of the pottery was taken from these historical sites by amateur archaeologists and treasure seekers. Even the scientific staff working on the Manhattan Project from Los Alamos only a few miles away, came to Bandelier during the war to search for pottery and other artifacts. It seemed as though no one could just leave them where they found them. Soon hundreds of basements and attics became repositories for priceless ancient pottery. Eventually some pottery made its way back to museums. The reason why so much pottery was stolen was that in the old west people believed in the law of 'finders' keepers.'"

Rolly interrupted the guide and asked her, "Why couldn't they stop people from taking these artifacts? Couldn't archaeologists just step in to prevent this plundering?"

"That is an excellent question which really raises the ethical and moral issues of archaeological exploration," the guide explained.

"How so?" Rolly asked. Rachel being an archaeologist herself was familiar with this aspect of her work and remained silent.

"Well, to answer your question, I refer to Craig Childs' book called *Finders Keepers*. He deals with the ethical question as to whom these artifacts belong in his book. Childs is an archaeologist who spent his life exploring several fascinating areas that generations of looters have stripped of precious artifacts. Many of them hold the secrets to the civilization of the Ancestral Pueblo people. And now much of this information is missing with so many artifacts taken by treasure hunters. We are left with a rather scarred picture of their ancient culture."

"Shouldn't those artifacts be left strictly for archaeologists?" Rolly inquired.

"Well that's debatable too," Cheryl said, shifting uneasily.

"So is an archaeologist that excavates a tomb or pueblo a hero or a villain? On the other hand, if someone steals a relic from a museum and returns it to where it was found, is he a thief? Until 1906 when the Antiquities Act was enacted in the United States the rule of 'finders' keepers' applied. After that, the law prohibited the activities of grave robbers, pot hunters, and treasure seekers in an effort to preserve remnants of a civilization from long ago. In spite of this law, many pot hunters still follow the principle of 'finders keepers.'" The parks guide was well informed with this aspect of archaeology and Rachel was now more than a little intrigued.

"Do people ever return the artifacts?" Rachel asked.

"Oh yes. Many who have taken the ancient relics have experienced death, accidents, and suicide in their families and many believe that some of the stolen items bring a curse to the new owners. Perhaps these things are just coincidences, but we are seeing more and more people bringing pottery to the interpretive centres all across New Mexico and Arizona because of the calamities in their personal lives. Other treasure seekers return relics from fear or from guilt after years of keeping them in their possession."

"That's incredible that people believe that sort of thing."

"Well, it's not just ordinary people who believe that. There are many on staff here who feel that there is a curse on relics taken from their sites of origin. Fortunately, vast collections of Anasazi artifacts now reside in half a dozen major institutions including the Field Museum in Chicago, the American Museum of Natural History, and the National Museum of the American Indian in New York City. Using museums to separate the artifacts from their sites of origin may, sadly, be the only way to keep them from ending up in someone's basement as archaeological plunder," the guide explained.

"But wouldn't it be easier to understand the reason why the Anasazi left if their artifacts could be studied? Is there anything left that might explain their sudden disappearance from this beautiful canyon?" Rachel asked.

"To simply state that they disappeared might be a misinterpretation of the past. Most archaeologists believe they migrated elsewhere. Just as many people arrived here from the northwest near the Four Corners area because of a prolonged period of drought, so too did they leave this place perhaps for similar reasons," the tour guide expounded.

"Where would they go then?" asked Rachel.

"They likely headed into the Rio Grande Valley. By the year 1300, this place and many other Ancestral Puebloan communities abandoned their homes. Environmental and social factors may have contributed to this exodus and they just moved on to new settlements."

The tour guide could tell that Rachel was interested in the history of Frijoles Canyon and invited her to the bookstore inside the centre. The two of them discussed further the mystery of why the Anasazi came to this beautiful canyon dwelling only to move on after a few hundred years. Rachel introduced herself as an archaeologist from Canada and that she was en route to Albuquerque for a job interview with the University of New Mexico, Department of Archaeology. Rachel asked the guide about what may have led to the forced abandonment of the Ancestral Pueblo people.

The tour guide launched into a brief explanation. Looking at her notes she read, "According to researchers, towards the end of the twelfth century, some cataclysmic event forced the Anasazi to flee their cliff houses and their homeland at Mesa Verde and Chaco canyon. Just what happened has been the greatest puzzle facing archaeologists who study the ancient culture. Many believe a mega drought spurred mass migrations throughout the region. Today's Pueblo Indians have oral histories about the migration of their ancestors although the details of these stories remain closely guarded secrets."

Rolly nudged his wife reminding her of what he had told her regarding oral tradition.

"Within the past decade archaeologists have wrung a new understanding about why the Anasazi left, and the picture that emerges is dark. It includes violence and warfare—even cannibalism—among the Anasazi themselves."

"Cannibalism!" Rachel exclaimed.

"Yes, you see after about AD 1200, something very unpleasant happens," said the guide dramatically. "Something mysterious happened that was a disaster for most of these people."

"Whoa, that's intriguing. My husband thinks it's possible that an epidemic of some kind could have driven them away," Rachel said.

"That's one possible theory, however, most of the really devastating diseases hadn't arrived by the time the Anasazi left. It's really anybody's guess but the general feeling among researchers is that it was probably a drought that drove them away around the end of the thirteenth century. Drought may have contributed to internecine warfare which resulted in isolated cases of cannibalism. Since you expressed an interest in pottery, I suggest that you go into our interpretive centre and check out some of the artifacts we have here from the Chaco Canyon area."

Rachel thanked Cheryl for her suggestion and entered the centre where several bowls and ollas featured behind Plexiglas caught her attention. She found it difficult to believe the dates on the pre-Columbian pottery dating back to the twelfth century and earlier.

Although she had been trained in Arctic and sub-Arctic native groups and fur trade history, she had not paid much attention to the stories of the American Southwest. Most of the pottery was plain black-on-white described as "Anasazi grayware". Rachel began taking pictures with her cell phone. She knew she wouldn't remember all the details presented in the various cases. Among the many bowls, jars, and cups featured on display, two things attracted her attention.

The first was a Lino Gray pitcher from the year 700 AD. At five and a half inches tall, the ancient relic looked just like her coffee mug back home, complete with handle and faded design. However, a few chips and scratches on the rim were a testimony to its vast age.

The second piece of pottery that caught Rachel's attention was a bowl labelled "Mancos black-on-white 4 ½ inches in diameter circa 1025 CE." In the centre of the intricate design at the bottom of the bowl, a little man with six-fingered hands was featured. Next to it was a photograph of rock art from the same area depicting a six-toed foot.

After visiting and taking pictures for half an hour in the interpretive centre Rachel purchased a few books from the bookstore and thanked the guide for her time and explanations. She found Rolly outside nursing a Thermos of beer at a picnic table in the sun looking very relaxed while munching on a bag of potato chips.

"I'm sorry to have spent so long in there with the tour guide Rolly; I find this stuff fascinating."

"I knew you would like this place. Boy, isn't this area perfect for community life? I mean you just use a sharp wooden stick to dig a hole in the volcanic tuff, carve out your cave home, plant your corn, beans, and squash on the top of the mesa with the same stick, and drink from the creek that flows down though the middle of the canyon. You can then go hunting at the top of the mesa or on the mountains on either side. An idyllic setting I would say. Come and sit beside me and have some beer Rachel," Boudreau said.

"Rolly, we're in a national park. I don't think open drinking is allowed." Rachel scolded.

"You're right sweetheart. That's why I poured it into a Thermos. Here, I've got a cool one for you too." Boudreau reached into a knapsack and pulled out another Thermos.

"Thanks, I am thirsty after that hike. What a great view from the top of the Alcove House. I'm not used to climbing at this altitude I'm afraid."

"I agree, it is a bit of a workout to climb at an altitude of six thousand feet. The Indians who lived here would have climbed up there several times a day. They were likely in great shape, and got used to this altitude," Boudreau said.

After basking in the sun for half an hour admiring the beauty of the canyon and the remains of its ancient stone buildings, they tried to visualize how several hundred people might have lived in the valley for almost four hundred years.

"I'd still like to know what drove them out of here," Boudreau pondered.

"Rolly, I bought a few books on the history of the Anasazi and the theories behind their disappearance from Bandelier and Chaco Canyon. They might give me some insights for the interview tomorrow. You know, Chaco Canyon is another place we really should visit. Did you know that several people from the Chaco Canyon area had six toes or fingers and that these people were given special status by their society? In fact, researchers have identified several handprints and footprints plastered into the walls and floors throughout the great houses."

Looking at his cell phone Boudreau said, "As a matter of fact I just googled that myself while you were in the visitor centre. I looked up an article online from the *National Geographic* magazine that depicts that unusual feature of the ancient Chacoans. Having an extra finger or toe automatically elevated you to a higher order of respect as if the gods favoured you. No one knows why, but according to this article the incidence of polydactyls was fifteen times more frequent in the Chaco natives than what we see today in the North American population."

"Polydactyly? Rolly you simply amaze me with your research. What else does that article tell you?"

"Well it discusses the Anasazi and six-toed people in general. Their handprints were clearly honoured elements in their society and probably held a ritual meaning. You know, I had a cousin who had six toes on one foot, so yes, I find this interesting. I also discovered that Halle Berry and Kate Hudson each have six toes."

"Rolly, that explains why you know about polydactyls. Admit it; you have a secret crush on these celebrities. I'll bet you have a fetish for polydactyl women. Shame on you!" Wagging her finger at her husband, Rachel was grinning from ear to ear. Rolly blushed at his wife's accusations.

"Look, I'm trying to be academic here, sweetheart; but you might be partially right.

And don't forget this isn't my first time at Bandelier National Monument. I came down here years ago when I was still in my twenties with two friends who were history majors at the University of Winnipeg. That's when we met Victor Lewis from Acoma. So yes, I am familiar with Southwestern Indian history, polydactyls and gorgeous women like you. But not necessarily in that order."

"Boy, you weaseled out of that corner pretty smoothly. You'd better take care not to slip on your own slime trail when we leave the park," she laughed, shaking her head.

"Thanks, I'll try. But I agree with you about going to Chaco Canyon. I've never been there and it's definitely on my bucket list. Bandelier just whets your appetite for more Ancestral Puebloan history. Let's plan a trip there this week depending on how your interview goes." He raised his Thermos with beer as a toast. Rachel clinked his Thermos with her own and blew him a kiss.

"Who knew my husband likes six-toed women?" Rachel laughed. After finishing their beer under the mid-afternoon sun they headed west on the Jemez

Springs scenic highway, one of New Mexico's more scenic routes passing through the historic town of Jemez Springs. Looping through the Santa Fe National Forest to the Valles Caldera National Preserve, they drove past a breathtaking expanse of mountain meadow and forest, part of the 33,000 acres of steep-walled canyons and mesas of the Bandelier National Monument wilderness. After Jemez Springs, Rachel fell asleep while Rolly drove on the undulating mountain highway past pine forests, cacti, and red rocks towards Albuquerque. A few hours later, they arrived at their hotel just as the early evening sky turned to a soft pastel blue over an orange horizon.

Chapter 5

The Raven—
Master of Time

*The desert owl and screech owl will possess it; the great owl
and the raven will nest there. Thorns will overrun her citadels,
nettles and brambles her strongholds. She will become
a haunt for jackals, a home for owls.*
~ Isaiah 34:11, 13

Through the heart of Shadow Dancer's community ran a seven and
one-half-mile long arroyo. Following a monsoon, water ran from
southeast to northwest, emptying at the end of the canyon into a
larger river.[4] North of the canyon stood towering sandstone cliffs
topped by wide, slick-rock terraces. The south harboured irregular
high rock bluffs. On a ledge on the canyon wall nestled a hiding
place behind a stone wall, indiscernible from the ground below. It
was accessible only by a rocky trail that switch-backed up to the
rim. This was where Shadow Dancer spent most of his waking hours

---

4. The Chaco wash cuts through Chaco Canyon emptying into the San Juan River
in northwestern New Mexico. Most of the year it is merely an intermittent stream
or arroyo.

beneath a lip of red sandstone. It seemed to be the loneliest place on earth for the seventeen-year-old native.

He tried relieving his boredom by leaving the cave to climb the cliffs above him and by carving small animals from any scraps of wood that he could find. Otherwise the weight of loneliness bore on him like the darkness of a moonless night. He began to feel imprisoned within his own body, serving the shaman in this solitude and he became envious of the raven and its lofty freedom.

Through cracks and small gaps in the irregular stone wall, shafts of pale light burst through, revealing soft pastel hues of the emerging dawn in the great canyon below. Sunrise spilled over the canyon rim striking the cobbled walls of the cliff side, casting a thousand fleeting shadows throughout the vast arid valley. Peering through a space between the stones, Shadow Dancer could see the enormous canyon stretching westward into a 3000-square-mile landscape of sandstone canyons, mesas, and massive formations of weathered red rocks.

A lone raven soared overhead, scouring the eroded waste of the desert floor for small animals, eggs, and carrion as the soft glow of twilight gave way to the day. Only the fading speck of the morning star remained in the northeast sky as a remembrance of the night. As the sun's rays struck the enormous hovering bird, its plumage reflected a metallic purple sheen, alternating with iridescent blue.

The barren desert soon began heating with the sun, sending huge updrafts of air. Powerful steady thermals lifted the raven to even greater heights, allowing it to soar tirelessly in elegant spirals without flapping its wings for several minutes at a time. Several other birds also coiled slowly upwards, higher and higher until they were only small black specks against the lazuline sky. Scouting the red rocks for incautious rodents, one desert predator aimed its large snouted beak ominously downwards as if pointing to its prey below.

Shadow Dancer stirred from his rocky hideaway 150 feet above the canyon floor, a nearly invisible wrinkle of ledge just below the canyon rim. Squinting against the brightness of the sun, he gradually lifted himself onto one elbow from his soft bed of deer hide and snake grass. He followed the raven's slow elliptical path over the canyon below, mesmerized by its graceful flight. He never ceased to be fascinated by its elegant and effortless soaring over the immense spaces and eerie silences of the canyon.

How can they do that? I wish I could fly like that.

His people knew the raven as the *Master of Time* and Shadow Dancer's mentor, Grey Elk, the medicine man taught him that those "who walked the path of the Mysteries" were often sought out by the raven. For years he paid little attention to these birds and had hardly noticed their presence in the canyon, being distracted by playing games with his childhood friends. But now he had little to do except to observe them from his quiet vantage point.

Does this raven wish to share some secret with me? What is he trying to tell me?

This same bird had awoken Shadow Dancer every morning for the past week with low, gurgling croaks punctuated with alarming shrieks that shattered the quietness of the canyon. With a startling suddenness a harsh *kraaa* echoed as the hovering bird hesitated for an instant before diving downwards towards its scurrying prey in the stunted scrub and tufts of buffalo grass below. Squinting against the morning sun, Shadow Dancer followed his tormentor's flight over high rocky precipices and flat mesas.

Is this bird a messenger of some kind? What is it doing here every day?

His secret hiding place high up on the rock was almost undetectable from the canyon floor. The stonewall protected him from sight of other humans yet somehow it always failed to hide him from the raven's morning flight as it ascended with its vast wing-span only metres from his rocky sanctuary, chasing its shadow along the rimrock.

How does it know where I am hiding?

Several smaller birds attacked the rook in mid-flight, diving, pecking, and chirping which the great bird acknowledged with loud and raucous caws. Their shrill quarrelling attracted other birds to the chase.

Shadow Dancer was a seventeen-year-old member of the huge clan of Native Americans who, in the year 1198, inhabited the series of huge rock palaces that stretched throughout the water-less desert canyon now known as Chaco Canyon in northern New Mexico. He painfully recalled that only two moons previously he had survived the worst experience of his life when he was engulfed by the desert flash flood, almost drowning. Although his abrasions and cuts had healed, he slept poorly since his frightening experience. Much of his time had been spent brooding and pining to be with other members of his people instead of following the medicine man's instructions in his lonely cliff-side vigil.[5]

Shadow Dancer lived with his parents and his sisters in one of the rooms of the great house. His people had laid a massive network of roads, many of them thirty feet wide, across deserts and through canyons connecting other native communities with their own. Whenever he was bored he traced these roads from the mesa and wondered as to where they led. His people also built sophisticated

---

5. Situated in the high-altitude of the Colorado Plateau, numerous splendidly masoned stone buildings housed a civilization that had endured for seven centuries. It would take another seven centuries before any Europeans would come upon this mystical place in the American Southwest and give it its curious name.

observatories from which the elders could determine the cycles of sun and moon.[6]

The young apprentice had painfully learned how the Chaco wash could unexpectedly turn into a raging torrent from unseen storms miles away. These unpredictable floods left only a few stranded junipers and stinking piles of litter along the edges of the wash.

Most of the time the river was just a quiet trickle throughout the alluvial canyon floor, providing just enough water to sustain its inhabitants. Narrow runnels of water often spilled down from the canyon walls after a monsoon or from thawing snow. Shadow Dancer's people made numerous dams to conserve this water. Women also collected as much water as possible in ollas and other vessels which they cleverly designed from clay found in the canyon. This water was cleaner than the water in the wash, which was often filled with the refuse of flash floods. Large shallow depressions in the rocks atop the canyon on the smooth wind-polished rock preserved more water in large natural cisterns following the rains or the spring melts. These various methods of water storage paid off in times of drought for the Nation and they could withstand years with very little precipitation. Apart from the nearby wash and infrequent rains, there was otherwise little water in this harsh environment to sustain life. And yet Shadow Dancer's people mastered the art of water preservation, enabling them to survive and prosper in this dry climate for centuries.

But this morning Shadow Dancer was tired and cold. He awoke in a mood as black as the raven that was presently harassing him. He

---

6. In fact, their knowledge of astronomy was so advanced they were able to develop a perfect east-west axis along their great houses that perfectly captured the passages of the equinox sun. This would confound twentieth century archaeologists and spawn a subculture of ufologists who felt these findings were "evidence" of space alien involvement that endowed the Chacoans with their superior knowledge of celestial science.

raised himself onto his elbow to get a better look at the annoying bird of prey which he was convinced bode ill for his people. Unable to see it, he left his cave and clambered up a series of felled trunks, notched at intervals by stone axes to provide primitive footholds. The hardened leather-like skin of his bare feet enabled him to grip onto the notches in the rough-hewn log ladders.

He climbed to the flat-topped lava butte to obtain a better view of the valley below which held the great houses of his people. Sure enough, the raven soared over the largest of the magnificent great houses, shrieking and flapping excitedly for no apparent reason. A few minutes later it reappeared, carrying a dead mouse in its beak, which it released right over the mesa top where Shadow Dancer stood. The rodent spun in the air for a moment until it struck the ground with a soft thud a few feet away from the frightened young man. As he watched the bird fly away, he wondered whether this gesture held significance for his people.

What does this mean? What is going on?

Gazing down at his six toes on each foot, he wondered whether he should share his premonitions with Grey Elk, his mentor who lived in the Great House. Perhaps he would understand the meaning of the raven's behaviour. The medicine man had sent him up to this rocky ledge to acquire knowledge of the spirits in the canyon. Shadow Dancer felt he could no longer contain his feelings regarding the raven. Walking over to the dead mouse, he turned it over with his foot then kicked it over the edge of the cliff watching it tumble and spin as it plummeted to the rocks below.

Chapter 6

University of New Mexico

If we wonder often, the gift of knowledge will come.
~ Arapaho

The next morning Rachel and Rolly drove to the University of New Mexico campus for her interview with the Department of Anthropology. She found the Office of Contract Archaeology in the Maxwell Museum on the edge of a well-groomed campus with gardens and walkways surrounding a large pond. A central fountain spewed scattered rainbows in the morning sun. Large overhanging shade trees ringed the pond, mainly Siberian elm and honey locust trees. Sitting on a park bench near a one-hundred-year-old ponderosa pine, they watched numerous students rushing to classes carrying their backpacks crammed with text books and tablets. Several students wearing hoodies cut across the grassy park as a buzzer sounded, indicating the beginning of the next class.

"Rolly, don't you just love this place? I never imagined a place in New Mexico could look like this. I love how they maintain a desert motif in the construction of their buildings. Just look at the administration building over there. It looks like a large sandstone adobe," Rachel said as she took several pictures of the campus buildings.

"Absolutely. You know, I think I could live in this state. I wonder if they get much snow in the winter."

"Rolly, my interview is in about ten minutes in the OCA building over there. I'm feeling a little nervous. How do I look?"

Rachel twisted a strand of her hair around her finger compulsively as she looked into her compact mirror.

"Rachel, you're drop-dead gorgeous as always. You certainly don't look like a nerdy archaeologist to me."

"Aw, thank you sweetheart, but I hope I'm hired on the basis of my résumé. Why don't you look around some more and I'll meet you here in about an hour?"

"Okay, sounds good. I might just check out the Maxwell Museum while I'm here. I'd like to learn more about the Anasazi and see what kind of artifacts they have in there. I know you'll do well on your interview, Rachel, but I'll say a prayer for you anyways."

Boudreau kissed his wife and the two separated. Rachel took one last look at the notes she had made on Chaco Canyon and the Ancestral Puebloan people. Rolly strolled through the museum and bookstore, reading from several of the exhibits. He was amazed to learn that the Chaco Collection housed up to one million artifacts from over 120 sites within the canyon and the surrounding region.

He was intrigued by a display that featured an article from *Scientific American* that described an FBI sting operation in 2009 in which three hundred federal agents swooped in on twenty-three people indicted on charges of stealing archaeological artifacts from public lands and Indian reservations in the Southwest. A display case showed photographs of several of the relics taken during the operation in the town of Blanding, Utah.. A sign below the photograph read,

"The arrests were made following a two-year operation code named 'Cerberus Action', after the multi-headed dog in Greek mythology that guards the underworld. The case involves 256 Native American artifacts including woven baskets, pots, sandals, and an axe, which the Federal Bureau of Investigation values at $335,685. Defendants were charged with violations of the Archaeological Resources Protection Act (ARPA), which prohibits the excavation and sale of artifacts from public land or Indian land, and the Native American Graves Protection and Repatriation Act (NAGPRA), which requires items retrieved from burial sites and other sacred objects to be returned to Indian tribes."

Boudreau was shocked to read further that a sixty-year-old physician arrested in the raid committed suicide the next day. A week later, another of the raid's defendants, a man from Santa Fe, also committed suicide.

Shaking his head at the disastrous outcome of the Blanding raid, Boudreau was reminded of the guide's comments about pottery thieves and the "curse" that seemed to befall many of them. He checked his watch and decided it was time to meet Rachel. Two hours later, they met in front of the fountain again. Rachel was beaming.

"Rolly, I got the job!"

Boudreau embraced his wife affectionately and whispered, "I knew you would. Way to go, sweetheart."

"Well before you get carried away, I was the only person they interviewed so it wasn't that difficult. The administrator who interviewed me said they have had very few applications for this job and mine is the only one they took seriously. I wonder why?"

"Probably because you're the most qualified for the job. So where do we go from here?"

"The administrator suggested we grab some lunch and then afterwards we can meet up with the team of archaeologists that I'll be working with. She gave me a campus map and suggested we go to Mitchell Hall for lunch."

"Sounds good to me. I'm starved."

Walking through the OCA building, they passed by a small lunchroom with an old picnic table with peeling paint. A brief glimpse into the room revealed three employees wearing work boots and stained Tilley hats, eating together from a plate of sandwiches. An old ghetto blaster on the floor blared Santana music from the early seventies.

Reddish dust covered their clothes and an older male wore coveralls; the others wore faded blue jeans. Shovels and assorted tools lay scattered on the floor. Rachel and Boudreau could not ignore the faint hint of body odour as they walked past the room.

"Those guys must be construction workers doing renovations or something," Boudreau whispered in his wife's ear. "Pretty grubby looking buggers, I should say." Rachel frowned and shook her head at her husband's crassness.

After finding the cafeteria and eating lunch, they headed back to the OCA building and found the administrator. Rachel introduced her to Boudreau.

"Rachel, we're so glad you will be joining us here at the University of New Mexico. We haven't had Canadians work with us before but your résumé is outstanding and we're looking forward to having you on our team. I want you to meet some of the people with whom you will be working here at OCA. In fact, they're finishing their lunch break just down the hall."

"Uh, oh!" Boudreau muttered under his breath. Rachel rolled her eyes, smirking at her husband.

The administrator walked them down the hall to the room they had passed earlier. One of the workers was sleeping on the picnic bench while the other two were busy on their cell phones. The ghetto blaster had been silenced.

"Rachel Thompson and Rolly Boudreau, let me introduce you to one of our archaeology teams here at OCA. They have just returned from the field and need to be here in our offices to catch up on their paperwork this afternoon."

"It's a pleasure to meet you gentlemen, I'm sure," Rachel exclaimed. "I'm looking forward to working with you."

The administrator smiled. "Actually Rachel, one of these gentlemen is a woman."

"Oh, I'm so sorry!" Rachel blushed.

The shortest of the three removed her hat and let her long black hair fall. She had keen dark earnest eyes which peered through a pretty face powdered with thin orange dust.

"Hi. No problem. I'm Isabella Sandoval. I guess I do look like a man when we're doing field work."

The two women shook hands. It was obvious which woman had been working as a field anthropologist and which one was in administration and research. Sandoval's blunt fingernails were unpainted and uneven with rough calloused hands whereas Rachel's glossy French manicured nails were long and smooth. Both women smiled at the contrast.

"Rachel, you need to know that once you start working with us your husband might not recognize you anymore. Outdoor work in the desert will soon ruin your make-up and your nails so you'd better get used to it. Since you're an archaeologist too, I'm guessing I don't have to tell you anything new. Let me introduce you to the two men on our team, Dr. Jack Nesbitt and Dr. Stan Brown. Gentlemen, make the lady feel welcome. I'm no longer outnumbered so you'd better be nice," Isabella quipped.

Jack Nesbitt was a tall middle-aged male, bronzed, bearded, and covered with reddish dust. His penetrating hazel eyes peered through dusty bifocals. His cheeks were highlighted by a delicate arbour of capillaries beneath heavy grey eyebrows. Despite his rugged appearance he carried an air of academia. Removing his soiled Tilley hat, he bowed slightly in courtly fashion and announced,

"Pleased to meet your acquaintance, Rachel. We have all been wondering who the new member of our team might be. Yes, it appears Isabella will no longer be outnumbered. Stan, we will have to be on our best behaviour from now on. Rachel this is Dr. Stanley Brown, professor and head of our Field Division. Technically, he is our boss. Out in the field however, we tend to function as co-equals."

Stanley Brown was a younger, lanky, and somewhat gangling man with a thin bony face. Adolescent acne had left his face and forehead with several scars which pocked him with dozens of small facial craters that were now filled with the same dry orange-brown dust. His eyes were as blue as tempered steel. He wore a faded red shirt, worn denim jeans, and a matching denim jacket that was full of holes and covered with dust. Without removing his hat he shook Rachel's hand and said, "Howdy. Want a Coke?"

"No, thanks, we just finished lunch. This is my husband, Rolly Boudreau, by trade a bush pilot but also a self-taught historian who knows more about American natives of the Southwest than I do. He and I were married just last Christmas."

After informal greetings all around Rachel asked, "When do I start work?"

"Work?" uttered Isabella. "Not yet Rachel. You have to attend a few orientation sessions and some lectures on Southwestern archaeology first. In anticipation of your arrival we've set up a program for you that shouldn't take more than a week just to bring you up to speed on our current project. We also need your clothing and hat sizes as you will need coveralls and a hard hat when working on some of our projects. In the meantime, gentlemen, we have arranged dinner for this evening so we can get to know each other better. Do you like Mexican?"

They both smiled and nodded.

"Great. We'll meet you at six at El Patio de Albuquerque. It's just a few minutes from here. Oh, and bring your tablet. You may want to take a few notes. In the meantime gentlemen we have to clean up if we're going out for dinner."

After Rachel and Boudreau left, Isabella sat down on the picnic bench and frowned at her calloused hands and her uneven fingernails.

Chapter 7

Tail Feather

Raven is the messenger of the void.
~ Native proverb

Born with an extra toe on each foot, Shadow Dancer immediately caught the attention of Grey Elk who knew from his birth that he was special. In the Chaco culture of this era, divine powers were attributed to polydactyls like Shadow Dancer; several medicine men in the valley also had six toes. This unusual feature bestowed an exalted status by his people. Having an extra toe on each foot garnered respect for Shadow Dancer from the people of the Nation and he wondered whether he would also become a medicine man someday.[7]

Yet Shadow Dancer wasn't so sure he wanted to be a medicine man; he felt lonely and depressed ever since he had begun his spirit journey on the cliff. There were times when he felt imprisoned within his own body serving the shaman in this way; he became envious of the raven and its lofty freedom.

---

7. Eight hundred years later archaeologists puzzled over the frequency of this unusual anomaly in the skeletons of Chaco Canyon. Petroglyphs and pottery from the thirteenth century featuring six-toed creatures likewise intrigued anthropologists.

In spite of his elevated status, Shadow Dancer's world was confined to his alcove overlooking the great houses of the Nation. His people, formerly hunter-gatherers had settled in this canyon, growing corn, beans, and squash for the past two 250 years. The canyon and its sere landscape were the entirety of his world. He had heard of other people from the south who occasionally traded with his people bringing shells and turquoise pendants, but he had never met any of them. Only the stories passed down from his parents through oral tradition taught him that the world was bigger than the canyon itself. He had no idea that the continent of North America extended for thousands of miles in either direction.[8]

Sensing the greatness of his people, Shadow Dancer believed his canyon community was invulnerable. Crops flourished, food and water were abundant, massive buildings five stories high were built from quarried red stone rocks and huge wooden beams; it seemed as if life for the Nation in the canyon would go on forever unmolested, undisturbed. After all, was Chaco not the centre of a huge social, ritual, and economic system? People travelled hundreds of miles to trade and worship at Chaco centre and to admire the wonderful architecture of the great houses of his people.

Yet for some reason Shadow Dancer felt uneasy with this irritating rook. He was certain its portentous appearance was to foretell a great loss for the Nation.

What do you want from me, you wretched bird? What are you trying to tell me?

Shadow Dancer followed the elegant flight of this scavenger from the canyon rim.

---

8. Shadow Dancer was also unaware as to the enormity of his own community. The valley of Chaco Canyon contained the largest numbers of people in one site on the North American continent during his lifetime. At Chaco, as many as 30,000 souls dwelt in the comfort of the canyon and its outliers.

Immediately the bird flew directly toward his hidden refuge, at the last second wheeling around with a harsh whisper, its feathered wingtip delicately ticking several of the stones in the rock wall before disappearing in the canyon below. A large tail feather flicked off as the bird swerved gracefully away. The feather wafted briefly towards the stonewall until it found a space between the stones high above the ground, lodging itself as elegantly as if a human hand had placed it there.

Watching this aerial display from the rim, Shadow Dancer's mouth opened as if to scream at this assault against his sacred ledge.

Why is he doing this to me?

He tensed himself at this unusual activity and recited to himself incantations taught to him by the medicine man in an attempt to ward off the spell that he felt the ravens were casting upon him. Shadow Dancer knew that the medicine man watched the behaviour of ravens in order to tell the future. Perhaps he should be aware of this raven.

Soon other ravens rode on upward drafts to more lofty ascents, climbing gradually on invisible columns of air, circling continuously, scarcely striking a wing-beat as they flew. They soared over rocky precipices, rusty crags, and rounded scarps, gliding gradually down to the uneven desert floor. Several landed on the mesa top, strutting with their mouths open, jerking their heads awkwardly towards their prey which lay scattered everywhere.

After spending several hours perched on a rounded hump of sandstone observing the ravens, Shadow Dancer finally decided to climb down to the great house and consult Grey Elk regarding the significance of the strange bird's behaviour.

Surely he will know.

Unexpectedly, one of the ravens swooped down like a black arrow near his head and then pulled up, soaring aloft with unearthly shrieks. The bird immediately became lost in the late afternoon light as it reflected off the broken sandstone surface of the Chaco cliffs. Shadow Dancer quietly uttered a curse against the obnoxious bird. In the distance, mesas and buttes endlessly stretched across the open plain, each paler than the last one, until they faded into a distant dull haze.

Chapter 8

Dinner at El Patio de Albuquerque

Listen, or your tongue will make you deaf.
~ Tribe Unknown

That evening they met at the El Patio de Albuquerque, a charming little restaurant with yellow clapboard sidings and a tall blue picket fence surrounding a small outdoor patio. Several large terracotta pots lined the yard. Inside the wooden ceilings and floors gave the restaurant a rustic appearance. A large floor-to-ceiling adobe oven sat in one corner with clumps of dried green and red peppers hanging from ceiling beams. A table near the oven was set for five and when Rolly and Rachel arrived, the three archaeologists were already into their second round of Coronas. A septuagenarian with a handlebar moustache sat at the next table with a woman half his age wearing tight blue jeans and a large set of turquoise and silver lever-back earrings. A tattoo of a coiling snake on her arm stretched upwards, disappearing through the sleeve of her blouse towards her ample breasts. Country music blared in the background with a Waylon Jennings song.

"Oh dear, we're late. We're so sorry!" Rachel said pulling up a chair.

"Oh no, we always get a head start when the university is paying for it. You're right on time," said Isabella. "What would you like to drink?"

Isabella looked much different with lipstick and make-up and without her dust-covered blue jeans and work boots. She had applied a clean looking set of pink acrylic fingernails which she proudly held up for Rachel to see.

"Nice. I'm impressed. Where did you find the time?" Rachel smiled at the transformation.

"In this job you learn to do these things quickly, girl. But after a day of digging your nails will be destroyed, too," Isabella sighed.

"So we had a few things to discuss regarding our current project and we felt a short meeting before your arrival might kill two birds with one stone. we've finished our discussion and now we want to focus on our newest member and get to know you and your husband." Jack Nesbitt raised his beer as if to toast the two Canadians as the waitress arrived at their table with menus.

After ordering beer and reviewing the menu, Rachel decided to order a chicken fajita. She was curious as to the type of work she would be doing with this interesting group. However, she felt it might be inappropriate to ask too many questions at first. She decided just to wait for an opening which came sooner than she anticipated.

"What would you like to know about our current project, Rachel?" Nesbitt inquired. "You must have lots of questions I'm sure."

"Yes, I do, but why don't you tell me what the project is all about and where do you see me fitting in?"

"Certainly. Well, we're working in the Chaco Canyon area and at an outlier called Pueblo Pintado. We are searching for clues that might help explain the sudden and mysterious disappearance of the people from the area around the year 1200 CE. Of course we know that they really didn't disappear. They likely just migrated to different areas such as Bandelier and other sites along the Rio Grande area. The modern day Pueblo Indians such as the Hopi and the Acoma believe they are the direct descendants of the Anasazi. Only they prefer to use the term *Ancestral Pueblo* people which is a bit of a mouthful," Nesbitt explained.

"Yes we still call them *Anasazi* so I guess we're not that politically correct. Besides, it would be impossible to change all the textbooks after so many years of research on them," Isabella added.

Rachel and Rolly nodded, being familiar with this controversy after exploring the ruins at Bandelier only a few days earlier.

"Is there anything specific you're looking for to explain why they left the Chaco area?" Rachel asked.

"For example, we've heard that the common explanation is that a prolonged drought drove them away when they were forced to look for water."

"Nah!" Jack Nesbitt erupted. "We know from the growth patterns of tree rings from that era that they managed to survive years of drought. Besides, if the drought was so bad, how would they manage to travel hundreds of miles in the desert to escape and look for water? They would all be dead and that would have been the end of it! No, the drought theory is too simplistic. If these people could build five-storey great houses out of thousands of spruce timbers and sandstone blocks, they had to be smart enough to store enough water for a prolonged drought. They were experts at building dams and reservoirs to capture run-off that would last years. There's even evidence that a huge dam at the western end of the canyon may have made the whole canyon a fertile plain for a century. No, I think there has to be another explanation."

"Some archaeologists believe that internecine warfare caused them to flee," Isabella added. "However, I agree with Jack. There have been several studies that have cast doubt on the drought theory as the main cause for Anasazi migration from the central San Juan Basin. It's a convenient way for the park docents to give tourists a quick answer, but it's more complicated than that, I'm afraid."

Stan Brown who had remained silent on this discussion pursed his lips and inhaled at the same time, a habit that showed itself whenever he became upset or engaged in academic discussions in which he disagreed.

"I don't know. Drought answers a lot of questions and the tree rings from that era clearly demonstrate a prolonged thirty-year drought, which I think would finish off any civilization, so I guess we agree to disagree on that subject. I believe people can only live where there's water," Brown added.

"Could they have ever suffered from a disease? Some kind of epidemic say?" Boudreau joined the discussion. He was thinking of the smallpox epidemics of the past that had decimated so many societies. He was also acutely aware of his own encounter with that devastating disease just a year earlier.

"Well, yes, that's an idea that I have often considered and it remains a possibility but again we have no evidence of such. If it did happen then oral tradition has kept it a secret over the centuries. Besides, most of the really lethal diseases were still in Europe and beyond. There was no measles or smallpox in North America. There was probably no influenza virus either until the Spaniards arrived. I should say, however, that evidence of tuberculosis has been discovered in the bones of many skeletons prior to Columbus' time.

"In the Americas, people had been totally isolated from those diseases for ten thousand years before Columbus' voyage, meaning that they didn't have any of the defences that had evolved to deal with them. Certainly after Columbus, millions of North American natives dropped like flies from all the European illnesses, especially smallpox. After 1519, millions died within a few decades, largely due to the Spanish Conquest. Ongoing epidemics devastated the Americas, wiping out at least half of all North American Indian tribes, all the way up to Alaska over the next few centuries. Simply put, before the Europeans arrived there was probably very little disease among the Ancestral Pueblos," Nesbitt explained.

"So there's a diagnostic dilemma for you. I should add that our pilot friend here is quite astute to consider the possibility of a disease of some kind causing the Anasazi society to disintegrate. After all, in Europe the entire feudal system came to an end in the fourteenth century thanks to the bubonic plague. So whatever that disease could be remains a mystery with no Europeans here to infect people. Keep in mind that at the time of the Anasazi, no animals such as horses or mules existed. Nor were there tumbleweeds, starlings, pheasants, or house sparrows either, for they had not yet been introduced to the continent. Also many horrific European diseases didn't arrive until the sixteenth century with the Spanish conquistadors. As simple as life was for the Chacoan Nation, it was Edenic with few diseases and no enemies," Nesbitt added.

"In fact at Chaco, thousands of people lived in the comfort of the canyon. Their only predator was the searing desert sun that could dehydrate and kill an unprepared man within less than a day in the heat of Chaco's dry summer," Stan Brown added.

Isabella interjected, "Perhaps we should have explained to Rachel during our introductions this afternoon that Jack Nesbitt is a forensic pathologist and Stan and I are anthropologists. Stan is trained in dendrochronolgy, the study of establishing dates in the past with tree-ring growths. My field of expertise includes the baskets and pottery of the Anasazi. So I'm basically a ceramics researcher and analyst. Each pre-Columbian tribal group made their own distinctive types of pots and jars and many books have been written about each type. Every now and then we find another pot, or at least the broken shards, which we can re-assemble to get an idea of when it was made and who made it."

Rachel nodded and turned to Jack Nesbitt and asked, "After hearing your discussion on diseases, I am not surprised that you're a medical doctor. So, you trained as a pathologist and now you're doing desert archaeology?"

"Actually, I began my career as a family physician," Nesbitt said hastily pouring his beer into a large glass to ensure a full foamy head which he slowly and quietly slurped.

"What made you give up family practice?" Rachel was intrigued.

"Well, I got tired of patients phoning me in the middle of the night to tell me they couldn't sleep!"

"People did that?" Rachel asked wrinkling her brow.

"Yep. Plus just being on call in a small town never gives you much time for family life, so I decided to study pathology where my 'patients' couldn't phone me or ask silly questions about stuff they read on the internet. But until that point I did everything that you would expect of a small town family doctor. You know, babies, scabies, and rabies. Every day it was either guts, butts, or cuts." Nesbitt chuckled to himself. Everyone burst out laughing at his off-the-wall humour.

"Do you miss being a family physician?" Rachel asked.

"Nah, this stuff is way more interesting. Digging around in the desert in 105 degree Fahrenheit temperatures, inhaling dust and spores while trying to figure out what happened to an entire ancient civilization over eight hundred years ago is way more fun."

"Really?" Rachel asked.

"Yes, but first allow me to share some of my own views regarding the field of archaeology. It's what I call *Fuzzy Science*. Archaeology is to real science as psychiatry is to real medicine. An archaeologist will interpret the culture from a prehistoric site as easily as a shrink will interpret your dream. It's all very subjective and archaeologists will develop great theories and write all sorts of books about a small discovery that can be interpreted in a variety of ways. Intense rivalries have been generated in the past century over the theories that have been spawned by investigations done in the canyon. For example, archaeologists have been studying Chaco Canyon for well over a hundred years. Yet they still differ in their views as to how the people lived, how they were able to build such a robust community in such an austere environment, and why they left without leaving a forwarding address.

"I mean, you could hardly find a more inhospitable place to sustain a large number of people who were able to support themselves and build such a unique civilization. Never mind the mystery of what made them leave; think of the mystery of how they survived and built such remarkable structures over several centuries." Nesbitt paused to drink his ale.

"But getting back to the Fuzzy Science. There are as many guesses as there are structures in the canyon as to how many people actually lived there. According to various experts in the field, it's been estimated that as few as two thousand to over thirty thousand people made their homes in Chaco Canyon. It seems the more you learn about Chaco, the less you really know, you know?"

Dr. Nesbitt reminded Rachel of her colleague back in Canada, Dr. Wojiech Jaworski, whose knowledge of medical history was vast. She enjoyed the seminar-like atmosphere that this collegial group created and she found the various theories fascinating.

"The problem with archaeology", Nesbitt continued, "is that it is a science of generalization. An archaeologist will often dig a site and then extrapolate his findings into what he interprets as a description of that culture. Archaeologists seldom take into consideration what the abnormal could have been. Ignoring catastrophes such as plagues, warfare, and cannibalism they dwell on the normative and explain the collapse of the civilization by a gradual means such as prolonged drought or repeated crop failures.

"In other words they don't think outside the box to consider the darker side of human nature. For example, there's lots of evidence of cannibalism at numerous sites in the Southwest yet little academic research has been done on this activity which might explain why an entire civilization disappeared. They believe that most systems remain stable over time leaving out the fact that history is replete with sudden acts of violence and war. Just consider the Holocaust, engineered and managed by what had been considered a 'sophisticated culture' in Germany prior to the Second World War. If we have seen cultures suddenly fall into depravity in our own day and age, why not back then? Just ask yourselves, were there no sociopaths back then? No megalomaniacs such as Hitler or Stalin? No, I think there has to be a paradigm shift in archaeological thinking and we need to look for other causes," Nesbitt explained.

"Okay, but getting back to the disease theory, what about something as simple as the flu? After all it killed millions a hundred years ago, right?" Rachel asked.

"Well, it's doubtful that influenza was even here prior to the Spanish Conquest of the Americas. Influenza is believed to have originally been an avian disease, which then spread to swine. Without domesticated animals, there was probably no influenza in the New World before contact with Europeans. Influenza could have devastated aboriginal populations early on but we don't have any records which tell us one way or the other," Nesbitt stated.

After a long pause Nesbitt asked rhetorically, "So if influenza has been ruled out where does that leave us? If there was some kind of an epidemic before Columbus arrived, what caused it?"

"I don't know, Jack, you're the doctor. Remember, 'rabies, scabies, and babies!'" Isabella quipped. Rachel smiled at the camaraderie her new associates displayed.

"Could it have been a disease that we don't see anymore, just because no one lives there anymore for it to be contagious?" Rachel asked.

"Good question. Very few people live in the Four Corners nowadays, but in the eleventh and twelfth centuries there were likely as many as thirty thousand Anasazi living in just the Chaco area itself. Many more lived in dozens of outlier settlements and at Mesa Verde, 140 miles away. So with that many people, yes, an epidemic could have devastating consequences. All we know is that they mysteriously just disappeared around the year 1200. It was as if the vanished inhabitants just walked away only a few hours before, leaving everything in place. Archaeologists have discovered granaries littered with seven-hundred-year old, perfectly preserved corncobs. Everything they left in their homes and kivas remained intact for centuries, perfectly preserved in the dryness of the desert air. So something sudden and drastic had to have happened to these people. That's why a prolonged drought just doesn't cut it with me," Nesbitt said, pausing to refill his beer mug.

"So, we reach a dead end in our knowledge about these people, and what led to their forced and, should I add, sudden abandonment of the hundreds of ancestral sites. This is the grand mystery that all the cultural anthropologists and amateur historians write about," Nesbitt added.

"Yeah. This is an interesting medical question and unless there was a New World virus around which we don't know about, then the whole infectious disease theory is down the drain, too. Which is why I stick to the drought theory," Stan Brown added.

"But I have a friend who lives at Acoma who told me that there are cases of bubonic plague cropping up every year in the Southwest," Boudreau asked. "Could the Anasazi have died from the plague?"

"Nope. There was no plague in the New World back then. It only arrived in the Southwest in the last century. The disease likely hitched a ride to America from flea-infested rats, which had boarded steamships in Asia. They likely docked in San Francisco where the disease spread, making its way to New Mexico, infecting mainly rodents, prairie dogs, chipmunks, and squirrels. Since then, it seems every year some poor trapper or hunter gets infected. Fortunately we can now treat the plague with antibiotics if it's caught early enough. But plague is definitely an Old World disease that only arrived to North America in recent times," Nesbitt explained.

"Enough talk of death and disease. Let's order. I'm starved." Isabella waved her menu at a passing waitress who came to their table. Everyone placed their order and resumed the discussion on the Chaco Canyon mystery. A waitress brought a tray with water and tortilla chips with three different flavoured salsas to the table.

"The fact is, we just don't have enough information on these people even with all the digging and research that's been done in the past forty years or so. In the 1960s, only a handful of archaeological sites in all of New Mexico existed, whereas today there are over thirty thousand and likely thousands more undiscovered. Hundreds of thousands of artifacts have been discovered at these sites in the past seventy-five years, from minute flakes to large intact ollas and cooking pots. And every artifact at every ancient site has its own story, ghosts from the past," Stan Brown added.

"That's incredible. How did they manage to survey so many sites?" Rachel asked. "Well, it took over fifty years of fieldwork to find this many. Keep in mind that New Mexico is the fifth largest state in the union with hundreds of canyons and thousands of acres of forests where the Anasazi could build settlements. Most of these were small scattered pueblos of a dozen rooms or so, hardly worth mentioning, but there are several pretty impressive sites, too, Chaco being one of the largest," Nesbitt added.

"But we get paid to delve into the tantalizing mysteries of the past. How cool is that, Rachel?" Isabella raised her palm for a high five.

Stan Brown, ignoring her exclamation carried on with his theory. "There's been so much digging since then, you'd think we would have discovered by now what caused this civilization to mysteriously come to an end in the Chaco valley. But it's not just Chaco and its outliers that baffles researchers. Many other sites like Mesa Verde and Canyon de Chelly likewise. just came to a grinding halt. That's why a severe and extensive pronged drought offers the best explanation."

"Just how long was the drought?" Rachel asked.

"It depends on which drought you're talking about. There was one from 1130 to 1180 and another lasting about twenty-three years from 1276 until 1299. This last one has been referred to as the *Great North American Drought.*"

"How would they know all this so precisely?" Boudreau asked.

"Dendrochronology. Also called tree-ring dating, The size of the rings tell us how much moisture the trees were exposed to in any given year. It's a precise method with each tree having the same growth ring for any given year," Stan Brown explained.

"But how far back can scientists go with this method of dating?" Boudreau asked. "Well, there are 1600-year-old Angel Oak trees in South Carolina. In California, the bristlecone pines have been in existence for over four thousand years. This has provided scientists with a record of wet and dry seasons for centuries, allowing for an extremely accurate system of dating. The Anasazi helped us tremendously by building their great houses with a quarter million trees. You can imagine how much that tells us about their construction activities over the years. Each tree can be dated according to its growth rings, when it was cut down for a roof beam, and how long it has been supporting the great houses. Furthermore, tree-ring dating is accurate to the exact year whereas carbon 14 dating can be out by fifty to one hundred years," Brown added.

"While Stan is right about an extensive drought, it appears that the Anasazi had already disappeared from the Chaco settlement as well as many other places before the last drought set in. Archaeologists don't always agree on the exact causes leading up to the Chacoan decline. While drought was prevalent in the twelfth century, there may have been other factors at work such as religious upheaval, internal political conflict, or even warfare, all of which may have combined to exacerbate the effects of the drought. Few societies collapse because of only one thing going wrong," Nesbitt pronounced, quaffing his beer.

"So could they have left for religious reasons?" Rachel asked.

"Yes, they were likely very religious with their worship of kachina dolls and the numerous kivas where we think they held their religious ceremonies. It's possible they developed differences of opinion as their religious views developed, sort of like the conflicts in Europe during the Reformation or with the Spanish Inquisition. If sophisticated European religious groups could kill each other over their differing theological points of view, then it is entirely possible that the different Anasazi groups could fight over how many kachinas could dance on the head of a pin," Isabella explained.

"But wouldn't one sect predominate leaving the others to go elsewhere?" Rachel asked.

Isabella shook her head and threw up her hands. "We just don't know without a written record. But never underestimate the ability of man to destroy his own kind."

"Why would they build a huge city in the desert in the first place?" Boudreau asked. "Well, Los Angeles and Phoenix were built in the desert totally dependent on the scarce water available to them at the time. People don't always accept what the environment tells them. I mean, you folks are from Canada and are familiar with the extremes of cold, and yet hundreds of Indian and Inuit groups have lived there for centuries under austere conditions," Isabella said.

"Besides, as I said, there is good evidence that the canyon was once occupied by a reservoir which irrigated their farmland and provided drinking water possibly for centuries," Nesbitt added.

"Archaeological evidence suggests that the Chacoans completed a dam with masonry sometime in the early eleventh century. They also built an accompanying reservoir lined with stones that was still visible until 1920. The dam helped raise the water table in the canyon, aiding Chacoan farming and this may explain how so many survived in such an arid desert environment."

The waitress brought a tray with fajitas, a green chili-slathered cheeseburger, blue corn enchiladas, and sopapillas — crispy Mexican flatbread deep-fried to a golden brown, served with honey. Rachel could not believe the variety of New Mexican cuisine; it seemed everyone had ordered something different this evening. Another pitcher of Dos Equis beer appeared on the table.

"While this is all fascinating, our dinner just arrived," interrupted Isabella. "I think our guests would like a break from all this history."

"Oh no! This has been most interesting and if I am going to be working with you in Chaco Canyon I need to know all these theories. And I definitely want to learn more about the ancient pottery that you are studying. Besides, Rolly is just as interested in the history of American natives as I am."

"Why is that, Rolly?" asked Isabella turning to him.

"Probably because I'm part Indian myself and also because I came down here when I was in university many years ago. In fact, I hope to connect with a friend from the Acoma Pueblo while I'm down here."

"Well, you'll definitely have to check out the pottery they make there. Several families have been producing some spectacular pots and jars since the last century. We believe they acquired some of their designs and skills from their ancestors, the same Anasazi that we are researching. One of the frequent design motifs is the parrot which must go back centuries to when the birds were brought here as trade items from Meso- American tribes."

"I will definitely look into that if I get there."

Nesbitt became aware that he may have pontificated too much on his own theories and felt he should lighten up a little. Turning to Rachel he asked her, "Know any good archaeologist jokes?"

"Not really. Why? I suppose you're going to tell me one?" Rachel asked.

"What did Richard III say when a planning proposal was submitted for building a parking lot?"

"I don't know, Dr. Nesbitt. What did he say?" Rachel smirked.

"Over my dead body!" Everyone groaned except Nesbitt.

"Did you hear the archaeologists from the University of New Mexico had a big party at one of their sites near Chaco Canyon? They were searching for a missing lower limb. It was quite the shindig," Nesbitt deadpanned while the rest groaned.

"Well, maybe I do have one for you, Dr. Nesbitt," Rachel said

"Let's hear it."

"Why do females make the best archaeologists?"

"I don't know. Why?"

"Because they absolutely love digging up everything that has happened in the past." Isabella burst out laughing. "I haven't heard that one before."

"Why is it you never laugh at my jokes Isabella?" Nesbitt asked.

"Because I've heard them all before! But I've got one more for you Jack," Isabella smiled. "Why did the archaeologist go bankrupt?"

"I dunno, why did the archaeologist go bankrupt?"

"Because his career was in ruins!" Isabella gave another high five to Rachel who shook her head at the adolescent humour of her new academic associates. Stan Brown remained silent without cracking a smile.

After several hours of eating, drinking and discussing the various theories behind the Chaco Canyon civilization with a few more jokes thrown in, the group left the restaurant in good spirits. As they drove to their hotel Rachel could barely contain herself.

"Boy, aren't they an interesting group, Rolly? I think I'm going to enjoy working with these people."

"Yes, a bright bunch of nerds for sure, but their jokes are pretty bad. It's interesting that after years of study on the subject even they can't seem to agree on what caused the collapse of the Chacoans. Maybe you might find something that could shed more light on the subject while we're down here."

"I doubt it. There have been thousands of digs in the area dating back to the 1890s and everything still remains a mystery. No, I'm afraid I have a lot to learn Rolly. They sure don't waste any time here though. Isabella told me that I start classes tomorrow morning with a bunch of undergrads. As humbling as that sounds, I'm looking forward to it."

"Great. While you're studying here, I'm going to fly home and do some work. I have a few contracts flying for Parks Canada which works out well as there's not much for me to do here. You're off to a great start and I think you're gonna be fine with this group Rachel. I'll text you before I return, but it might be two or three weeks," Boudreau said.

Rachel yawned and soon fell asleep in her hotel room while reading the notes she had made from the evening's discussion. Boudreau leaned over to close her laptop, kissing her goodnight. He knew he was going to miss her a lot during the next two weeks.

Chapter 9

Grey Elk

Everything on the earth has a purpose, every disease
an herb to cure it, and every person a mission.
This is the Indian theory of existence.
~ Mourning Dove Salish

Shadow Dancer knew he had to speak to the medicine man imme-diately regarding the raven. Although he respected the medicine man for his knowledge, he was seldom impressed with his answers, always mystified with the long spiritual explanations he was given. Whenever he felt he was about to learn something of great signifi-cance from the medicine man he ended up disappointed. Whereas he hoped for something that would explain everything, he was invariably left with even more questions than answers. And yet Grey Elk had shared several of his visions with Shadow Dancer who found them fascinating.

It didn't take long for the agile adolescent to descend the long cavernous passage along the cliff to the canyon floor. He ran to the great house in search of Grey Elk. Stumbling through one of the wooden door frames, he encountered several women in one of the outside rooms weaving baskets. In another room, women ground corn maize with their *manos* and *metatae,* stones that crushed the kernels to a fine powder that filled the air in the room, covering their arms with a yellowish-grey dust. In fact, the air was hazy from the same yellow powder which covered the walls and the ladders leading up to the next floor. While they were grinding, a man sat at the door playing a six-holed flute made from box elder wood; the women moved their stones, keeping time with the music, singing together.

Another large room contained potters who skilfully coiled large ollas and jars from the reddish clay taken from the wash. Many of their cleverly designed jars and pots would survive eons in the dryness of the desert only to reappear undisturbed in the nineteenth century when pot hunters and collectors scavenged the ancient settlement for treasures like these.

A young woman named Spotted Deer carefully painted intricate zigzag designs on a series of coiled pots with a black dye obtained from boiling wild onions before they were fired. Her pottery was made by coiling thick ropes of clay and piling them on top of each other in such a way as to create large ollas and bowls.[9] Spotted Deer was one of the better artists and had painted hundreds of thin-walled pots with angular fine-line geometric designs with parrots, deer, and rainbow bands. She made bowls, seed jars, effigy pots, and drinking pots which her people used for storage, drinking, eating, and ceremonial purposes. Her work was considered so valuable that much of her pottery was traded to other clans and Anasazi communities over an area of several thousand square miles. Lately she had been

---

9. This clever method precluded the arrival of the potter's wheel in the Southwest by several centuries.

experimenting by adding red ochre to some of her bowls but she hadn't completely mastered the technique at this point.[10]

Spotted Deer looked up at Shadow Dancer as he raced from room to room searching for the medicine man. She quietly arose and left the other women in the ceramics room to follow him as he searched the great house. When he finally encountered Grey Elk, the medicine man was disturbed to see his young protégé away from his ledge. Spotted Deer quietly stepped behind the wall in the next room to listen. She wiped the wet clay and black stain from her lithe fingers on her apron which was made from yucca fibres.

Grey Elk was a short barrel-chested shaman who wore a necklace of animal bones and a leather medicine pouch, which smelled of desert herbs. A pair of recently snared rabbits hung bleeding from his belt, which looped under his slight overhanging paunch. Thick blue veins on his forearms protruded like a cluster of knobby worms. Short stubby bloodstained fingers emerged from thickened and gnarled knuckles, grasping a grey quartzite knife. Red sandstone dust clung to the sinuous fissures of his wrinkled cheeks giving his face the appearance of a cracked gourd. His thin mouth was as straight and featureless as if a hatchet had split his face sideways; his stained teeth were brown from chewing on cacao that visitors from the south had brought to the Nation. A high peaked forehead and a strong nose gave Grey Elk a look of authority. His long grey hair hung in thin wisps to his shoulders with small pieces of dried snake grass projecting from various angles as if he had just awoken. A large scarlet macaw feather arose from the back of his scalp. He wore a cape made from turkey feathers, a common accoutrement for shamans. He smelled of sweat and wood smoke and dead rabbits.

---

10. Yet eight hundred years later her reddish tinted corrugated ware with her intact fingerprints on the dried clay became known as *Anasazi polychrome*. A pot of this type currently commands tens of thousands of dollars for collectors and museums.

His gaze was penetrating with dark transfixing eyes and Shadow Dancer immediately felt uncomfortable.

"Why have you left your sacred ledge, Shadow Dancer? You were to stay there until I summoned you," he said gruffly.

"I'm afraid of the signs the raven has left. I fear he is a bad omen for the Nation," Shadow Dancer responded nervously.

"What signs?" Grey Elk huffed. The young man went on to explain the strange behaviour of the bird with the mouse and his own premonitions.

"Why, this valley has many ravens and they all make a loud noise in the morning.

They often wake me up early, too. Why do you think this one is so special Shadow Dancer?"

As Shadow Dancer proceeded to describe the unusual bird and its antics, the old sage listened with increasing interest. His high forehead furrowed with consternation at hearing the young man's anxious tale.

"Perhaps you were having a vision of some kind and you were not even aware of it," he said. Grey Elk knew this was not the time to scold him. Under his rough exterior, Grey Elk was sensitive to ordinary lives that, beneath their surface, held a wisdom that might rise to shine at some future moment. He tried not to be judgmental. He admired his young apprentice in such a way now and felt he was destined for great things but he also knew that he needed a word of explanation.

"My son, you must know that the raven is the most honoured among birds and animals to the shamans because of his ability at shape-shifting. They bring clarity to the things that we cannot understand. For you see, the great mysteries of life are enfolded within the wings of the raven, only to be revealed to those who are ready for such enlightenment. You must learn from observing and not allow yourself to be distracted."

Grey Elk felt that perhaps Shadow Dancer could be experiencing a revelation of this type from his spirit chamber high up on the cliff. After all, ravens seldom flew alone.

"My son, you must return to your ledge and listen to the spirits if you think they are trying to tell you something. It takes patience and solitude to hear what the *Master of Time* is saying to you. But do not come back until your vision is complete. Do not allow yourself to be frightened when you should be listening. Watch the raven and listen to what he is trying to tell you instead of running away. Don't let his cries upset you. If you believe this bird is a messenger then you must pay heed. When you learn of his message then you must return and tell me. Now go."

Shadow Dancer quietly bowed before the medicine man who gave him a pouch filled with cacao beans and piñon nuts. He returned to his small isolated chamber in the cliff clambering up the precarious rocky stairway behind the great house. He felt dejected that he had displeased the old man. Meanwhile, Spotted Deer had been secretly listening to the entire conversation from behind the wall. She was fascinated by the story that Shadow Dancer related to the shaman about the raven and his dark premonitions. She made a decision that would change the course of Shadow Dancer's life.

Chapter 10

Walter Etcitty

If a man is as wise as a serpent,
he can afford to be as harmless as a dove.
~ Cheyenne

Following a week of orientation which involved attending lectures in the Department of Anthropology at the University of New Mexico, Rachel was hooked on the subject of pre-Columbian indigenous people of the Southwest. She was excited and more than ready to begin work for the Office of Contract Archaeology. She joined her project group in the OCA building the following Monday where she donned her working gear and climbed into a white Chevy Suburban with her colleagues. Stan Brown was behind the wheel with Jack Nesbitt in the passenger seat. She sat in the back with Isabella Sandoval. She wondered whether there was sexism with the seating arrangements with men in the front and women in the back. However, she quickly dismissed this concern when she recalled how tall both men were.

Isabella handed her a briefing package regarding their project which she opened and immediately read. She could barely contain herself knowing they were headed to one of the greatest archaeological sites in America.

"I have a million questions but I suspect many of them will be answered by the end of the day," she quietly said.

"Don't worry Rachel. We have a million questions too. That's the nature of our work," Nesbitt reassured her. "When you stop asking questions, it's time to get a new job. By the way, we're pulling over at Grants for breakfast where we'll pick up one of our field workers. His name is Walter Etcitty and he lives in Window Rock. He hitched a ride early this morning to Grants and should be waiting for us at the restaurant. Like many of the employees at the Chaco Canyon Centre, he is a full blooded Navajo Indian. He's a quiet and conscientious worker and does most of the heavy lifting at our work sites. He's been assigned to our team for the next month by the OCA. I think you'll like him but don't expect to get too much conversation from him. He's rather soft-spoken and seldom looks you straight in the eye but he listens carefully to everything you say."

"Why do you suppose he is like that?" Rachel asked,

"Dunno. I guess he's shy and we probably intimidate him with all our archaeology discussions. Besides, Navajo people tend to be like that. To many people eye contact is considered polite and important, but among Navajos it is considered the opposite. From childhood they are taught not to talk too much, be loud, or be forward with strangers.

That kind of behaviour is considered impolite or showing off. If you are speaking to a Navajo they will often look down and away, even though you have their full attention."

"Hm, he sounds like an interesting character," Rachel said.

"Although Walter has a few university courses behind him he's not an academic but don't let that fool you. He has a mind like a trap with an excellent memory and a dry sense of humour. He once got a cheque from the payroll department at the university payable to 'Walter Ethnicity' which many of us thought was hilarious. When we asked him how he felt he just said, 'Stupid white people. They should know my ethnicity is Navajo.' And then he cashed the cheque anyways without bothering to correct them. As far as I know he is still getting 'Ethnicity cheques.'"

Cupping her hand over her mouth Rachel chuckled and said, "That's too funny!"

"He's also very sensitive about any racial comments and he expects to be treated as an equal. Many of our colleagues seem incapable of doing that so I'm giving you a heads- up Rachel. But I recall your husband at the restaurant last week saying he was part Indian so I'm sure you will have no difficulty relating to him."

"Thanks for telling me this in advance. Yes, I know I will find him interesting and I also know Rolly would relate well with him too if he were here. I'm already looking forward to meeting him."

After driving for an hour and a half the Suburban passed Mount Taylor on the right and pulled off the I-40 at Grants, driving onto the parking lot at Denny's. Rachel took several pictures of the snow-capped peak. Walter Etcitty was waiting for the team inside, drinking coffee in a booth.

"Ya' at'eeh. Have a seat."

Walter Etcitty was a tall laconic Navajo with shiny black hair streaming back into a long pony tail with slight greying at the temples. He wore a black cowboy hat with a broad brim and a high crown. A hat band glowed softly with several sterling silver conchos, hammered discs embedded with polished turquoise ovals. Like many Navajos, he had high cheekbones with a narrow straight nose, heavy eyebrows, and a wide mouth. He was broad shouldered and appeared fit although prominent crow's feet and weathered skin suggested he was likely in his late forties. A small jagged scar indented his right eyebrow. His penetrating almond-brown eyes were fixed straight ahead during much of the breakfast conversation. The entirety of his right index fingernail had turned a dark purple from a recent injury.

He moved his knapsack from the bench to the floor to make room for the rest of the team in the booth, stood up and shook hands with everyone. Rachel could not help but notice the faint hint of Brute cologne, something that her husband often used.

Following brief introductions, everyone crowded into the booth where coffee was served and their orders were taken. Rachel chose to sit next to Walter who said nothing. She wondered if Walter felt uncomfortable in the presence of so many educated white people or if he was just shy. After several minutes of silence she initiated the conversation with a simple but awkward statement.

"Well, this is the first time I have ever met a Navajo person."

After a brief pause and to everyone's surprise, Walter looked straight ahead holding his coffee and answered, "Well, this is the first time I have ever met a Canadian person. By the way you may call me an Indian instead of a person. It sounds friendlier, don't you think?"

Rachel, caught by surprise, was at a loss for words. "Um. Yes, I suppose so but not where I come from."

"Why not? You have Indians in Canada don't you?" Walter frowned briefly sipping his coffee, still staring straight ahead.

"Well yes, we do. Lots in fact. My husband's mother was Indian but we don't call them that. You see our indigenous people prefer to be known as *First Nations* and they consider the term *Indian* to be derogatory."

"Derogatory! That's strange. Why is that?" Walter continued to focus straight ahead, his jaw tightening.

At this point breakfast arrived and a pause in the conversation took place. Remaining silent, the three other researchers looked at each other with raised eyebrows wondering how Rachel was going to get out of this situation. They had never seen Walter in such an animated conversation before and Isabella quietly prayed that the issue of race would not blow up in Rachel's face. Rachel quickly resumed the conversation over breakfast.

"You see in our country, the Indians, as you call them, consider the term *Indian* as derogatory because that's the word the Europeans used to describe the native people they met in the New World. Recall that Columbus thought he was in Asia when he arrived on the shores of whatever Caribbean island he discovered. Our country has lots of immigrants from India and they are the true *Indians*, not the indigenous people that were living on the continent for centuries before Columbus. They were here first so they refer to themselves as *First Nations*. Since that's how they prefer to be addressed, most Canadians are sensitive to this and we avoid using the old term *Indian*. In fact, we don't even talk about *Indian summer* anymore. I know things are different down here. So as a Navajo does that make any sense to you, Walter?"

Walter looked straight ahead, slowly chewing on a piece of toast. After an uncomfortably long pause he turned and looking at Rachel nodded slowly. "Yes. I think it makes great sense. I think I see where you are coming from. Brilliant actually."

"Walter, it's not where I'm coming from. It's what almost one million aboriginal people in Canada have decided to call themselves. You see, they refuse to be labelled as *Indians* which historically is really a European term. Which begs the question, what do you want to be called?" Rachel nervously picked up her coffee.

"Just call me Walter. Call me *Navajo* or you can call me an *Indian* because that's what I've always known myself as. But I kind of like this Canadian *First Nations* thing. It makes sense."

Walter smiled warmly and looked directly at Rachel who quietly breathed a sigh of relief. She wished her husband was with her. Rolly always had the knack of putting people at ease with his biracial background.

"By the way, I just remembered you are the second Canadian I've met, not the first," Walter said.

"Oh, who was the first?" Rachel asked.

"A guy named Adam Beach. He was an actor from Manitoba, I think. He said he was a Salteaux guy playing the role of a Navajo in a war movie. It was years ago and I didn't get to talk to him much. He seemed like a nice guy. He was the only Indian from Canada that I ever met."[11]

"Wow, Rachel is also from Manitoba. What movie was he in?" Isabella asked.

"It was called *Windtalkers*. It's a story about Navajo code talkers in the war against the Japanese. They hired Navajos to send messages and create a code in their own language that the Japanese couldn't figure out. It was based on a true story. The Navajo people are very proud of their code talkers."

"Did you like the movie Walter?" Rachel asked.

"Not really. It was supposed to be about the Navajo but as usual the white guys got all the glory. Besides, it's a violent movie and

---

11. Adam Beach is a member of the Saulteaux (Plains Ojibwe) nation. He was raised on the Dog Creek Reserve near Ashern, Manitoba. He failed his high school English exam but excelled in drama to become a popular actor featured in numerous Hollywood films taking on Native roles.

I found it disturbing. I don't know why they have to do all that killing, but that's Hollywood, I guess. Anyways, that's how I met Adam Beach. They only spent a short time on Navajo lands during the filming. I guess they wanted to meet some real Navajo before they pretended to be ones in the movie." Walter stared into the bottom of his empty coffee cup, shaking his head.

After an awkward pause Isabella decided to propose a toast. Holding her glass of orange juice in the air she said, "Here's to a great team and a wonderful working relationship with all our racial and national differences."

Everyone raised their coffee cup or juice and clinked them together in agreement and finished their breakfast. Later in the women's washroom Isabella winked in approval at Rachel and whispered, "Feisty girl. You handled that nicely, I think Walter likes you."

Chapter 11

Spotted Deer

A maiden is also dancing around
Singing so softly it's you that she's found.
~ Robert Sutton

Spotted Deer, a distant cousin to the shaman's young apprentice had recently turned eighteen years old. Her long dark hair was braided with small polished nuggets of turquoise coiled at the ends. Thin leather straps stained by a rocky pigment of red ochre coiled around her thin wrists. The perfect ogee of her sculpted lips with her long eyelashes shielding her deep brown eyes gave her a beauty seen only in a few older women of her people. She wore a thin tan-coloured dress made from the soft hides of mule deer fawns that revealed the golden tones of her skin. The hem of her dress was dyed yellow from lichens; several small seashells that had been carefully sewn in the hem clinked softly when she walked. Her sandals were made of woven yucca fibres.

Around her neck hung a small pouch of wild flower petals, fragrant purple sand verbena, and claret cup cactus flowers. Dusky and graceful, she carried herself as a gazelle in movement. But she stood motionless as she eavesdropped, a handsome statue whose lustrous black eyes alone moved, glancing for others who might notice her clandestine undertaking. Spotted Deer decided to follow the young apprentice back to his alcove.

After Shadow Dancer returned to his ledge he fell asleep, having been rudely awakened earlier by the noisy raven. Following him from the great house, Spotted Deer slipped into the small cave-like structure behind the stonewall on the edge of the cliff through a slotted passageway. She found just enough room to recline quietly beside Shadow Dancer. She had no idea that he spent so much time confined to this hidden alcove so high above the canyon floor. She didn't want to wake him and she stared at him for a long time while he slept, admiring his youthful physique.

Shadow Dancer was lithe and sinewy from climbing the heights of the canyon each day to the vast plateau above where he hunted. His skin was deeply bronzed from clambering daily over the cliffs above the canyon. His young face was thin and sensitive and his high forehead was wrapped with a thin leather headband that held back his long black hair. His heavy breathing suggested he had fallen into a deep sleep.

Spotted Deer was surprised that she had never seen this ledge from the bottom of the canyon, so cleverly concealed by the interlocking shale. Most of the other young men of the great house were compelled to travel sixty miles away to haul large logs back to their treeless community, an exhausting trip that took over ten days. This was necessary following the complete disappearance of all the large evergreen trees in the Chaco area over the previous century.[12]

Much to his disappointment, Shadow Dancer had been assigned to a different kind of work with the medicine man in the Chaco community. This involved almost no physical exertion except for his daily climbs to the cliff ledge. At times he cursed his sixth toe which had consigned him to a life of boredom. There were times he had considered cutting it off with the obsidian knife that the shaman had given to him. One day he used it to etch an image of the shaman on the canyon wall with a sharp rock. It depicted him with large shoulders and stick legs, a mystic figure which he painted red and white colours.[13]

Shadow Dancer stirred in his sleep and rolled towards Spotted Deer so that their faces were opposed to each other. He began dreaming; his eyes rolled from side to side and he continued to breathe heavily. Spotted Deer wondered what he could be dreaming about and she soon became rapt by the young man's sleeping form and his sullen mouth.

Although she was a year older, he did not seem to be much younger than she was. She gently touched his forehead; his eyes continued to roll under his heavy eyelids. Listening to the deep rhythms

---

12. The numerous stone masonry structures of the Chaco community required an estimated 240,000 trees that were incorporated as roof beams, door and window lintels in the great houses and the roofs for the dozens of kivas. Although they possessed sophisticated architecture and astronomical observatories, for some unknown reason as with every other North American tribe, the Chacoans failed to invent the wheel. This fact consigned the people of the canyon to carry on their shoulders the rough-hewn logs each weighing over six hundred pounds from the forests of the Chuska Mountains over the span of a century and a half.

13. Modern archaeologists later invented all sorts of different theories to explain this pictograph, which became known as *the baseball umpire*, not recognizing it was merely the doodling of an angry and bored adolescent male from the twelfth century.

of his breathing, she remembered his sad face from the time he was rescued from the flash flood a few months ago. She wanted to kiss him but held back as she didn't know how he would react.

Is he dreaming about the raven right now?

While pondering what to do, Spotted Deer reacted to the dust in the small enclave and suddenly an uncontrollable high-pitched sneeze erupted. Immediately, Shadow Dancer awoke and shouted, standing up, trembling with fear. A collared lizard quickly scrambled across the red rock ceiling of their enclosed hiding place like a fish skittering through shallow water. Staring intently at his unexpected visitor, he exclaimed, "What are you doing in here? This isn't a place for girls!"

Chapter 12

Pueblo Bonito

One does not sell the land people walk on.
~ Crazy Horse

Following breakfast the team loaded Walter's gear into the Suburban and headed west on the I-40 to Thoreau for half an hour. Rachel focused on the landscape, savouring the rugged beauty of this part of New Mexico. She was mesmerized by the shapes of the cloud shadows on the hills, the broad escarpment of Old Red Sandstone which marked the southern boundary of the Colorado Plateau to the north, and the endless blue sky.

She was thrilled to see a roadside highway sign pointing the way to the "Historic Route 66", recalling the old television series of the same name. The Suburban passed a faded billboard that read, "Have a John Wayne Burger in Gallup, New Mexico." Rachel smiled as they passed through Grants. A homemade sign on the side of the road read "Rain dance scheduled for Friday evening, weather permitting."

Turning north at Thoreau they drove past single-storey houses with shallow roofs, and colourfully painted walls. A fenced-in lot next to a schoolyard held several yellow school buses. They travelled for another hour or so on well-paved roads deep into the Navajo reservation, past dusty houses and mobile homes, several with broken windows until they encountered a Navajo "service road" which was basically a meandering dirt road for the next twenty-six miles. Traversing twenty cattle-guards, numerous potholes, and masses of tumbleweeds piled several feet high along the barbed wire fences, they found themselves driving on a single-lane washboard road for miles. Rachel was astounded at the isolated stretch of remoteness and the roughness of the heavily rutted road. They hadn't passed another vehicle since Grants. She found the sudden jolts and jerks unnerving.

"This must be the roughest road I have ever been on," she solemnly announced.

"Yep. One of our colleagues poetically described this area as 'a desolate territory of wind-sculpted stone and brittle scrub'- and that's just the road. We are now entering a 30,000-square-mile blister of land so barren that you really have to wonder how anyone lived here. There are no services or stores within sixty miles of the Chaco Canyon National Historical Site, so we really are in the middle of nowhere here. Don't count on the GPS, and cell phone coverage is pretty sketchy out here and nonexistent in the canyon. These are all privately owned Navajo lands and they don't maintain the roads because they really don't want us here. Besides, they don't have the funding for road repairs at any rate so it's hardly ever graded. Right, Walter?" Nesbitt asked.

Walter stared ahead and grunted.

"Well, I grade it every time we come here and I never give it more than an *E*," Nesbitt quipped in an effort to lighten things up. Rachel smiled at his off-the-wall humour. They slowed down for a series of deep ruts where a flash flood had recently eroded much of the road for several hundred feet. A sign near a wash said-"Danger! Do not Cross if Wash is Flowing."

"This land is so dry and stark you can appreciate why Chaco Canyon remained undiscovered for so long. After the Mexican War ended, a U.S. Army detachment finally passed through here and surveyed the ruins in 1849. The canyon was so remote, however, that it was basically left alone for another thirty years until the railroad went through south of here in the 1870s," Isabella explained to Rachel.

"So after 170 years the road is still a bone-jarring ride, not much better than it was when the canyon was discovered by white men. In fact, there are several times a year when this road is impassable from flash floods, chuck holes, or the occasional sand dune," Nesbitt added.

"What are chuck holes?" Rachel asked.

"They're huge potholes that can ruin your suspension. Smaller vehicles have to be towed when it rains as the wheels just spin inside them. Having four-wheel drive certainly helps."

The vast, harsh tract of land stretched into the distant empty red desert like the backside of the moon as far as the eye could see in every direction. Scruffy patches of salt-bush and clumps of silvery-green sagebrush and snake grass lined the edge of the road. Small herds of sheep and cattle moved freely along, some crossing the access road through untended gaps in the barbed wire fences. When the group finally arrived, the Suburban was covered in red dust and Rachel's back ached from the repeated bouncing on the uneven terrain. They drove up to the interpretive centre on a well-paved stretch of the national parks road and entered the main parking lot near the centre. Rachel immediately noticed an older model mud-splattered motor-home in the parking lot next to several SUVs. It, too, was covered in dust and the fender wells appeared rusted and dented. She couldn't see a licence plate but noticed that the grille had been partly bashed in.

That wreck must belong to one of the local workers. It's certainly seen better days.

Rachel followed the rest of the team into the visitor centre where a young Navajo woman in a neatly pressed national parks uniform with a parks patch on her shoulder was giving a lecture to a small group of tourists. Thin and tall, she had long black hair and spoke clearly. Rachel and her colleagues with the OCA stood quietly at the back listening to her presentation. The others nodded, recognizing the docent as one of their own, a graduate of anthropology from the University of New Mexico.

"Ancient people of the Pueblo culture of Chaco Canyon often decorated their houses with six-digit handprints and footprints. We don't really know why these images were depicted in homes, but researchers suggest that having an extra finger or toe made that person more important and respected in their society. In the 1920s, American archaeologist Neil Judd found a six-toed skeleton in the ruins at Pueblo Bonito. You will find six-toed petroglyphs on the rock wall directly behind Bonito. And even today having polydactyly — an extra toe or finger — is regarded as a special gift among some Pueblos."

Being familiar with polydactylism from her conversation with Rolly at Bandelier, Rachel smiled. She wondered if the docent knew about Halle Berry and Kate Hudson. The docent continued her talk.

"One of the bodies discovered in the 1920s in the Pueblo Bonito great house had an ornate anklet around its six-toed foot, but carried no such offering on its five-toed foot. So it seems that polydactyls were given status in life and death and perhaps even mystical powers were attributed to them. In fact, the most highly decorated burials in the Southwest have been discovered here at Chaco Canyon in one of the many rooms of Pueblo Bonito." The docent paused for a drink of water.

"One richly dressed skeleton was found lying on a bed of 56,000 pieces of turquoise surrounded by fine ceramic vessels. It was covered by a sheet of ivory-coloured sea shells from six hundred miles away. He must have been someone of great importance."

After the docent finished speaking to her visitors she turned to welcome the team from Albuquerque.

"Welcome to the Chaco Canyon Cultural National Historic Park World Heritage Site. Isn't that a mouthful? We heard that you have a new member of your team and that she is from Canada. We have a guided tour for any of you who would like to take, it but of course most of you are quite familiar with this place with the work you have been doing here. I have been told for the benefit of our Canadian friend that I will be taking her and Dr. Sandoval on a tour of the centre here and then visiting Pueblo Bonito, the largest of the great houses built by the Ancestral Pueblo people. Following that you will be climbing to the mesa top for a terrific view of the ruins and the canyon. Then you will hike across the mesa to visit Pueblo Alto for a round trip of about three miles."

The docent shook hands with Rachel and after a quick tour of the visitor centre they went outside and drove to the great house known as Pueblo Bonito. Several tourists were purchasing books, videos, postcards, posters, and tee-shirts from the bookstore in the centre. Once outside, the group separated from the three men who headed to their project on the paved road further down the canyon in a separate park vehicle while Isabella and Rachel accompanied their guide. Nesbitt and Brown were quite familiar with the ruins and had to get to work. Isabella offered to accompany Rachel on the tour to explain more of the history.

Etched on the canyon wall behind the great house the Anasazi had left their creative imprints with a series of petroglyphs in a light brown patina. Images of animals, spirals, circles within circles, and strange rectilinear shapes suggested the bizarre scrawls of ancient artists. Despite eight centuries of weathering, the rock art still intrigued archaeologists even though they had no idea what they represented. Rachel stopped to take several photos of the petroglyphs.

The guide took them to the massive remains on what was for centuries the largest building in North America and as large as the Colosseum in Rome. The women climbed over a gigantic slab near the cliff face which had destroyed much of the back wall and several of the rooms.

"What on earth happened here?" Rachel asked.

"This is a thirty-thousand-ton wedge of sandstone that had once towered precariously behind Pueblo Bonito from the time it was built. After centuries of small undetectable shifting it finally came crashing down on January 22, 1942. It wiped out the north wall of the palace, destroying sixty-five rooms in the process. Now we just bring tourists on a trail built over the rubble. It was quite unfortunate, really," the docent advised.

"Good heavens, what a disaster. Could they not have prevented it?" Rachel asked "Not really. Engineers were powerless to stabilize a monolith of that size back then.

For years it was known as *Threatening Rock* but it's not threatening anymore. It's just a massive pile of rubble as you can see," the docent explained.

"Can you imagine how much larger Pueblo Bonito would look without that jumble of boulders covering much of it? But it's still huge. When Charles Lindbergh flew over here in 1929 he took aerial photos which give you an idea of what the great house looked like before Threatening Rock collapsed onto it," Isabella added.

"Charles Lindbergh of *Spirit of St. Louis* fame? What was he doing here?"

"After his famous transatlantic flight he and his wife flew out here to get away from all the paparazzi. They also worked with some of the early archaeologists here and took aerial photos for them. Lindbergh's photograph of Pueblo Bonito may be one of the last ones taken before Threatening Rock collapsed onto it."

After exploring the remains of the ancient pueblo, stepping through numerous doorways under greyed wooden lintels, they were ready to explore other great houses. Rachel was impressed with the perfect masonry in the construction of the walls and windows with squared corners and straight lines.

"These people took such pains in their construction of this building. Remarkable!" Rachel exclaimed.

"Yes, everybody who comes here feels that same sense of awe. How much attention was lavished on this place. And that's what pulls you in. You just want to know more. Soon you're hooked on Chaco Canyon," Isabella replied.

The two women thanked the docent who then showed them the way to the trail-head that would lead them to the overlook at the top of the mesa.

"I'll leave you ladies here to explore the stairway to Pueblo Alto. I have another talk to give back at the centre. Please be careful climbing this path. It's uneven and steep in many places but I think you'll enjoy the view once you get to the top."

Looking up to the mesa top Rachel paused, and seeing the steep stony trail that led to it, she wondered if this might be too difficult for her. She gazed upwards to the blue vault of the sky where a pair of red-tailed hawks circled lazily near the cliff – a sheer wall of red sandstone rose four hundred feet high. Steeling herself for the difficult climb Rachel uttered a quiet prayer.

Chapter 13

Message of the Black Feather

Feathers appear when angels are near.
~ Anonymous

Still caught in a frenzy of sneezing, Spotted Deer was unable to answer Shadow Dancer's angry interrogation. Fanning the air with her delicate hands, she finally looked up and said, "I followed you from the great house after you spoke with Grey Elk. I wanted to know why you're hiding here lately while all the other boys travel to the sacred mountain for logs. I'm sorry if I frightened you. I didn't mean to wake you." Her lips trembled.

As she stood up Shadow Dancer eyed her shapely form and didn't know what to say.

He had always admired this young woman but was too shy to approach her. Now she was standing beside him in the confines of his hidden alcove right next to him. All at once, his mind became a kaleidoscope of thoughts. Although he had known Spotted Deer before she always seemed to be a young girl, not worthy of his attention. Now, she was all of a sudden so mature, so fine and different.

She's beautiful. What am I supposed to I say?

After a long, awkward pause he finally spoke. He was unable to look directly at Spotted Deer, so distracting was her beauty.

"Grey Elk sends me here to listen to the spirits. I have to spend several days a week here by myself. It's very boring except when that cursed raven comes by every morning and screams his face off."

"Why did Grey Elk send you, Shadow Dancer? Why not any of the other boys? Why don't they all take turns?"

"Because he believes I will become a medicine man someday and he wants me to listen in solitude to the spirits of the canyon including the raven."

"Oh. Is that because you were born with six toes?" She gazed down at his bare feet and smiled.

"I guess so. There are others with the 'sign of the feet' living here too you know. But for some reason he chose me as his student. I'm not so sure I'm happy with the idea but my parents are proud of me for being chosen. I really don't think I can become a medicine man though."

"And why is that, Shadow Dancer? I know people who think you should." Spotted Deer's smile was alluring.

"Because it's too lonely staying here day after day by myself. I go up to the plateau and look down the valley and over the great houses whenever I can but I'm still alone. I often see the men carrying the logs from the holy mountain when they are still miles away and I wish I could be with them."

"But that is such hard work, travelling so far and carrying those heavy timbers. Those men are exhausted when they return."

"I know, but at least they are together and they can talk to each other and sing the songs of our Nation. Up here I have no one to talk to."

"But I'm here now. You can talk to me," Spotted Deer said coyly. "Yes, but you couldn't stay here all the time."

"Why not?" she said indignantly. "You don't remember me do you?"

"Remember you from what?"

"From the time you were rescued by my family during the desert flood two moons past. My mother covered you with a mat and I was the one who sang to you and helped you back to the great house. It was a very hot day if you recall and you almost drowned in the river."

Spotted Deer looked disappointed that he did not know her.

"That was you?" Shadow Dancer exclaimed. "Yes, I remember someone who sang to me and held my hand after I was pulled from the water but I had no idea who it was.

I've often thought about that day and how comforting it was to have someone near me. I have never been so frightened in all my life as I was in that flood. So that was you?" he repeated.

"Yes, that was me. You never even thanked me for staying with you, Shadow Dancer." She pouted slightly as if to feign hurt feelings.

"I'm sorry. Yes, thank you for your kindness," he said sheepishly. "You're welcome."

"But you can't come up here to stay with me."

"Why not?"

"Because they need you to grind corn and weave baskets and whatever else women do in the great house."

"Actually, I paint pottery. But you wouldn't notice these things would you?" Spotted Deer rolled her eyes and sighed. Shadow Dancer again at a loss for words, stared down at his dysmorphic feet.

"But I don't have to be there all the time. I could come and visit you and stay here with you, couldn't I? Why I can just as easily paint pottery here as anywhere."

Shadow Dancer was stunned. Never in his wildest dreams could he imagine that a girl as beautiful as Spotted Deer would want to stay with him on this small secret ledge peering out through cracks and holes in the stone wall at the canyon below day after day. He liked the idea but was hesitant to break the rule that Grey Elk had made about no visitors being allowed to the sacred site.

"Could you ask them to bring my food up here and I could see you then?" he asked.

"Of course, and I could sneak away at other times to see you. I could also bring grasses to weave baskets here and no one would notice my absence," Spotted Deer enthusiastically suggested with her large expressive eyes.

"All right, I guess, as long as Grey Elk doesn't hear about it. I would like that very much if you were to come and visit me. It gets lonely here. Some nights in the midst of my loneliness I feel like a spider swinging on a thin thread trying to find a place to land," Shadow Dancer said, smiling at his own shameless attempt to elicit sympathy from this lovely young woman.

Ignoring him, Spotted Deer faked a slight shiver. "It's kind of cool in this place. Don't you ever get cold at night?"

"It's not too bad. I have these deer hides to keep me warm."

"Can you show me?" Her long eyelashes batted as she pretended to shiver once again. "Okay, I guess." Shadow Dancer lifted the soft deer hide and wrapped it around them both while they stood in the coolness of the cave, shafts of daylight breaking through the small cracks of the stone wall. A small rainbow of colours reflected off a chunk of quartz in the wall illuminating Spotted Deer's soft cheek with spangles of coloured light. As soon as he placed the hide over Spotted Deer's slender shoulders and around himself, she drew closer to him. She smelled of wildflowers and new leather and yucca root soap.

Their bodies quickly found each other as her long black hair brushed softly against his face. He felt her breasts pressed against him, gentle shudders emanating from her rib cage. He placed his hands around her thin waist while she nuzzled her face sideways into his neck.

At first, the ground seemed to sway beneath him; all at once it was as if he was thrown off a cliff, tumbling, twisting, and spinning headlong into a dizzying abyss of sheer ecstasy. It was an exhilarating and frightening feeling holding Spotted Deer in his arms. He felt himself in the embrace of a deep tenderness and for a vertiginous moment, his heart was beating and pounding as if it would burst forth from his chest and he began to perspire. Shadow Dancer was completely lost in his longing to comprehend his own intoxicating emotions, strong yet vulnerable, joyful yet fearful. For him Spotted Deer was a fragile desert flower opening to the warmth of spring.

What is happening to me?

If this was the "spiritual experience" that Grey Elk told him to seek, Shadow Dancer was happy to enjoy it for the rest of his life. Looking into Spotted Deer's eyes, the colour of burnt umber, he saw wells of deep, enriching, and transforming love. He wondered if he would ever be able to drink enough from these wells to satisfy him. Any feelings of inadequacy or loneliness he had experienced while in his alcove melted away in the arms of Spotted Deer.

Spotted Deer sighed and looked away towards the cracks in the stone wall. Reaching out she grasped the large black tail feather that had fallen between the stones. Extracting it, she then twirled it tantalizingly in the air before Shadow Dancer, her eyes dancing before him. The black feather gleamed with a blue fire in the slanting light.

"Is this feather from your friend the raven, Shadow Dancer? Is this the omen you were looking for? Maybe this sign is about you and me and not about the Nation. Could it be you didn't think of other possibilities when the raven was diving and shrieking? He was warning you about me, wasn't he? And now it's too late!"

Spotted Deer smiled with a coquettish smirk, tiny beads of perspiration collecting along the delicate philtrum of her upper lip. Shadow Dancer remained silent at her mockery and just slowly shook his head.

"Now you have to bring the message of the raven back to Grey Elk and that message is me," she laughed, giving the feather to Shadow Dancer.

Then she gently kissed him on the lips, pressing her soft breasts further into the firmness of his chest; she held him behind the nape of his neck, firmly twining her hands around his long black plaited hair, pulling him gently towards her inviting mouth.

At that instance, Shadow Dancer knew her argument was invincible, and he instantly sensed his utter transformation, a rebirth that dramatically introduced him to the power of obsessive love. Perhaps the raven had indeed been warning him about this beautiful young woman. Grey Elk was right when he said, "It takes patience and solitude to hear what the *Master of Time* is saying to you." He closed his eyes and felt the wonderful softness of Spotted Deer in his arms, as if a sweet wind was blowing over him.

I just didn't listen long enough, but now I understand.

Chapter 14

The Overlook

I have been to the end of the earth, I have been to the
end of the waters, I have been to the end of the sky,
I have been to the end of the mountains, I have found
none that are not my friends.
~ Navajo

Leaving the docent at the base of the escarpment, the two women climbed the rough stairway to the clifftop above Pueblo Bonito on the North Mesa. The climb to the top involved laborious clambering over a steep pile of rocks, frequently requiring them to grasp rocky handholds in the cliff wall for support. The ancient Chacoan stairway began as a narrow ribbon of trail that seemed to disappear into a large stand of boulders near the bottom of the cliff. Looking skyward through the chasm, only a thin spear of daylight appeared above them as they ascended between the cliff face and a large sandstone monolith. Climbing over a series of awkwardly placed stepping stones, Rachel was surprised once more at how difficult it was to breathe.

"I have to start working out, Isabella. I had no idea how out of shape I am."

"Well, we are over 6500 feet above sea level here, so don't beat yourself up until you get acclimatized to the Colorado Plateau. Plus, we are climbing over three hundred feet above the canyon floor," Isabella explained.

After reaching the mesa top Rachel looked down on the ruins of Kin Kletso, another of the other great houses in the Chaco complex. She could see the rest of the canyon with the Chaco wash meandering into the distance. She could also see the remains of other great houses in the distance where a few tourists studied the various park signs. The women hiked across the mesa for about half a mile until they were right over the great house of Pueblo Bonito which covered almost four acres. Several of the eight hundred rooms of this great house were open to the elements, their roofs having been destroyed eons ago. Twenty circular kivas were clustered within the great house which was shaped like the letter *D*. From their vantage point three hundred feet up, the entire intricate complex with its honeycomb of rooms and kivas had the appearance of an enormous pocket watch cut in half with all its mechanical components, cogs, and gears and wheels exposed to the desert sun. Its enormity and complexity in such a remote region was overwhelming; it reminded Rachel of an English garden maze only made from sandstone. She took several photos of the great house with its labyrinthine circularity.

"My goodness Isabella, I've seen numerous photographs of this place but I never expected anything quite like this. This is absolutely spectacular. I can't believe the size of the great houses. And to think these ruins are over eight hundred years old. I don't think I've ever seen so many massive ruins in one place. And such elegance in its design. This was totally worth the effort."

"Yep. We're actually in the architectural heart of the Anasazi civilization. Can you imagine what it looked like in its heyday with five-storey buildings, walkways, gardens, and roads radiating for miles in all directions? After the base was built, second and third stories were added to create a huge complex of room**s**. And if you look down the canyon you'll see there are a dozen more great houses. It boggles the mind to think there could have been up to twelve thousand people living in 'downtown Chaco' and as many as thirty thousand living within the confines of the canyon. Back then in the twelfth century most people in England were living in wooden hovels or huts with thatched roofs."

"This is simply amazing. Such a view."

"I get tingly every time I come up here and look down on these grand buildings.

There's no doubt that these are the most sweeping ruins north of Mexico. And yet not a single person has lived here for centuries in a place that was once swarming with Anasazis. Think of all the planning and labour that went into the construction of these buildings. If you look at the configuration of the kivas in Pueblo Bonito you might notice a similarity to the constellation Pleiades with its seven stars. Some archaeologists feel these kivas were designed to represent that constellation although personally I think it's a bit of a stretch. Still, it's an archaeologist's dream, Rachel."

"No kidding. It's so quiet up here. Not even the wind is blowing. Makes it kind of eerie, doesn't it?"

"Yes, definitely eerie especially when you run across a group of New Agers who bring bus tours here for 'meditations and activations' where they try to channel the spirits in the canyon. Many claim to have made contact with the ancient Pueblo people through their spiritual journey. One of them told me it was 'as if they were time travellers, channelling to become Anasazi themselves.'"

"Really? That's just crazy talk, Isabella."

"I agree, but to them this place is 'numinous' and they keep coming back."

"Numinous? I've never heard that term used."

"It means *spiritual* or *supernatural*. It comes from the Latin word *numen* which refers to the influence of a spiritual force. The New Agers throw the term around a lot and they say that they 'sense a numinous energy' here. It's easy to see why, don't you think?"

"Yes, there is a certain mysteriousness here, but really Isabella, 'channelling to become Anasazis'? They must be nuts!"

"Yep, I was astounded to hear these educated people claiming they had actually deliberated with the elders regarding when to leave their village and migrate south over eight hundred years ago. These ancient ruins are a huge magnet for these people who bring their crystals and Navajo spiritual guides. One of my Navajo friends knows a *wisdom keeper* and a *story teller* who described how some of the Navajo actually walked through a gateway into another world. They claimed they saw native children with unusual haircuts. Some members of that group followed the children through a stone passageway and found another civilization."

"Incredible! I wonder if they bothered to ask them what happened to make the Anasazi leave this place."

"Well, yeah, that's the million-dollar question, but no, they will just tell you that they migrated elsewhere but never explain exactly why they left in the first place."

"Kinda makes you a bit skeptical, doesn't it?"

"We believe the Anasazi were profoundly spiritual and lived in harmony with nature.

Nowadays many of those involved with the New Age movement see themselves as *spiritual descendants* of the Anasazi and so they come to Chaco Canyon to worship and meditate. The site had to actually be closed at one time because the New Agers were burying crystals illegally. Some even had their ashes scattered here."

"Oh boy, that's getting kind of creepy, don't you think?"

"For sure, but think of what the canyon must have been like in the eleventh or twelfth centuries. People shouting, dogs barking, babies crying, the repetitive rasping sounds of women grinding corn against rock slabs. Hundreds of people coming and going in all directions. The place would have been just humming with activity."

"But now there's just the occasional tourist and a few crows. I can certainly see why it's a UNESCO World Heritage Site."

"Yet in spite of being one of America's greatest national heritage sites, Chaco barely gets over one hundred visitors a day, except in peak season as it's so far off the beaten path. The park guides are happy to see anyone during the slow season," Isabella added.

Rachel looked down into what was now a dry and desolate canyon with its stark sandstone land forms. She tried to envision what Pueblo Bonito might have looked like eight centuries ago. She stood near the exact spot where Shadow Dancer once embraced his young bride as they watched the sunsets each night. Her mind raced as she considered all the theories as to what caused these talented people to leave what was once a small city. Looking into the canyon the few tourists appeared as small insects clambering over the sandstone slabs in the distance. Parked in the small lot near the entrance to the great house was the same rusted recreational vehicle that she had seen earlier. An open side door suggested someone was inside instead of exploring the ruins as other visitors were doing.

Atop the mesa, Rachel was exposed to a striking panorama of the canyon's great houses with the mountains and square-topped buttes in the distance. She could see the ancient caldera of Mount Taylor to the south, the Chuskas to the west, and the rugged canyons that led up to the Rockies to the north. From here she could also see sections of the prehistoric road system which the Chacoans developed that linked them to various other sites throughout the canyon and to places like Mesa Verde and Aztec Ruins. She took several photos from this vantage point.

It is so beautiful up here. This was truly the centre of a fascinating ancient culture.

Rachel could not help but admire the graceful soaring of several large black birds near the cliffs and she wondered what they ate. A sudden whoosh overhead from a pair of raven's wings broke the silence and her reverie.

This place is certainly numinous, all right.

Chapter 15

Divine Messenger

All dreams spin out from the same web.
~ Hopi

*The old ones say you can feel your spirit
during a vision quest.*
~ Harman

In the cave, on the ground, wrapped in the canyon darkness, Spotted Deer and Shadow Dancer found themselves carried over plateaus and mesas, buttes and gullies, floating through colourful clouds over the sandstone colossus of the great house below to a pinnacle of mystical ecstasy. Locked in each other's arms they floated down to the canyon floor, suspended in space, sensing the earth's rotation under the warm glow of a pale purple moon where ponderosa pines, piñon jays, and horned lizards welcomed their slow descent with surrealistic colours. In those early morning hours, the two teenagers had glimpsed infinity from the confines of their hidden alcove. A coyote on the mesa top yipped twice, then released a full-throated wail. Its baying seemed to float down from the stars as if it were the echoing voice of a demonic hound, dispensing a dreary sadness throughout the canyon.

After their lovemaking the night before, the teenagers had shared the cacao beans and piñon nuts, that the medicine man, Grey Elk, had given to Shadow Dancer. However, Grey Elk had kept his peyote buttons in this same pouch.[14] Lying in the narrow confines of their rocky chamber under a soft deer hide, Spotted Deer and Shadow Dancer had fallen under the spell of the peyote.

Feeling a distorted awareness, their relationship had begun dramatically, both physically and psychologically. Neither one of them ever forgot that night. Coming down to earth from the effects of the drug, they slept soundly well past dawn. By noon, they finally awoke feeling bewildered and exhausted, questioning each other on what they had experienced. Everything seemed to be shrinking and expanding at the same time. Confused as though they were in a void, they finally awakened to reality, awake yet still dreaming, aware but still dazed, with smothered memories and jumbled thoughts.

"Spotted Deer, are you all right?" Shadow Dancer's voice seemed to drip like water in a cave echoing into the labyrinth of her hearing.

"Mmmmph," was all she could say.

"I had such vivid dreams last night with wonderful colours and shapes. By the look of the sun's shadow, I think we've slept til noon. I don't know— but I had visions of animals and birds that were so

---

14. Found in several cactus species, the active ingredient of peyote is a naturally occurring psychedelic that causes a dreamlike state, a drifting delirium that the shamans used to stimulate inner reflection and mystical experiences. Taken from the Aztecs, the word *peyote* appropriately means *divine messenger* because of the powerful visual hallucinations it produced. Structurally related to adrenaline, the naturally occurring alkaloid would accelerate neurological impulses in the adolescent brain, bringing on visions with strong hallucinogenic experiences. In young adults, naive to the drug, peyote would cause them to hallucinate for hours.

real. It seemed the whole world and all the stars were going round and round and we were flying without wings over the canyon."

Spotted Deer stirred and opened her eyes and lay there for several minutes trying to re-orient herself. Shadow Dancer began talking again.

"Shh! Be quiet. I heard something just now." Spotted Deer was now fully awake, her senses heightened from a tapping sound as if someone was sending a signal.

"I heard that, too," Shadow Dancer whispered, "only it seems to be coming from outside the stone wall. How is that possible?"

Tap, tap. Tappety tap — tap, tap. Like a child playing with two rocks against each other, the sound reverberated within their heads like an echo chamber. They both looked at each other wondering if this was part of their peyote-induced delusion.

"It's very close and I think it's coming from somewhere outside the stone wall," Shadow Dancer repeated himself.

Spotted Deer licked her lips, trying to get rid of the metallic taste still in her mouth from the peyote. She peered through the cracks in the stone wall and muttered, "Ra-Ra-raven." The sunlight blinded her for a moment and she winced in pain. "I think it's your special raven out there, Shadow Dancer."

With a residual feeling of euphoria, Spotted Deer blinked several times and began to yawn uncontrollably from the ongoing effects of the peyote. "That's the last time I let you give me cacao beans to eat, Shadow Dancer. I've never felt like this before."

"I've had cacao beans many times before and I have never dreamed so much as I did last night. No, it must have been something else. I wonder whether Grey Elk gave us peyote with the cacao beans. I've heard it can do strange things to you. But can you see the raven?"

"Yes, it's perched on a rock and pecking at something. Maybe it wants its feather back." She smiled and touched him gently on the arm. Shadow Dancer tried to stand but his heavy limbs would not support him and he fell against the wall of his rocky chamber. Standing on wobbly legs, his surroundings confusing, he slid down beside Spotted Deer who was off balance herself and could not help him. Everything seemed to move in slow motion. The tapping soon stopped and all they could do was to lie there focused intently on the reflecting light from the quartz as if all the secrets of the universe were immersed in this singular beam of light. Distorted images and feelings of euphoria continued on and off for the next hour, until at last they emerged from the effects of the peyote and ventured outside the chamber.

Descending the rocky trail to the canyon floor they held onto each other to avoid falling. They sheepishly entered the great house avoiding the smiles of the many women weaving and preparing food. Several cast knowing glances toward the young couple. An elderly woman offered them each a bowl of warm cornmeal with piñon nuts. They both sat down and ate heartily in a separate room by themselves. Shadow Dancer could not help but notice the dozens of large clay ollas in this room filled to the brim with beans, flowing over and spilling on the ground. Never had he recalled seeing such an abundance of food in one place. Other rooms likewise served as granaries for squash and several held racks of dried meat from various animals. One entire room held corn cobs stacked to the ceiling like cordwood.

Times were good for his people, and Shadow Dancer knew that he wanted Spotted Deer at his side forever. With an average lifespan of only forty years in the Chaco culture, they both knew they were not too young to marry at seventeen. In fact, as he thought about it, his life at this point was almost half over. All he could think about now was how to approach Spotted Deer's mother and see if they could live with her parents after they married. He had forgotten entirely the advice Grey Elk had given and the warnings of the mysterious raven. He was still trying to interpret the strange pecking sounds on the stone wall of his chamber earlier this morning. How would he explain his extraordinary dreams and visions to Grey Elk now? Would he believe the visions he experienced with Spotted Deer? Would the shaman grant permission to marry her? His thoughts were confused as he tried to make sense of things.

Chapter 16

Isabella Sandoval

For he shall give his angels charge over thee, to keep thee in all thy ways. They shall bear thee up in their hands, lest thou dash thy foot against a stone.
~ Psalm 91:12

The two women hiked across the flat rock mesa until they came to a set of stairs carved right into the rock face, which led up to a higher level where the remains of a smaller great house stood.

"So this great house is at the highest elevation at Chaco known as Pueblo Alto. It probably housed twenty families in the eleventh and twelfth centuries," Isabella said. Rachel took a few pictures and then they walked back to the Pueblo Bonito overlook.

"This is amazing, Isabella. After our conversation in the restaurant last week it just makes me wonder even more, what caused them all to disappear?"

"Well, that's a difficult question for sure and we may never learn the answer. But drink in this magnificent vista before we leave to join the men at our excavation site where we will put you to work. Then you can wreck your lovely fingernails for a change." Isabella smirked.

"That's fine with me. I've been looking forward to working here for some time and I'm just happy to be with such a great team at this remarkable site. But I'm curious about where you all come from. All we've discussed so far is the history of the Anasazi. Um, I still know very little about you," Rachel said inquiringly.

"Okay, for starters my educational background includes a PhD in anthropology as well as an MA degree in anthropology from East Carolina University. I also studied classical archaeology from the University of North Carolina at Chapel Hill. I'm currently a research scholar at the Ronin Institute and a teaching assistant professor in anthropology at the University of New Mexico at Albuquerque. I'm single and thirty- three years old. What else do you wish to know?"

Rachel had developed an interest in religion since her near brush with death a year earlier in Winnipeg. Smallpox had motivated her to pray and read her Bible and look at things differently since then. She had also taken a liking to this woman who was her own age and felt a kinship with her. Both women had excelled in the field of archaeology and both worked with men with whom they constantly felt the need to prove themselves. She hesitated to ask her the next question.

"Wow. That's a pretty impressive CV. I'm guessing your background is Hispanic? Are you Catholic?"

Isabella hesitated for a few seconds. "Sort of. But not really," she replied sheepishly. "I'm sorry if I'm being too nosy, Isabella. Forgive me if I'm too personal. It's just that if we're going to work together I'd like to know more about you."

"Not at all. Before immigrating to the United States my mother grew up in northeastern Mexico and worked as a librarian at a small university. She told me this story about four years ago which changed her life and mine. Her own parents identified as Christian, so she never understood why, by family tradition, they abstained from pork, washed their hands thoroughly before and after meals, and covered the mirrors in the home after someone died. It seemed that they had to do this but never knew why. She eventually suspected that she might have Jewish roots so she spent as much time as she could in the municipal archives of Mexico City. She sleuthed out old church records as well as a very old document from the year 1610. It was a property record bearing the name of her great-times eleven grandfather. She discovered that her ancestors were Sephardic Jews who came to the New World probably to get away from the Inquisition. She always knew there was something different about us."

"Isabella, that's amazing that your mother discovered documentation on your family tree going back four centuries."

"Yes, my mom was smart. She began her research after the Spanish Parliament passed a law in 2015 that granted citizenship to the descendants of Sephardic Jews. Within a few months the Ministry of Justice received more than 130,000 applications. By the end of the year six thousand of those applications had been approved including our own family. So now I can claim Spanish citizenship if I want. And it only cost me six thousand dollars to do this. How crazy is that?"

"Well, for six thousand dollars it sounds like a Spanish tax grab if you ask me. Are they doing this for the money or is this a way of saying 'sorry' to ease their collective conscience about the Inquisition? I'm sorry if I sound cynical, Isabella but if Spain was truly remorseful for the way it treated Jews, why would they make you pay to be repatriated? It makes you wonder about their motives don't you think? And have they ever made a public apology for the Inquisition? But don't get me wrong, I don't think it's crazy at all for you to discover your roots."

"Well. It may be a tax grab, but it does make Spain the only nation aside from Israel to grant 'automatic citizenship' to the descendants of Jews."

"Automatic citizenship for six grand? Oh well. At least they're trying to make up for the past. How does it make you feel, Isabella?"

"Well, it's still sinking in. Last year I visited the archives in Mexico City to see that ancient document for myself. I was actually able to touch it. I always wanted to know who I was as I never seemed to fit in with most of my friends. You may be right about Spain's motives, but it was liberating to learn this and I'm still processing this information. It does make me feel rather emotional at times."

"Knowing this about your ancestors, has it changed your faith at all?" Rachel asked. "Not yet, but it has introduced a lot of introspection and some confusion. While I am still Roman Catholic, finally knowing my roots is kind of haunting me. As you can see from this vantage point over Pueblo Bonito, the beckoning power of history can be almost overwhelming and you always want to learn more."

"I can't argue with that. That's why we're here," Rachel said.

"After 1492 about one-quarter-million Spanish Jews converted to Christianity under threat of execution by the Inquisition. They were called *conversos,* but many still clung to their Judaical traditions in one form or another. Many came to the New World to escape the intense scrutiny in Spain and Portugal, and thousands more were expelled from those countries. Like Jews during the Holocaust, they lived in constant fear, something I have never known."

"Hmm, I can only imagine. But why cover the mirrors after someone dies?"

"So if a Jewish family is holding services for a deceased person in their home, they need to cover the mirrors so that no one sees their own reflection during the service. Jewish law forbids worshipping in front of an image regardless of whether it is an icon or an image in a mirror or a picture. I had witnessed this as a child but of course I never knew any of this until I started researching Sephardic Jews in the New World."

"Have you told anyone else about this, like your co-workers?"

"No. I'm not sure how they will respond. There's still a lot of anti-semitism out there. Besides, what good will it do? We all have secrets that are better kept to ourselves. I hope you won't share this with any of the others, Rachel. I don't know why I'm even telling you this but for some reason I feel I can trust you to keep this to yourself."

Rachel gazed out over the flat slickrock into the canyon which widened as it turned westward revealing the soft desert pastels of an ancient land. She didn't know what to think. She certainly had her own secret about her encounter with smallpox the year before and wondered just how many people knew about it. She still carried feelings of shame and guilt regarding her York Factory experience as well. She decided that this was a secret better kept to herself for now.

Isabella is right. What good would it do?

"Of course, Isabella. You have my word," she reassured. At this point Rachel decided to change the subject. "Tell me how you got involved in the study of Southwestern native pottery?"

"Certainly. Pottery is one of my favourite subjects. Archaeology has been called *the study of the ancient* and pottery plays a huge role in that. From the ancient Greeks to modern times, pottery tells us lots about a society. I think the study of pottery is without doubt one of the most important tasks taken on by any archaeologist."

"Okay, but where did you learn about it?"

"Actually, right here on the job. And in museums and from books, of course. In our own museum we own some beautiful pieces of pottery from a thousand years ago that remain unbroken. You should tour the Maxwell Museum at the campus next time you are there and check out some of the stuff they have."

"I will, but tell me, how do you think the Anasazi learned how to make pottery?"

"Good question. By trial and error, I suppose. They had no potter's wheels as the ancient Greeks and Romans had; they just made all their jars and ollas by coiling long strands of clay which they had to find locally. Some of the pottery from Chaco Canyon was made from clay along the wash. Then they would burnish or polish the rough pot with a smooth rock and then paint the designs with plant dyes using a yucca paintbrush. Finally, they would fire it in the open air or in a kiln made from rock slabs. Historically, women made all the pottery in Southwest tribal groups, but today both men and women are accomplished artists among the various Pueblo groups."

"Do they still coil pottery today or have they advanced to using the potter's wheel?"

"Actually they do both. There are purists who still resort to the ancient art of coiling pottery just as their ancestors would have done. But it is too imperfect for some of the high-end stuff that you see for sale in the shops and boutiques, especially the Navajo pottery that sells mainly to tourists."

"I can't wait to see some of this stuff," Rachel replied.

"Well that may happen sooner than you think. I'll let you in on another secret, Rachel.

Our team has just recently discovered a burial site with dozens of pots and jars that are exceptionally well preserved after lying under several inches of sand, likely buried from a flash flood centuries ago. Collectively they could be worth a few million dollars.

They're still there for a few days while we take photographs and measurements."

"Great. When do we go?"

"Right now, if you like. The guys will be waiting for us at the site and they'll be wondering what happened to us. Just be careful on the way down. It's much easier to stumble going down than it is going up."

After about a fifty-foot descent, Rachel tripped, suddenly losing her balance. She was about to fall headlong down the steepest part of the stairway. She immediately felt an invisible arm hold her back until she regained her balance. Isabella who was right behind her reached out and grabbed her backpack, pulling her back so that she fell on her buttocks. Rachel gasped as she looked down and saw how far she might have fallen. A few stones that jarred loose from her fall bounced down the path disappearing over the edge of the escarpment.

"Omigosh!! You just saved my life, Isabella. I can't believe I almost tumbled head first into the canyon. And you just warned me about it. I'm such a klutz."

"That's okay, but perhaps I should go first. I would hate to lose you on your first day on the job."

"Let me just sit here for a moment, please. My heart is just racing. Oh dear. If you hadn't grabbed my arm I would be lying on the canyon floor right now. Thank you Isabella."

"But Rachel, I never grabbed your arm, I just caught the strap on your backpack."

Without responding, Rachel closed her eyes and uttered a silent prayer. She recalled a verse about how angels often protect people from falling. She began to tremble slightly and fidgeted with a strand of her hair twisting her finger around it as she did when she was nervous or upset. After a few minutes she got up, turned around, and gave Isabella a hug.

"All right, I'm all right. I guess I wouldn't make a very good Anasazi, would I? I promise to be more careful. Thank you again."

"Rachel, I think you'd make a lovely Anasazi. But I honestly didn't touch your arm," Isabella replied, laughing nervously.

Chapter 17

Of Mice and Love

Listen to the wind; it talks. Listen to the Silence; it speaks.
Listen to your heart; it knows.
~ Native proverb

Just as Shadow Dancer was wondering how to approach Grey Elk to tell him that he had fallen in love with Spotted Deer, he noticed a movement out of the corner of his eye along the floor. A darting grey streak, a fleeting shadow. Perhaps it was a residual effect from the peyote, he thought to himself. Then something moved again and Spotted Deer shrieked, "There are mice in here!"

It wasn't that she hadn't seen mice in the canyon before, but mice were always kept away from the food in the storage rooms of the great houses. Teams of boys with sticks monitored the storage rooms to keep the mice away. Somehow, they had missed this room.

"Those boys should be told about these mice," Spotted Deer said. Instantly two more mice scurried across the floor. Shadow Dancer picked up a pottery shard and tried to hit one of them, but his aim was off and the mouse was too fast.

"Let's get out of here. We can eat somewhere else," Shadow Dancer suggested.

Just then, several young boys with large sticks entered the storage room beating the floor around the ollas and in the corners killing mice with almost every blow. It seemed as soon as they killed one, a few more would appear out of nowhere. The boys moved a large storage jar and several more mice skittered out. Numerous mouse droppings and spilled corn lay near a small defect in the wall revealing an entry point for the opportunistic rodents.

Shadow Dancer was astounded at seeing so many mice in one room. Holding Spotted Deer's arm with one hand and his bowl of corn meal with the other, he quickly left the room. "Let's go up to my ledge where it's quieter and there are no mice," he suggested.

"Fine with me. I hate these creatures. They are so disgusting, but why are there so many here? I've never seen so many before."

"I don't know why. I'll ask the medicine man later. He'll know."

Shadow Dancer had no idea of the tremendous reproductive power of deer mice.[15] However, the elders were aware of their destructive abilities and tried to guard the storage rooms with teams of boys with their sticks. Yet Shadow Dancer wondered whether the mice had the upper hand in this great house.

After climbing up to the secret ledge the young couple finished their meal in solitude and talked at length about their future together. Spotted Deer knew she had to obtain her mother's permission to

---

15. With a gestational period of only twenty-one days and the capability of producing litters up to a dozen, a pair of mice with sufficient food can produce up to two thousand offspring in one year. The mother is fertile immediately after her pregnancy so she can have a new litter of young every two months or so.

marry Shadow Dancer. If they married, then Shadow Dance would become a member of his wife's clan.[16]

After finishing their meal they climbed to the top of the mesa on the overhanging cliff to enjoy the canyon sights together. Hundreds of feet below, dozens of people were farming, entering Great Kivas to worship, digging irrigation ditches, and hiking down the wide roads that connected the various settlements in Chaco Canyon. A group of laughing children raced across the plaza, dogs barking and leaping at their heels.

Numerous master masons worked on buttressing the five-storey stone walls of the great house while two old men sat idly by, watching the construction project. Dozens of wild turkeys pecked away in a large coop made from willow branches.

Suddenly black shadows raced across their path as flocks of ravens and other soaring birds of prey swooped and dove to the canyon floor, each time scooping up a squealing mouse. The shrill cries of a hawk echoed along the canyon walls accompanied by the loud and egregious caws of the ravens. Several birds dropped their prey on the mesa top as Shadow Dancer's raven had done yesterday.

"Look at all the birds, Shadow Dancer! And they're all catching mice. Why are there so many? And why are they dropping them here?" Spotted Deer exclaimed. No sooner had she said this when a large owl flew down and stood right beside them staring and hissing, seemingly unafraid and apathetic to their presence. From its mouth a mouse's tail projected, still writhing like a small disoriented snake. Spotted Deer turned away and clung to Shadow Dancer. He embraced her for several minutes as they both surveyed the activity in the canyon below.

16. It is generally believed the Anasazi held a matrilineal society as did most of their descendants. It meant that women were involved in the decision-making process for the greater good of the tribe.

Later that evening they found Grey Elk in one of the great subterranean kivas. They quietly climbed down to the base of this religious centre where a fire burned. Several people quietly meditated, sitting on seats along the walls of the massive cylindrical chamber. A row of baskets and pots stood along a short section of the wall. Sparks rose and blinked out before they reached the blackened roof beams.

Grey Elk looked shocked to find the young couple together and he immediately scowled. Without saying a word, Shadow Dancer showed the shaman the raven feather from his spirit ledge and pointed upwards, his finger making a circular motion. Leading them up the ladder, Grey Elk took them outside away from the kiva entrance.

"What's going on? And what is she doing with you?" he growled.

Shadow Dancer nervously explained how Spotted Deer had followed him to his ledge and spent the night with him. He told the shaman that they wanted to marry. He then asked for Grey Elk's permission knowing this might require a release from his apprenticeship as a medicine man. Shadow Dancer explained that there had been peyote buttons mixed in with the piñon nuts that Grey Elk had given him.

Grey Elk's eyes lit up with curiosity and he cracked a brief smile. "Yes, I had forgotten to remove those buttons. What did you experience in your ecstasy?"

As a medicine man, Grey Elk had often entered a trance-like state under the influence of peyote. He pressed the young couple to learn what the spirits revealed to them in their trance.[17] Grey Elk was curious to know whether Shadow Dancer and Spotted Deer

17. Shamans believed that these plants enabled the extra corporeal flight of the shamans and that the ecstatic religious experience induced by the peyote allowed them to enter the spirit world. Shamanism was dependent on the messages received from the mysterious world of the spirits.

had likewise entered this realm as he himself had done so many times before.

The teenagers reluctantly described their strange experience from the night before when they had been under the spell of peyote. They explained how they both knew from their magical journey that they were destined for each other. This was all that the spirits revealed. It was why Shadow Dancer needed Grey Elk's permission to marry Spotted Deer and to free him from his apprenticeship with the medicine man.

To their great relief, Grey Elk announced, "Yes, you may marry, but you must still attend your duties each day in the spirit ledge, listening to the spirits until I think you're ready. Your wife can spend the nights there and bring you food, but she must continue to work with the other women during the day. Her mother must arrange a ceremony for you which will bind you together. I will speak to her for you both. Yes, you may marry Spotted Deer and still become a medicine man."

Heaving a sigh of relief, Shadow Dancer awkwardly thanked his mentor. He still had several questions for Grey Elk regarding the unusual activities in their community and in particular the erratic behaviour of the birds of prey in the canyon.

"Please explain to us the meaning of why there are so many ravens and why they drop mice on the clifftop. Is this not most unusual? Is this not a sign for the Nation?" Shadow Dancer was nervous in asking this question to his learned master. He presented Grey Elk with the raven feather, which was considered to be sacred, a symbol of knowledge and creativity.

"You are wise to make these observations, my son. The raven is a playful hunter," he said, holding the sacred feather in the air twirling it between his thumb and forefinger.

"There are many mice infesting our lodges and storage rooms and they have overrun our community. The ravens are catching the mice but there are so many that they drop the mice on the cliff so they can catch more. They are saving them to eat later. They are very wise birds, my son. Think of them as harvesting their food just as we do, to be eaten at another time."

"But why are there so many mice, Grey Elk?"

"Because we live in a time of abundance. There was much rain last year which blessed our crops but too much food attracts mice and they grow rapidly in numbers. So you see, we have fallen victim to our own prosperity. It may get worse. But don't fret about these things. You will have a young bride to look after soon."

The shaman smiled weakly at Spotted Deer and handed the feather to her as a gesture of friendship. Blushing and lowering her gaze, Spotted Deer accepted his gift. She immediately began to twirl the feather nervously between her finger and thumb. The teenagers then ran back to the ledge to continue their lovemaking.

Their yearning for each other had become incandescent; they began meeting frequently in their secret aerie, grasping and groping as if their very lives depended on each other. Shadow Dancer had no more chance of focusing on the spirits in his cliff chamber than he did of returning the raven feather to its elusive owner. Times were indeed good in the valley of the great houses.

Sharp-faceted quartz edges, honed by the sand-ladened winds reflected hundreds of vermilion sparkles in their alcove as the sun slowly set, and a calm, still darkness sank down on the great houses of Chaco Canyon. The piercing trill of a screech owl broke the endless canyon silence as sheet lightning flashed in the eastern horizon. A full moon brimming with albescent pearl soon rose in the south like a pale, unblinking eye.

Chapter 18

Desert Reliquary

I am the same as you in God's sight;
I too am a piece of clay.
~ Job: 33:6

After descending slowly to the canyon floor, Isabella and Rachel hiked to the Suburban for a ride to the work site where they joined Brown, Nesbitt, and Walter Etcitty. Leaving the paved part of the park road at the western end of the canyon, they travelled over a bumpy gravel road for a few hundred feet where two "No Trespassing" signs and several old sawhorses were placed at intervals on the road. They parked their vehicle beside a second white Suburban from the university which the men had used to drive to the site. They had been photographing and labelling pottery that had been recently unearthed. A large pit excavated to a two-foot depth revealed numerous ollas, corrugated jars, pitchers, and bowls, all of the typical black-on-white style and all at least nine hundred years old, and most of them still remarkably intact.

The glint of several shards of shattered pots nearby caught Rachel's attention and she noticed the broken ring of a corrugated jar. Carefully picking it up and turning it over in her hands, she admired the black zigzag design with triangles painted in an almost perfect symmetrical pattern. She was astounded to find a human fingerprint impressed on the bottom of the jar as if it were a signature. Several intact cylinder jars with handles lay nearby in the sand.

"Well, Rachel, what do you think of our find? It was a stroke of luck as the site wasn't on the team's original survey area. By the way, you are the second person to have held that jar in nearly eight hundred years. Stan discovered it just a few weeks ago. This is all classic Anasazi corrugated cookware. Most of the pottery in Chaco Canyon has been removed over the past century so this is indeed a rare find," Nesbitt said.

Rachel carefully picked up one of the cylinder jars and held it by the handle as if she were drinking coffee, while Isabella took her photo.

"By the way, that cylinder jar was probably used to drink broth made from maize or water. DNA studies of the residue in a similar mug found here revealed chocolate," Nesbitt advised.

"Chocolate?"

"Yep. Cacao was likely imported from Meso-America along with parrots, macaws and little copper bells."

"This is unbelievable. How did you protect it from being looted out here in the open and why are they buried so far from the great houses?"

"Well, to answer your first question, we had two of our undergrads camp here for the past few days keeping an eye on things. The park employees were also asked to keep visitors away. We'll be removing most of the artifacts today for further analyses and more pictures will be taken at the university where they will eventually end up in the Maxwell Museum. To answer your second question, we can only speculate that they were buried under several inches of sediment from flash floods over the centuries.

There's probably a lot more nearby. But we're not sure why they're way out here away from the great houses. Doesn't make any sense."

"But how did you know they were here? How did you find them in the first place?" Rachel asked.

"Actually, we were experimenting with some new ground penetrating radar equipment in the area and by chance we found a disturbance in the soil strata here. A few hours of brush and trowel work and voilà. This is where you come in, Rachel. We need to excavate this whole area which could take awhile. This desert reliquary has somehow eluded archaeologists and pot hunters for over a hundred and fifty years. So say goodbye to those lovely fingernails. In a week or so you'll have 'archaeologists hands' complete with callouses and broken fingernails. Here, maybe these will help," Nesbitt added.

He grinned and threw a pair of new leather work gloves towards Rachel with her name written on each one. Picking up the personalized gloves she noticed the right glove had the word "Right" written on it in large black letters and the left glove was similarly labelled with the word "Left."

"We weren't sure if you knew your right hand from your left being a Canadian and all, so we thought we would help you out a little," Nesbitt joked. The two women looked at each and broke into laughter. Rachel smirked while playfully throwing the gloves back at Nesbitt.

"Thank you so much!" Rachel deadpanned, rolling her eyes. "I suppose this is what you were discussing at the restaurant that evening before Rolly and I arrived?" Rachel asked.

"Well, as a matter of fact, we haven't stopped discussing it since this discovery was made a few weeks ago. We were debating that evening at the restaurant how to write up a paper for presentation to the *Journal of Anthropological Archaeology.*"

"What else do you hope to find with this project?" Rachel asked.

"We'll just have to get our trowels into the ground and see what other relics from the past reveal themselves," Nesbitt replied.

The team quickly got back to work. Wearing her new work gloves, Rachel began at one end of the pit, carefully brushing the sand away, scooping soil up with her trowel and depositing it in a large wooden frame. At the bottom of the frame was a screen used to sift for smaller pieces, flakes, and tiny ceramic fragments which would give information regarding the creator of the pottery. This was a painstaking procedure and she realized how it might take months to cover the entire area. Meanwhile, Isabella began packing the labelled pots and cylinder jars into wooden boxes with packing foam pellets. Stan Brown wrapped duct tape around the boxes and Walter placed them carefully in the Suburban for transport back to Albuquerque. Everyone worked methodically and slowly with the precious Chaco pottery. By the time the sun was beginning to disappear at the western end of the canyon, they had finished their work for the day and were heading back to the campground located around the corner from the visitor centre. Not far away a pair of white trailers with the University of New Mexico logo were lined up near two portable toilets each labelled "men" or "women".

"Welcome to the Chaco Canyon Hotel, Rachel. Wait til you hear the coyotes howling later this evening. Some nights it's almost impossible to sleep but we do have ear plugs," Isabella advised. "You and I share the trailer on the right."

After unloading their gear into the trailers they sat in lawn chairs around a small fire pit. Nesbitt brought out a cooler of beer while Stan played country music from the same old ghetto blaster Rachel had seen at the Maxwell Centre. Walter started a fire and fed it mesquite logs which he unloaded from the back of the Suburban.

Rachel hadn't felt this peaceful and contented in a long time but she felt that something was still missing. She wanted to share the excitement of the day with her husband. She wanted to tell him about her near brush with death on the rocky trail with Isabella earlier that day, and the mysterious arm that held her back. She pulled out her cell phone to text her husband but it couldn't pick up a signal in the canyon, so she reluctantly turned it off and put it away. She opened a bottle of Corona and sat near the fire.

The wind picked up slightly and a lone tumbleweed rolled through the campground, rustling past the group as if it were a StarWars android, intent on some secret mission known only to itself, disappearing across the road into the endless scrublands. A few gritty swirls of sand blew between the trailers, fanning the fire to a bright crimson flame.

While sitting outside sipping her beer, Rachel watched the sun slowly leave the sky, spewing streaks of pale blue luminescence, catching high in the cirrus clouds over the canyon. A coyote whisked out of the wash and chased a small animal across the asphalt road into the snake grass. She watched the setting sun's purple-red reflection off the distant mesas as it congealed over the horizon.

If only Rolly could be here. He would love this.

Chapter 19

Outbreak

What is life? It is the flash of a firefly in the night. It is the breath of a buffalo in the wintertime. It is the little shadow which runs across the grass and loses itself in the sunset.
~ Crowfoot

Remember that your children are not your own, but are lent to you by the Creator.
~Mohawk

Following approval from each of their clans the young couple were soon married. Shadow Dancer joined his wife's clan as custom dictated. Shortly following their wedding ritual, Spotted Deer and Shadow Dancer took up residence in a room on the fifth floor of the great house as newlyweds, an apartment next to her parents. Each day they were able to look out of a window onto the Chaco community from the highest point of the great house.[18] From there they watched the canyon come alive each day.

---

18. They had no idea it was the tallest building in North America, perhaps one of the tallest in the world at that time.

Early morning the sun sliced through the drifting haze of woodsmoke from a hundred fires that were lit for the day's cooking. Then they followed the busy swarm of people carrying out their various chores like water beetles circling on a stagnant pond.

Shadow Dancer still spent several hours of the day in his spirit ledge on the nearby cliff face at the behest of the medicine man. Grey Elk was determined that he learn about the spirits in the solitude of the canyon sanctuary.

Yet on most nights, Spotted Deer slept with him on the ledge. She had become uneasy while sleeping in the great house with so much noise coming from the hundreds of families living in such close quarters of the labyrinthine structure. She also didn't like the fact that there were still so many mice living in the honeycomb complex of rooms in the great house.

Before she married Shadow Dancer, Spotted Deer had been living in one of the rooms with her parents, her older sister Morning Bird and Morning Bird's husband Lone Eagle. It was a relief to live in less crowded quarters now with her own husband.

Morning Bird supported Spotted Deer during her wedding ritual; she made a turquoise pendant and a shell bracelet for her as a wedding present. Lone Eagle had gone to great lengths bargaining for the precious turquoise with traders from the southeast where the valuable stone was mined. The blue stone had become a status symbol for the Nation; it was mined in vast quantities for its beauty.[19]

Her family also gave Spotted Deer a coveted parrot feather for good luck. Shells and feathers also were bartered from southern

---

19. Over the years, archaeologists discovered more than 200,000 turquoise pieces at various sites in Chaco Canyon. The gems, which are often embedded into jewellery and figurines, are important to the Puebloan culture to this day.

traders. It pleased her family to see Spotted Deer so happy and they all approved of her choice of a husband.

A few weeks following the wedding rituals, Morning Bird became ill. For several days she was tired and felt dizzy and light-headed whenever she stood up. She then developed a fever, chills, and head-aches. She was no longer interested in eating and vomited several times. A persistent cough left her short of breath and she breathed rapidly. Soon, Lone Eagle developed similar symptoms, accompa-nied by muscles aches and blurred vision with intense headaches. He, too, became short of breath with even mild exertion.

Abdominal pains were severe and he could no longer eat. Spotted Deer left Shadow Dancer in his spirit ledge to come down and minister to her sister and her husband, feeding them a cornmeal broth and tea made from juniper berries and rose hips. As Morning Bird grew sicker by the day she asked Shadow Dancer to call for the medicine man to minister to them both.[20]

Grey Elk came to their room with several pouches of herbal medicines and a handful of eagle feathers.

"Hmm!" was all he could say when he examined the nineteen-year-old girl who by this time had developed a rash. Grey Elk held out one of the feathers, a charm used in healing ceremonies and waved it over the stricken woman.

"She should be in the kiva where others can minister to her," was all he could offer, but Morning Bird was too weak to move. In fact, she had to sit up in order to breathe. Her husband likewise lay in a

20. What was taking place within the stricken natives' blood cells was a hijacking of sorts. The young Anasazis were infected with a virus to which they had never been exposed. In this case the virus had a preference for lung cells which once infected allowed body fluids to enter the lung interrupting the exchange of oxygen. Once this process began the lungs quickly filled up with serum causing pulmonary edema, a condition in which the patient basically suffocates, drowning in their own fluids.

state of languor in their small room within the great house, unable to eat or move. Other clan members living in adjacent rooms also became sick and soon the sounds of coughing and hacking echoed throughout the great house throughout the day. After a week the entire complex stank of death and several bodies were piled up outside the stone wall of the great house. Several women of the great house were kept busy washing, dressing, and handling the bodies of the dead. It was a gruesome task but it was necessary to keep the corpses outside the great house because of the smell and because of the fear of the lingering spirits that needed to be released away from the abode of the living.

Days passed with no improvement, and one night Lone Eagle's breathing became so laboured that his chest rattled and gurgled as if it were full of water. His cough deteriorated to a shallow rasp and his face became dusky, his nail beds blue. His eyeballs had sunk into their sockets. The medicine man, helpless to do anything, gave him some peyote to chew on and an extract of Osha root, which he used to treat various respiratory ailments. He halfheartedly waved an eagle feather over Lone Eagle's head.

In spite of the kind care he was given, Lone Eagle's skin turned cold and grey; within a few hours he passed away in the arms of his sick wife, who wept until morning.

Morning Bird slowly recovered from her sickness largely because of the care and comfort provided by Spotted Deer, who stayed at her side night and day. Many others in the great house were not so fortunate. The smell of sweet sage smoke permeated the air to overcome the stench of death.

Weeping and mourning carried on for days and still more people became ill with "the coughing sickness." Dozens of children likewise succumbed to this unusual desert malady. The elders didn't know what to do; some talked of bad spirits in the Chaco community and they discussed whether or not they all shouldn't just pack up and leave, establishing themselves elsewhere. Others felt they should stay, as there was much food to be harvested along the wash before the coming winter. Besides, the dead needed to be buried. The elders determined that they would be buried as far away from the great houses as possible. Teams of men dragged the corpses on travoises into the local side canyons for burial. Only the bodies of elders and sages were allowed to be buried within the great houses, but space was running out even there, and so several were removed for internment deeper in the canyon with the rest of the dead.

Making mental observations, Grey Elk recognized that whatever this illness was, it seemed to be characterized by a brief mild illness followed by a rapid decline in breathing. He knew that with this illness the lungs often filled up with water. He noted this was a bad sign since four out of ten of those who were so afflicted would die. Those who survived the plague remained debilitated with cough and fatigue for weeks. Some never stopped coughing.

Grey Elk was puzzled and disturbed over the high number of young people who were still dying. He sadly realized that none of his medicines worked. His countenance gradually assumed an aura of stagnating doom as he watched more bodies being carried out of the great house and he felt like a failure as a medicine man. He questioned whether witchcraft was behind this epidemic. He asked other medicine men this question and several felt that the coughing sickness was caused by the intervention of a supernatural being or perhaps one of their own people who held special evil powers, a sorcerer of sorts. They felt a thorough search of the Nation might expose such a troublemaker. Others believed it was a dead ancestor as the cause of this mischief and that a search of this type would be fruitless. In any case, the shamans agreed that some type of spiritual intervention was necessary to combat the powers behind the illness.

The next day Grey Elk arranged for a ceremony in the Great Kiva with other shamans in which chanting and prayers were uttered. Beginning in a high and descending pitch, Grey Elk repeated the same prayers, dancing before a fire in the centre of the massive room, calling out to ancestors with an urgency in his voice. A central fire cast an eerie orange light on the silent congregants whose shadows stretched grotesquely upwards like a bizarre carousel within the cylinder of the kiva. After several hours the crowd quietly dispersed, returning tentatively to their rooms in the great house.

Shadow Dancer feared for his young bride and himself. After seeing so many of his people die, he insisted that Spotted Deer stay with him as much as possible, away from the great house where many of the sick people seemed to be clustered. They spent much of their time up on the cliffs, sleeping in the alcove, wondering what they should do.

"Let's just stay up here for now. This is where the shaman wants me anyways. I think we're safer here, Spotted Deer."

"But what's causing so many of our people to get sick and die?" She trembled at the thought of losing more family and friends.

"I wish I knew. If it gets any worse we may have to leave the Nation."

"Where would we go? We can't just leave our people because they're sick."

"If we don't leave soon, then we will all get sick and die like the rest of them. We could head south towards the holy mountain where they harvest the logs for the buildings here. It might be safer."

At eleven thousand feet above sea level, the mountain was snow-covered much of the year, its base covered in piñon pine, ponderosa pine, and spruce that were harvested for the construction of many of the beams in the Chaco great houses. Following the prayers and

ceremonies in the Great Kiva, people continued to die of the mysterious ailment. Grey Elk looked to the mountain as a place of refuge
for his people and several elders of other great houses also talked
about leaving the Chaco community to escape the ravages of the
brutal epidemic that was devastating the Nation.

Many elders felt they should migrate east, others south towards
the holy mountain while others were determined to venture west
towards the Chuska Mountains, where many of the massive spruce
and fir timbers were harvested for the great houses.

After a lengthy discussion, the sage held a second ceremony in
the Great Kiva and called to the spirits of the ancestors for guidance.
In the end, the community broke up and divided itself into several
clans, each heading in a different direction just to get away from the
deathly scene that surrounded them. Shadow Dancer was now convinced the raven had been warning him about this tragedy unfolding
among his people and told Spotted Deer that his predictions had
come true.

Over the course of ten weeks, a third of the Chaco community
had died of the strange malady. The elders concluded that a great
evil had come to their community to drive them away and that they
should leave as soon as possible before more people died. After dwelling in this remarkable area for centuries, it was difficult to just leave
en mass but they had no choice. Several families banded together,
leaving their ancestral home for the first time, many leaving their
food uneaten. Meanwhile mice continued to proliferate, consum-
ing much of the stores of corn and beans in spite of efforts to keep
them away.

Mice seemed to infest every crack in the ground and every nook
within the great house walls, leaving the Chacoans powerless to
eradicate them. At times it seemed as if the ground was moving,
such were their numbers. Condors soared daily overhead, savouring

the smell of death. Shadow Dancer asked the shaman why this was happening.

"There is much more in life than we can directly see, my son. This coughing sickness is a mystery to me. It is as if a curse were laid upon us."

Shadow Dancer knew that shamans were considered as prophets and priests, operating as a secret society in which the arts and practices of each medicine man were kept from others including the uninitiated members of his own tribe. He was aware that a prolonged apprenticeship was required from those who would become members of this elite group. Still, he found it extremely frustrating when his mentor failed to give him any clear answers. He was disappointed with Grey Elk's lack of any demonstrable curative powers over this epidemic, despite the fervency of his prayers. But he knew Grey Elk was right about one thing. It was not poverty or famine, but rather their prosperity and the abundance of food that was bringing about the imminent and tragic end of their sophisticated society.

Chapter 20

The Dig

We know our lands have now become more valuable.
The white people think we do not know their value;
but we know that the land is everlasting, and the few
goods we receive for it are soon worn out and gone.
~ Canassatego

Leaving Rachel and Isabella with Walter at the excavation site the next day, Nesbitt and Brown drove back to Albuquerque to the University of New Mexico to bring their newly discovered treasures from Chaco Canyon to the Maxwell Museum.

"Rachel, we have thirteen well-preserved pots, cylinder jars, and ollas from the Anasazi era circa 1150 from this site. They are an absolute godsend for the Department of Anthropology. They must be worth hundreds of thousands of dollars and there may be even more in that site. Walter is staying with us as he has a very sharp eye for pottery shards," Isabella said.

"That's fantastic! I can't wait to start working on it."

"This type of pottery would have been common in the Southwest 140 years ago, but pot hunters have left few undiscovered ceramic relics especially in the Chaco Canyon area," Isabella explained.

In an effort to find more pottery, the two women began working on the site which had yielded such highly prized artifacts. Walter quietly worked with them.

Rachel continued to be intrigued by Walter and his unique cultural background as a Navajo. Working alongside each other the next day Rachel couldn't resist asking him more questions.

"So, Walter, how long have you been working with the Department of Anthropology?"

"About ten years or so, on and off," he replied as he carried two pails of soil to the large wooden tripod sifting box, which contained the metal rocker screens of different-sized mesh. Occasionally he would pluck a small shard from the screen and call Isabella to identify and label it. Most of them were angular black-on-white pieces of Anasazi pottery of little value.

"How do you like working at this particular site?" Rachel asked

"You mean here in Chaco Canyon? Well, I've been to about fifty sites in New Mexico, but this one is definitely the most interesting."

"Really? Which other sites have you worked at?"

"Well for starters, Mesa Verde, Canyon de Chelly, and Aztec to name a few."

"How does it feel to be working where your ancestors lived and worked so long ago?"

"Not my ancestors. You forgot I'm Navajo and these people were all Anasazi. By the time my ancestors came here there was nobody around. They had all left the scene three hundred years earlier. My people just found abandoned great houses and kivas. No, these people were the ancestors of the Hopi, the Zuni, and the Acoma. Probably all the Pueblo groups in New Mexico can trace their ancestors to this area."

Immediately Rachel remembered Rolly's description of the native history of the Southwest and she bit her lip. She was embarrassed to have forgotten this important information about the Navajo people.

How stupid am I? Of course the Navajo came later.

"I'm sorry. I forgot about that, Walter. Now I recall that your ancestors came from Canada around the year 1500, right? They were the first snow birds to New Mexico."

"I guess so. But they didn't like what they saw here and they stayed away at first."

"Hm. Why do you suppose they did that? Why didn't they just move into the great houses themselves? After all, the buildings were probably still in good shape at that time, don't you think?"

"They stayed away from this place because they thought it was haunted. Evil spirits and dark forces, you know? In Navajo we call it *chindi*."

"*Chindi*? Do you believe in that stuff Walter?"

"Yes, I do, but I'm not afraid of this place. I don't think it's haunted. Neither do all the employees in the cultural centre who are Navajo. I think we're more enlightened than we were in 1500, although some of my people are still afraid of the *yee-yah* associated with the Chaco ancestors."

"*Yee-yah*? Is that another Navajo expression?"

"Yes. It means scary or dangerous. Whatever it is that makes you afraid."

"So what is it about this place that spooked the first Navajo people who came here in the 1500s?"

"Nobody knows for sure, but imagine if you came to a place like this five hundred years ago with all these magnificent buildings, some of them five stories tall without a single soul in sight. I think it would seem a little creepy even for white people to find so many massive great houses completely abandoned. Many of our people still believe the spirits of the 'ancient ones' live here in the canyon, and that's what makes it spooky for them."

"I understand what you're saying, Walter. I find the place a little spooky myself." Rachel was beginning to appreciate Walter's common sense approach to history. He certainly wasn't as quiet as Nesbitt suggested and he showed remarkable insight into the history of the Chaco complex.

Walter scooped up another shovelful of sandy soil from the pit and carried it to the sifting box. He then rocked the screens for several minutes quietly looking for artifacts in the soil before returning to the pit.

"So, Walter, what motivates you to work here? The money? The history?"

"I like working outdoors. I also like to work at this site because the canyon is sacred to my ancestors. The Navajo have lived in this area for about five hundred years and I want to preserve it from development. I come here every year to celebrate the season of the summer at the solstice ceremony because we believe the canyon has spiritual powers."

"Um, what do you mean 'preserve it from development?'"

"Haven't you heard? The Resources and Development Committee wants Congress to cut its Chaco Canyon Protection bill by half. That means that the ten-mile buffer zone around the Chaco Canyon

Natural Historical Park will be reduced to five miles and the oil companies will be allowed to enter the area and do their fracking and drilling."

"They can do that?"Rachel asked incredulously.

"Sure. It's all federal land. They do whatever they want with federal or Indian land," Walter replied.

"That's insane. Why would they request a law like that?"

"They say that it will benefit the Navajo who live within the ten-mile area to provide them with royalties, but many people think it will cause a lot of damage to the area. They want to buy us off to get their oil even if it means violating sacred grounds. Frankly, I don't see how all the fracking and drilling helps the communities at all. We know there are many people without running water, but there's going to be lots of water used at the fracking sites. Why won't the gas and oil industry help people more?" Walter asked. "They do nothing for the Navajo community!"

"Gosh, Walter, just how much area is involved with this bill?" Rachel asked.

"They say that the legislation would open up over 300,000 acres for oil and natural gas development. We need to protect the history and culture of both the Pueblo and Navajo people. Having university archaeologists like you working here is important in opposing this bill. Think of the thousands of undiscovered artifacts in the area that would be destroyed with this kind of activity."

The late morning was heating up. Walter put his shovel down and took off his hat, pouring himself a few sips of water. Isabella had been quietly digging and listening to this conversation. She had never heard Walter open up quite like this. She decided to weigh in on the conversation.

"Walter, this is incredible. I can't believe this committee is serious about passing this bill." Isabella exclaimed.

"Well, we Navajo have a long history with the white man and his laws. We have never trusted them to this day after they removed us from our lands in the last century. It's the way of the *bilagáana* I'm afraid to say."

"As you might have guessed that's Dineh for *white man*, Rachel," Isabella interjected.

"Right. I'll have to tell Rolly I'm getting a real education on the politics of the Southwest and it doesn't sound very good. In fact, it's rather depressing."

"No, this bill affects us all, not just the Navajo, Rachel. Think of the artifacts that could be destroyed. We have years of work still to do in this area. Of course our department is currently actively lobbying against this bill and we're supporting a piece of legislation called the Chaco Culture Heritage Protection Act which would prevent this sort of thing from ever happening. Like Walter said, this act would protect the heritage and culture of both the Navajo and Pueblo people," Isabella explained.

Walter put his equipment aside, pulled out a knapsack containing his lunch, and sat down on a nearby rock in the shade. The two women followed suit and lifted a cooler with drinks and sandwiches which they had made the night before. Sitting close to Walter they both wanted to continue the conversation regarding the legislation since it affected their jobs as well.

The sudden sound of a loud ricochet startled them as several fragmented pieces of rock blew off in all directions only a few feet away. Simultaneously, a streak of blood revealed itself on Isabella's left leg, a red gash from a small rock shard that embedded itself in her calf.

Isabella let out a cry. Two seconds later the sharp crack of a gunshot reverberated in the canyon, releasing a series of booming echoes.

A piñon jay exploded from a juniper near the wash in a burst of black-and-white feathers, while a roadrunner darted from a tunnel in the nearby sage.

Chapter 21

Exodus

Take nothing but memories,
leave nothing but footprints.
~ Seattle

The population of entire cities moved
into other worlds never again to return.
~ Navajo Elder

Shadow Dancer and his young wife joined a group of several hundred other natives on a late summer day as they headed south. Clutching their worldly possessions in large yucca fibre baskets and food in clay ollas, they traversed the canyon, looking back at the magnificent great houses where they had lived all their lives. Several women wept bitterly for they were not only leaving their ancestral homes, but also several of their loved ones who had died. Buried in shallow graves along the wash, the bones of the dead would be swept away by flash floods into the San Juan Basin over the centuries.

Several of the elders who died of the infection were entombed under the floors of the great houses with thousands of turquoise beads and macaw feathers. Their bodies were buried in a fetal position to better prepare them for their entry into the next world.

Setting out with their families and leaving behind the dead and dying, Shadow Dancer's clan pulled dozens of travoises made of poles and hides. Several were hauled by dogs but most of them were drawn by hand, making this migration exceedingly difficult for everyone. Nevertheless it was possible for a man to transport more weight on a travois than could he could carry on his back.

Spotted Deer wrapped several of her pots and mugs in deer hides and tied them to the travois with leather thongs. After barely a mile it was obvious that their trip was going to be more difficult than they had planned with the added weight of the pottery. Shadow Dancer could not see how they could travel the sixty miles to the sacred mountain with all his wife's pottery on the travois.

"We'll have to leave some of your pots here, my love. We need to take enough beans, corn, and water with us for the journey. I'm sorry but we must leave some behind. They're just too heavy."

Spotted Deer wept at the thought of leaving her prized ollas and jars behind. Shadow Dancer tried to comfort her and put his arm around her.

"I know you're right. It's just that I spent hours coiling and firing and painting them. These were my favourite pieces. It's a shame to just leave them here out in the open desert for others to take, Shadow Dancer."

"We could bury them here in case we ever come back. We can place some stones as markers to help us find them in the future."

Spotted Deer had no choice. They hastily dug a long shallow pit into which they placed a dozen cylinder jars and pots, covering them with a few inches of sand. Shadow Dancer placed marker stones nearby. They could not foresee that after only a few years, flash floods would wash away the marker stones and cover the pottery with several more inches of sand and stones, leaving them buried and undisturbed in the valley floor for the next eight centuries.

A flock of piñon jays flew across the canyon rim and glided downwards towards the young couple as if to bid them farewell with their harsh nasal calls before flying away towards the chunky buttes in the western horizon. Spotted Deer turned around to see the great stone desert city for one last time.

Chapter 22

Rogue Assassin

Coyote is always out there waiting,
and coyote is always hungry.
~ Navajo Proverb

The stony fragment that struck Isabella's leg was split off from a larger rock by a bullet travelling at 3200 feet per second. Less than two seconds later it was followed by its own sound travelling at 1100 feet per second as it left the muzzle. Walter quickly calculated the shooter must be almost half a mile away.

Could be a thirty-aught-six. Or maybe a thirty-thirty to fire from that range.

Dropping their lunches, all three quickly dove for cover behind several large rocks against the cliff-side. For an instant Isabella thought she had been shot. She panicked when she realized they had no idea from which direction the shot had been fired. She looked at Rachel who sat frozen, her mouth open in shock. Within a few more seconds another bullet zinged past them, smashing into their cooler, exploding pieces of blue plastic casing and splashing water into the air. Again, a short interval before the harsh blast of the rifle could be heard like thunder after a lightning strike. Looking up to the cliffs, Walter could see the glint of reflected sunlight several hundred yards high up on the mesa top, a brief flash betraying the shooter's position.

Two seconds, all right — must be an HK three-oh-eight coming from the cliffs. He's using a tripod and a telescopic sight with that light reflection.

Walter felt that the shots were coming from a Heckler and Koch PSG1 semi-automatic sniper rifle, at one time claimed to be one of the most accurate semi-automatic sniper rifles in the world. He knew that with a muzzle velocity of almost three thousand feet per second, the 300 Magnum was deadly accurate from as far away as six hundred yards with a range of twice that distance.

"This is not good," he whispered.

"Where the heck are those shots coming from?" Rachel asked, scanning the canyon rim.

"I think it's from the cliffs up there behind us to the east. We need to head for cover up the rincon," Isabella shouted, holding her leg which by now was covered in blood. Rachel had no idea what a rincon was but she quickly followed Walter and Isabella into the angular recess of a large cleft in the cliff face that extended inwards for sixty feet.

Another bullet zipped overhead, bursting open Walter's knapsack, shattering his Thermos, sending coffee and glass flying everywhere. Scrambling as fast as they could, the three found themselves huddled in the alcove within the cliff face, out of the line of sight from the cliff tops where they figured the shooter must be.

"Damn, I just bought that Thermos this past week. Whoever is shooting at us has pretty good aim," Walter said wearing a taut expression.

"Aim? Good grief. He missed us three times! His aim isn't so good, Walter," Isabella exclaimed.

"I don't think he was trying to shoot us or one of the bullets would have connected by now. I think he's trying to scare us away by hitting our stuff. Those are warning shots."

"But he shot Isabella in the leg. Omigosh, Isabella, are you all right? Let me see your leg," Rachel said.

"I'm okay. It's just a laceration from a small piece of rock that ricocheted. It's not a bullet. But boy does it sting."

"But it's still bleeding a lot. Walter, we need to put a tourniquet on that leg," Rachel said with panic in her voice.

Walter didn't answer as he focused on his knapsack lying on the ground which was now covered in coffee and pieces of glass. He then looked at his purple fingernail for several seconds and then turned his gaze back to his knapsack. Without warning he made a mad dash back to the work site for his knapsack. Grabbing it by the straps, he quickly wheeled around only to hear the rush of air as another bullet struck the sandy soil behind him with a loud *thwack*. A spray of sand and small rocks exploded into the air and a hand trowel flipped upwards and somersaulted several times. Panting and perspiring, Etcitty scrambled back into the rincon and dove for safety, landing on his elbows with a thud in front of the two women. He muttered something in Navajo as he managed to stand up and brush the red soil from his denims.

"Walter, you're crazy. Why did you do that? You could have been killed!" Isabella shouted.

Ignoring her, he sat on his haunches, resting on the back of his heels and carefully plucked several shards of glass and the remains of his Thermos from the knapsack.

Reaching down to the bottom he pulled out a small silver .22 calibre pocket revolver and a coffee-stained Navajo headband. After loading the gun and clicking the safety, he tucked it into his back pocket. He then tied the headband around Isabella's wound and cinched it tightly. The bleeding immediately stopped.

"How does that feel, doc?"

"It's tight and it hurts but at least you've stopped the bleeding. Thank you, Walter. But what do we do now? What if our shooter crosses the mesa and aims from the top of this rincon? We'll be sitting ducks. I don't think that revolver will help from this distance.

What else have you got in your backpack?" Isabella winced as she moved her leg to get a closer look at the contents of the Navajo's knapsack.

"Like I said, I still think if he wanted to kill us we'd be dead by now. Whoever it is, he's a professional. I have my cell phone here but there's no reception inside these cliffs. Anyways my battery is low so we'll have to think of something else," he said stoically.

"Oh boy, I thought this stuff only happened in the movies," Rachel said. "What do you think we should do?"

After staring straight ahead for several seconds, Walter emptied the entire contents of his pack onto the ground and mumbled, "Hm. The movies you say?"

A copy of the *Navajo Times*, a package of cigarettes, a bag of nacho chips, and a couple of Bic lighters tumbled out. Reaching around him, he picked up small pieces of sticks, snake grass, and leaves and piled them together in a heap. Using the newspaper he started a small fire near the outer edge of the rincon with one of the lighters. Rachel found a large tumbleweed and added it to the fire which immediately erupted into flames, sending up a crackling cascade of sparks. The leaves and the tumbleweed quickly produced a column of thick grey smoke, beaded with orange embers, which rose straight up into the air. A smoky incense of burning sage filled the air.

"Bravo, Walter! That smoke should get someone's attention soon," Isabella said.

"But why would anyone shoot at us?" Rachel asked. "And on federal land too? Who would do this?" Her fingers nervously played with her hair.

"*Bilagáana* most likely. I can't see an Indian shooting unarmed women, especially on sacred land. We're doing something that has pissed them off. Could be the oil company I suppose. They really don't want us here," Walter pondered aloud.

"Do you really think they would hire someone to shoot at archaeologists working in a federally run national monument? I mean that's just crazy!" Isabella was becoming angrier by the minute.

Walter remained silent for a few minutes, feeding the fire with whatever he could find.

He opened the bag of nacho chips and passed it to the two women. He reached for his jacket which he had left near the sifters and quickly retrieved it. He then spread it over the fire, holding the smoke from rising for a few seconds at a time, removing it to allow puffs of smoke to arise at intervals. In the distance another shot could be heard echoing in the canyon with a muffled sound.

"I think he's shooting at something else now. It sounds farther away."

"Why, you're sending smoke signals. Good for you, Walter. Is this a Navajo thing?

What exactly is the message you're sending?" Isabella asked.

"Darned if I know. I once saw this in an old John Wayne movie. Rachel gave me the idea. I just figured it's the thing to do in a situation like this. People might not pay too much attention to a plain column of smoke, but they might notice puffs of smoke, don't you think?"

Isabella smiled. "Hah! Some clever Navajo you are, Walter. And here I thought you were sending a secret message."

"Nah, I just don't know what else to do to be honest with you."

"But you're going to ruin your jacket!" Rachel exclaimed.

"I think losing my jacket will be worth saving two *bilagáana* women." Etcitty grinned as he continued to fan the fire which created a crude Morse code of the rising smoke column. After several minutes of doing this he pulled out his pocket revolver and crept to the edge of the alcove that protected them from the shooter. Looking up he could see nothing on the cliffs. He draped his smouldering jacket over a long stick and held it outside the edge of the rincon for several minutes, waiting tentatively for further gunfire. Silence. He waved the jacket back and forth several times. When no further gunshots were heard he decided to slowly creep back out to the work site. Turning around, he beckoned Isabella and Rachel to leave the safety of the rincon and start packing their equipment.

"We'll need to notify the people at the visitors centre and the state troopers as well. I might give my cousin a call at the Navajo tribal office in Shiprock to let them know about the shooting. The shooter would have to escape on Navajo lands, so the tribal police will be on the lookout. And you need to get that leg treated. I'll have to drive you to the hospital in Farmington. You might want to let Brown and Nesbitt know what happened when we get back to the centre."

Walter drew out his cigarettes and a lighter from his tattered backpack and lit one, inhaling deeply.

"Walter, I didn't know you smoked," Isabella said.

"I don't smoke. But you know that we Indians do use tobacco for religious purposes from time to time?" He paused and inhaled again.

"Yes?"

"Well, after the events of this morning I'm feeling a little religious aren't you?" Both women smiled and nodded. "Absolutely!" Isabella exclaimed.

"Okay, let's get out of here, *asdzaa nizhoni*." Drawing his revolver he cautiously led the women to the Suburban and started to head back down the six mile road to the visitor Centre all the while scouring the cliffs to his left.

"What did he say Isabella? He uses too many Navajo words for me to keep up with him."

"I think it's something like *pretty women*. Don't worry, you'll get used to it."

With a startling suddenness, the full-throated roar of an airplane engine echoed from the cliffs. Within seconds a Cessna soared over the canyon rim, rocking its wings from side to side. As soon as the plane flew over the mesa it performed a barrel roll in the canyon, its engine droning loudly overhead. Walter stopped the Suburban for a closer look at the airplane.

"That's Rolly! That's my husband!" Rachel exclaimed with a weary smile. "He always does a roll like that when he sees me."

"Cool," Walter said. "What's his name again?"

"It's Rolly, short for Roland."

"Rolly? I guess that makes sense, the way he flies that plane," Walter deadpanned, watching the aerial acrobatics above the canyon. "But he's going to have to land that plane on the paved highway in the canyon. There's nowhere else for fifty miles. The old landing strip at the other end of the canyon near Route 57 and Route 7980 is in pretty rough shape."

"He could probably land there with his eyes closed. I can assure you, Rolly is an outstanding pilot," Rachel said.

Afternoon storm clouds cast the canyon into a steely grey hue as the three researchers watched the Cessna circle westwards and begin its descent for a rare highway landing within the confines of the red sandstone cliffs onto the shimmering asphalt road of Chaco Canyon.

Chapter 23

Diaspora

I cared for you in the wilderness,
In the land of drought.
~ Hosea 13:5

Following a day's travel the clan encamped near an arroyo, a dry creek bed in the middle of the desert. After starting a fire, several of the young men screamed and howled together across the echo-less plain in a vain attempt to hear their voices returning to them. They had always heard even a faint return of their voices when living in the canyon, but now only an immense brooding quiet drifted over the vastness of the open desert. Several of the elders sat amused by their youthful antics as they tried in vain to create an echo where none existed. In the distance the mountain appeared to be suspended over the desert by a current of shimmering air, a desert mirage that mystified many who had not travelled this far before.

Without the shade provided by the canyon walls, the sun rose earlier than they were used to, and they realized their lives were about to change forever. Looking south, the familiar upthrusting silhouette of the Turquoise Mountain was now only about thirty miles away.[21]

But for the Anasazi migrants wandering in the desert, this mountain was their goal and they hoped it would become their salvation. That night Shadow Dancer and Spotted Deer slept fitfully in their strange new environment on the open plain, without the protective walls of their canyon great house. Camping near the wash, an expanse of silvery chamisa bushes with a scattering of sage offered them meagre protection. Two skeletal junipers a few yards downstream clung tenaciously to the eroded bank, managing to sink their roots in deep enough to survive. The teenagers snuggled into the warm softness of the deer hides and stared into the darkness for a while before falling asleep.

They both awoke in the middle of the night and found themselves embracing each other as they listened to the nocturnal desert orchestra; coyotes yipping and insects chirping, punctuated by the occasional hoot from a desert owl. Shadow Dancer reached for his wife's breasts but Spotted Deer winced. She softly whispered, "My love, I think we are going to have baby."

Shadow Dancer stiffened momentarily and his wife sensed his unease at her unexpected announcement. He paused, realizing the

---

21. The snow-covered peak of Mount Taylor rises four thousand feet above the desert floor. It was considered a sacred mountain for the Anasazi and in centuries to come their descendants; the Acoma Pueblo group knew it as *Kaweshtima*. Later still, the Navajo knew it as *Reaches for the Sky*. In years to come it would become known as *Mount Tsoodzil*, the blue bead mountain by the Navajo. This mountain was active from 3.3 to 1.5 million years ago during the Pliocene Epoch, and is surrounded by a field of smaller inactive volcanoes. Repeated eruptions over eons produced lava domes, ash plumes, and mud flows. Like Mount St. Helens in Washington, the mountain eventually became surrounded by a great volume of volcanic debris, suggesting multiple major eruptions over the centuries. The Turquoise Mountain still marks the southern boundary of Navajo homeland and to this day is held sacred by its people.

---

weight of responsibility that was immediately thrust upon him by this news. Uncertain as to what to say to his wife he did what many men did in this situation and lied, "That's wonderful! When do you think the baby will come?"

"Seven moons from now if we ever find a place to live. I'm afraid for our child with all that's been happening." Spotted Deer exhaled a series of short sighs before she began to cry. She knew her timing was bad but the tears flowed anyways.

Shadow Dancer comforted his wife with a kiss and tried to reassure her.

"Don't worry. We'll be safe away from the canyon and the coughing sickness. we've made it this far and nobody is getting sick anymore. Grey Elk thinks we will be all right once we make it to the holy mountain and that's only two more days for us to travel. Our baby will be safe. We'll start a new life together with our child south of the mountain."

Spotted Deer smiled weakly and embraced her husband once more. They made love under the stars while a thin crescent moon lay low in the south, grazing the distant dark blue rumple of the sacred mountain. Overhead a great river of over one hundred billion stars ran through the sky, illuminating the heavens in a thick scintillating swath of light.

Numerous shooting stars from a meteor shower streaked iridescence across the sky, creating a spectacular light show with the trembling canopy of stars hanging over them. The two youths had never been exposed to the vastness of the night sky, having lived all their lives within the confines of the canyon and the great houses. But now it seemed as though the lights of heaven had somehow found their voices; they felt comforted by these celestial signs in the night-darkness.

"I think these lights in the heavens are a good omen for us," Shadow Dancer whispered to his wife. Looking up he found the familiar constellation which the builders had incorporated into the design of the great house with its numerous kivas. Pointing to it he said, "Look, my love, the Seven Sisters."

But Spotted Deer was already asleep.

Chapter 24

Canyon Landing

The landscape of the American West has to be seen to be believed. And, as I say on occasion, it may have to be believed in order to be seen.
~ N. Scott Momaday, Kiowa

As the Cessna descended into the canyon it bobbed and buckled with the higher air currents like a canoe in rapids but as it continued its descent it found some gentler air. It slipped smoothly into the canyon as though its engine had been turned off, landing with ease on a flat stretch of the asphalt road. Fortunately, there were no tourists on that section of road and the prevailing west wind allowed an effortless landing. Ginger-coloured dust spiralled over the blacktop in loose swirls, chasing the aircraft along the road.

Immediately after touchdown the passenger door flew open and Stan Brown threw up on the ground, his Tilley hat fell out and rolled behind the plane in the light breeze. His seat belt prevented him from following the hat, which quickly blew behind the plane from the draft of the still rotating propeller.

After coming to a complete stop, Boudreau turned off the engine and hopped out, placing a pair of chocks against the wheels. He then helped Brown and Nesbitt stagger out of the plane to solid ground which they both seemed to appreciate. While Brown threw up again, Nesbitt bowed down dramatically to kiss the ground. Rachel just shook her head at the sight, knowing her husband was enjoying every minute of this spectacle.

Turning to Isabella she said, "He always tries to get at least one of his passengers to throw up in the plane. He knows I won't fly with him anymore if he tries that stunt on me."

"You gotta admit it looks pretty funny. Poor Stan. He takes himself so seriously," Isabella chuckled. "Let's go help them with their equipment. He looks absolutely green from that barrel roll."

Within a few minutes, a massive cumulonimbus cloud began building up in the west one hundred miles away close to the 9400-foot Chuska Mountains, along the Arizona-New Mexico border. Faint flashes of lightning blazed every few seconds within the rounded mass of the cauliflower-shaped clouds, scintillating upwards to the top of the thunderhead. Rolly ran towards Rachel; the two held each other in a warm embrace while the rest of the team watched in awkward silence. Nesbitt finally shouted, "C'mon, you two. Rent a room, if you can find one out here."

Rachel turned around blushing. "Sorry, folks. After the experiences of today I really needed a big hug. Besides, I haven't seen my husband in over two weeks. So give a girl a break, will ya?"

"What experiences are you talking about, Rachel?" asked Nesbitt.

"We almost got ourselves killed at the pottery site. Some guy was shooting down at us from the cliffs and scared the heck out of us. Isabella caught a sharp piece of rock when a bullet ricocheted. Thanks to Walter starting a fire, we managed to convince whoever was shooting at us to leave us alone."

"Fortunately Walter knows Indian smoke signals, which he learned from an old Hollywood western. He ruined a perfectly good jacket in the process. I think we all owe him a debt of gratitude and maybe a new jacket," Isabella added.

Ignoring Isabella's comments, Walter stood stoically watching the storm clouds brewing in the west. "I think we should all get over to the visitors centre right away with that storm coming," he said solemnly.

Turning to Rolly he added, "By the way, I'm Walter and that was a nice landing. I've never seen a plane land in the canyon before. Only helicopters. You are very brave to do that."

Walter shook hands with Rolly and mumbled something in Navajo to him. Rolly responded with something in Cree. Neither one understood each other but their eyes met and they nodded to each other and smiled.

"Thank you for taking care of my wife today, Walter. Dr. Nesbitt and Dr. Brown asked me to fly them here and we saw your smoke rising from the cliffs, so we changed course and flew over the mesa. I think we saw your shooter on the mesa top so we decided to fly over him to get a closer look, but then he took a shot at the plane.

"Fortunately he missed, but then he ran away. So who on earth would be taking potshots at a bunch of archaeologists working in a national historic site?"

"We were asking ourselves the same question, Rolly," answered Isabella.

"Walter thinks it might be a hired thug working for the oil company that wants to shrink the canyon's borders, which will increase drilling rights in the region. We have no idea but his shots came mighty close. Walter tied a tourniquet around my leg as it was bleeding a lot. Would you mind taking a look at it, Dr. Nesbitt?"

"Not at all, Isabella. Let's see." Nesbitt carefully removed the Navajo headband which was stained with coffee and blood. Isabella's wound had stopped bleeding, but a small puncture site was evident where the rock chip had entered her leg in the calf just below the knee. Nesbitt removed his glasses and frowned.

"You might have a small chunk of rock lodged in your leg, Isabella. If so, it will need to be removed or you'll get an infection. And it could start bleeding again if you walk on it," Nesbitt advised.

"But how will we know if there's a piece of rock stuck in my leg?"

"Well, we would have to get an X-ray somewhere. Maybe Rolly could fly you to Gallup or back to Albuquerque. That storm seems to be advancing this way so Farmington is out. What do you think, Rolly?"

"I agree. There's no way we can fly through that thunderhead. I'll take both of the ladies back to Albuquerque and we can get Isabella's leg checked there. In the meantime, I suggest you guys might want to head for your trailers before the storm rolls through," Boudreau advised.

"We'll have to let the parks people at the visitors centre know about the shooter. They'll notify the Tribal police as well as the state troopers," Stan Brown said, his normal colour returning to him. He glowered at Boudreau for making him sick.

Rachel helped Isabella into the plane while Boudreau loaded their knapsacks. After a quick inspection of the Cessna, he removed the chocks. The plane took off, ascending steeply westwards towards the impending storm as the din from the plane's engine echoed and reverberated against the wind. When he reached the elevation of the canyon, he veered south making a 180 degree turn towards Albuquerque away from the towering thunderheads. The rest of the team piled into the Suburban and drove east towards the visitors centre.

Rachel turned to her husband once they were airborne and asked, "Where did you get the plane, Rolly?"

"I'm renting it by the hour from a flying school at the airport. Today the university is paying for it since Dr. Brown wanted an aerial view of the canyon. We didn't plan to land in the canyon until we saw the shooter."

"I'm impressed. So what did you say to Walter when you met him?"

"I thanked him for taking care of you. I told him he was very brave."

"Is that all?"

"Well, he mumbled something in Navajo which I didn't understand so I said something to him in Cree, knowing he probably wouldn't understand either. I think he wanted to connect with me because of my native background."

"That's interesting Rolly. But you told me that you hardly remember Cree anymore.

So what did you say to him?"

"I said *miyo-manitowi-kîsikanisi*! I think he was impressed."

"And just what does that mean, sweetheart?"

"It means Merry Christmas. It's all the Cree I can remember." Isabella guffawed from the back seat.

Behind them heavy bruised clouds hung ominously in the western sky with the fading afternoon light. Sporadic flickers of sheet lightning pulsated within them causing the drifting clouds to blaze orange every few seconds. Below them the long shadow of

Fajada Butte stretched eastwards like a giant finger pointing the way to Albuquerque.

Looking down over the Navajo road from Chaco Canyon, Rachel saw a cloud of dust trailing behind the same motor-home that she had seen the week before in the visitor centre parking lot. The vehicle was moving quickly, jostling over the rugged washboard road heading south towards Crown Point. Pulling out her cellphone, she motioned to Rolly to fly over it for a photograph. He immediately complied, arcing the Cessna to the south over the jouncing vehicle. Rachel managed to take several photos of it before the plane resumed its course towards Albuquerque.

Far to the northwest the bastions of the Sangre de Cristo Mountains appeared as looming giants. Below, a panorama of deep canyons, sharp ridges, and coulees created elongated shadows which stretched as giant claws towards the soft vermilion cliffs of the Sandia Mountains, east of Albuquerque. Both Rachel and Isabella were spellbound at the beauty of the Southwestern landscape, having never seen it from this vantage point. They flew across the Chaco Mesa, past the volcanic plug of Cabezon Peak to their left, and snow-capped Mount Taylor to their right just as the sun began to set. Boudreau rocked his wings from side to side several times to allow the women to take better pictures of the spectacular land-forms below.

Rachel marvelled as the brown scrub of desert made the transition to green forest highland and escarpment over the great West Mesa. The shining ribbon of the Rio Grande River stretched southward as molten gold. The Cessna slowly descended, slipping through the scattered clouds above Albuquerque where the street lights sparkled in the twilight. Boudreau made an easy landing, unpacked his gear, and stored the plane in a hangar just as a light breeze from the west trundled a chain of menacing dark clouds over the city.

Chapter 25

Reaches for the Sky

He caused an east wind to blow in the heaven:
and by his power he brought in the south wind.
He rained flesh also upon them as dust, and feathered fowls
like as the sand of the sea: And he let it fall in the midst
of their camp, round about their habitations.
~ Psalm 78: 26-28

The group of migrants from the Chaco complex consisted of a clan numbering over eight hundred men, women, and children heading south towards the massive blue bulk of the Turquoise Mountain which loomed on the horizon as a giant sleeping bear. They fled to escape whatever was causing their people to die in vast numbers in the canyon. Meanwhile, thousands of other survivors of the plague departed westwards towards the Chuska Mountains and beyond. Other groups headed east establishing new settlements at Bandelier and eventually another twenty communities established themselves along the Rio Grande, in New Mexico.

Following another two days of travel the clan finally arrived at the base of the extinct volcano which was enveloped in a misty crown of clouds. It indeed seemed to "reach for the sky" when they looked up at the white cone above. Exhausted, they set up temporary living quarters in the open air after walking through waving amber grass filled with a vast expanse of weather-greyed stumps. Thousands of timbers had been harvested from this field for roof beams used in the construction of the great houses of the canyon. Axe marks imprinted like ancient runes remained on the dried stumps from the past century.

Shadow Dancer threw deer hides on a moss-covered area beneath a ponderosa pine and built a fire twenty feet away, near a small mountain stream. Spotted Deer fell asleep immediately. It was a unique experience for all of them since most Chacoans had been born and raised under a roof within the walled community of Pueblo Bonito. Over the next week only two more children sickened and died from the mysterious ailment.

Mourning mothers would not be comforted.

Subsequently there were no more new illnesses and it seemed that the plague had arrested itself once they were away from the canyon.

Although the sacred mountain afforded easy access to drinking water and ample wood for fires, it proved to be an impossible environment for growing squash or beans with its rocky and acidic soil. After several weeks the migrants resorted to snaring small animals and spearing the occasional mule deer. The elders knew that it would be impossible to stay for any length of time with the elevation contributing to snow and freezing temperatures for much of the winter; they decided to move further south where they knew that a group of Mimbres people had established a small settlement on a large mesa to the south of the mountain.

But before they could mobilize such a large group to embark on the thirty-mile journey, they had to be fed and food was becoming scarce on the mountain. What the clan needed now was a source of protein other than piñon nuts and the occasional squirrel. Grey Elk surveyed the situation and knew they needed a miracle. Several of their clan were starving after travelling so far and lacked the strength to proceed any further. The days were getting shorter and cooler. Moving on was not an option; neither was remaining on the holy mountain. They were not used to this way of life.

One night the clan encamped under a grove of evergreen oak trees for protection on the slopes of the ancient volcano. In desperation several people resorted to eating acorns that had fallen on the ground. Acorns remaining on the tree had been green in September but now had turned to brown, the colour of raw umber and they were less bitter to the taste especially if they were roasted. That night a strong east wind began to blow.

The next morning the pink glow of dawn greeted the clan. Many of those still sleeping were awakened by a sound like a tornado and a wildfire all in one; a cacophony of sounds with clucks, twitterings, harsh cooings, and the flapping of a million wings. This was soon followed by the snapping and cracking of hundreds of breaking branches from the oak trees.

Shadow Dancer jumped up and saw that some of the branches had fallen dangerously close to several of the sleeping families. He was immediately showered with white creamy guano that rained down from thousands of the birds perched overhead. He had never seen so many birds in one place and at first he felt threatened. Large oak branches the size of his wrist had been snapped off by the sheer weight of the flock of birds. The ground quickly became covered with birds in their midst, pecking and cooing and eating fallen acorns and piñon nuts. On the upper branches, birds piled on top of each other in their efforts to find a place to roost, such was the vastness of their numbers. Gnarled branches moaned and creaked under the weight of the enormous flock.[22]

An unusual eastern wind had blown this particular flock off course from its normal range and brought it west to the holy mountain. Using a stone axe, Shadow Dancer began clubbing those birds that had fallen to the ground with the broken branches. He quickly amassed a pile of dead birds in no time, and other young men began doing the same. Simply throwing a club into the air would invariably bring down a bird or two from the oak branches. Once they had accumulated sufficient food, the elders instructed the young men to stop clubbing the birds. Indigenous people managed to live in harmony with nature and these birds were no exception. They knew that they should only kill what they needed to eat or the next time they might go hungry.

Like numerous raw sores on the hide of a colossal animal, the base of the sacred mountain sparkled with hundreds of cooking fires as thousands of birds roasted on juniper branch skewers. The fragrance of burning sage drifted through the trees in the evening air. For the first time since they left on their journey, the voices of singing and laughter was once again heard within the clan. With full bellies, many of the children danced gleefully around the fires as their mothers sang and watched.

---

22. These were passenger pigeons, the most abundant bird in the world constituting forty percent of all North American birds until about 1850. They received their name from the French word *passager*, meaning "passing by" due to the migratory habits of the species. Alexander Wilson, the father of scientific ornithology in America, estimated that one flock consisted of two billion birds. The great American naturalist John James Audubon witnessed a flock of more than of three hundred million that took three days to pass. With its inestimable numbers, the passenger pigeon provided food for native tribes all across the eastern half of the continent sustaining them over millennia.

Later that week, with a sudden massive explosion of wings, the flock left the oak grove, rising to darken the sun for several hours as it flew southwards to warmer climes. This small flock of pigeons consisted of only thirty or forty million birds. In order to fly efficiently with as little weight as possible the birds needed to evacuate their cloacae as soon as they were airborne. As the flock ascended, tons of guano spackled the oak trees with a creamy white rain, leaving the ground as white as snow. Many of the Chaco migrants quickly hid under branches, others covered their heads with hides. Those who couldn't avoid the droppings appeared as old men with white hair. They laughed at each other as the roar of fluttering wings continued unabated overhead. The noise from the birds' wings was as the thundering of a waterfall, such that the Chacoans could not hear each other's voices until the bulk of the massive murmuration of birds had finally left.

None of the Chacoans would ever forget this experience. The elders deemed it a miracle, a sign that they had done the right thing to leave the canyon. Grey Elk smiled for the first time in months as he faced skyward with his eyes closed when the birds flew away, freely allowing himself to be doused by the foul-smelling ordure as if it were a holy unction from the gods.

Surely we are on the right path. This must be a sign to move on.

After a week of feeding on pigeons, the Anasazi migrants had sufficiently renewed their strength to move on towards the mesa that would eventually become known as Acoma. The clan reasoned they could survive the winter by following the flock south where they could once again plant corn, beans, and squash. But the flock returned east to its usual range. It took another century before the birds were blown off course again this far west.

A few days following the birds' departure a gentle rain washed the guano into the rocky soil, providing nourishment for the trees that covered the base of the mountain. Grey Elk washed himself in the rain and spent the rest of the day looking up to see if any birds remained in the trees. But there was only an immense, brooding, and motionless silence on the slope of the holy mountain; it seemed as if it had always been that way.

The immense flock of birds had scoured the oak grove of acorns and the piñon pine of their nuts and then left. Instead of the awful stench from the bird droppings, the refreshing smells of wet sage, piñon resin, and buffalo grass consecrated the mountain air after the invigorating rain.

For the next seven hundred years these "feathered tempests" thundered annually across the skies, eclipsing the sun, and resting on trees, indulging on the seeds and fruits of prairie and forest to empower their seemingly endless flight across the vastness of their range on the North American continent. For centuries they sustained man's survival as if it were a small thing. The sound of the flapping of their wings would split the air; they were invariably heard before they were seen. Flocks a mile wide and two hundred miles long landed in fields in crashing waves, terrifying hunters or anyone else nearby fortunate enough to witness this great phenomenon of nature. It was not until the arrival of millions of Europeans to North America in the late nineteenth century that this extraordinary bird was doomed to extinction.[23]

---

23. From being a wonder of the natural world, this bird of passage was totally annihilated within the span of a few years. Its propensity to concentrate in great numbers proved disastrous for the passenger pigeon as it enabled mass slaughter by hunters and farmers. The species was shot, netted, and clubbed into oblivion, often just for sport. From uncountable numbers its precipitous decline began in the 1870s. The last known specimen died on the first of September, 1914 in a zoo in Cincinnati, Ohio.

But in the late autumn of the year 1198, the passenger pigeon kept eight hundred wandering Anasazi alive on the holy Turquoise Mountain, enabling them to continue their search for a new homeland.

Chapter 26

Canyon Storm

Thunder echoes
through seven hundred
empty rooms,

a massive pueblo
of mud bricks
curved around sacred kivas,

perfectly aligned
with the cycles
of sun, moon, and stars,

keeping track
of heavenly journeys
for twelve hundred years.
~ Blue Raven

After the Cessna took off, Walter Etcitty, Stan Brown, and Jack Nesbitt drove east toward the Chaco visitor centre. The storm loomed in the west just as the sun began to set. Soon the darkened sky hung heavy with pendants of stratonimbus clouds that formed a grey blanket, covering the canyon great houses like a shroud.

After notifying the park staff and warning the Navajo Tribal police in Shiprock about the shooter, the men settled into their trailers just as the storm hit the canyon with all the ferocity of a tropical monsoon. Driving rain in thick sheets swept through the canyon, rinsing the desert dust off the millions of sandstone bricks of the sixteen great houses.

Water quickly drenched the roads and ditches, filling the Chaco wash by several feet. Lightning coursed across the sky and thunder rumbled and echoed between the canyon walls with such short intervals that it sounded like an artillery barrage. Water poured down from the mesa top, first in narrow runnels and rivulets over the slickrock terraces; then in cascades and heavy torrents that filled the numerous gulches, draws, and rincons that drained into the centre of the great canyon.

In the midst of the mounting gloom in the canyon, bright orange flashes reflected from the sandstone cliff walls every few seconds, exposing the ancient great houses as ghostly castles, otherworldly structures. A small herd of canyon elk huddled fearfully near the Kin Kletso great house, immobilized behind a sandstone wall in the lee of the storm. Their antlers glistened with every flash of lightning as they stood motionless, eerie phantoms sulking and cringing under the pelting rain.

Sitting safely in the trailer, the three men drank beer, munching on nacho chips while the metal roof reverberated with the thunder and clattered from the falling rain. It was a deafening tumult, like a thousand beating wings. Once the storm abated the men could finally hear each other and carry on a conversation discussing the events of the day.

"Boy, that's quite the storm outside. We didn't make it back here too soon, guys," Nesbitt announced.

"It's a typical desert monsoon," Walter Etcitty said dryly. "There's gonna be a flash flood in the wash, and then we could be stranded here for a few days while they fix the roads."

"Well as long as the beer and nachos last, we should be okay," Nesbitt said. "So who do you think was shooting at you today, Walter?"

"I don't know. I couldn't see him from where we were but he had a powerful rifle with telescopic sights. I saw a flash of light reflected from the lens so I think he meant business," Walter said stoically.

"Good grief! You're lucky he didn't kill any of you. Maybe his aim was off," Nesbitt said.

"I don't think so. Isabella said the same thing but he hit our cooler and my backpack bang on. No, I think he was trying to scare us off by hitting our stuff. But his shots were awfully close just the same," Walter advised.

"But who the hell would do that sort of thing? That's just nuts!" Nesbitt erupted.

"Beats me. All I know was that he was a good shot with a pretty sophisticated weapon. Nobody that I know has anything like that in Navajo country. I wonder if the oil company was behind this since they want to reduce the park boundaries for oil exploration. I think we may be in their way with the university project here in Chaco."

"You really think they would do this? Of course, who else would pull a stunt like that? You might be right Walter."

Walter Etcitty sat back nursing his beer, slowly shaking his head as he considered the sniper in the canyon and how close his bullets came.

"Stan, we need to talk to those oil people tomorrow after informing the police. Of course they will deny any of this, but we have to let them know we won't be pushed around even if we have to hire our own armed guards. But the idea of an oil exploration firm scaring researchers away from a UNESCO World Heritage Site sounds unlikely in any event. They must know this can't be good for publicity. Who knew archaeology could be so dangerous?"

Stan Brown looked frightened and remained silent during the entire conversation, merely nodding in agreement with Jack Nesbitt as the thunder continued. Walter meanwhile opened another beer.

Chapter 27

Outlier

*Don't be afraid to cry. It will free your mind
of sorrowful thoughts.*
~ Hopi

While Shadow Dancer, Spotted Deer, and their clan were camped out temporarily at the base of the sacred mountain, dozens of families back at the Chaco Canyon complex were wondering what to do, where to go. The "coughing sickness" continued unabated, and most of the remaining elders felt that only a complete and final abandonment of all of the great houses would save their people from the ravages of this great pestilence.

They concluded a curse had been placed on their people for some reason. Numerous ceremonies, prayers, and rituals performed in the kivas had not altered the mortality rates among the Anasazi.

An Anasazi stone mason and his wife, his wife's mother, and his two sons, set out east towards the great river to the east. They lived in the Kin Kletso great house which was close to Pueblo Bonito and where the mason worked on building the walls of this grand building. One of his boys had been assigned to rid the storerooms of mice. His son's hands bore many callouses and not a few blisters from wielding his club against the rodents over the preceding weeks. Walking along the wash with as much food and as many provisions that they could carry, the family arrived after a day of travel at one of Chaco's outlier great houses known today as Pueblo Pintado, twelve miles east of Pueblo Bonito.[24]

This great house stood almost empty of inhabitants except for several elderly Anasazi men and women. A few sick people were confined to the inner rooms of the structure.

Lying outside the masonry pueblo were the dead, strewn beside the wall in the shade. Most of its inhabitants had fled toward the great river to the east to settle in a large ancestral village named Tyuonyi which meant *place of meeting*. They dug their new cave homes into the volcanic tuft with sharpened sticks, and prospered under the massive cottonwood trees next to a small stream that flowed into the great river nearby.[25]

By the time the mason's family arrived at the outlier, his two boys had developed a hacking cough with fever, chills, and muscle aches. One of them also developed a rash. Their mother also became ill with shortness of breath and fever. With no place to stay they found a storage room inside the great house. It was built almost as an afterthought with a small T-shaped opening. Reluctantly, all five entered the small chamber with all their worldly goods and settled

24. As its name suggests, the Chaco Culture National Historical Park includes more than just the great houses of the canyon. While the Chacoan culture was concentrated within the canyon, Chacoan influence extended throughout the San Juan Basin and beyond. Numerous Anasazi communities have been discovered as far away as northern Arizona, southwestern Colorado and northern New Mexico. The entire region contains "outliers" or other great houses, with many similar features as those in Chaco Canyon, albeit generally on a smaller scale. These outlying great houses, and their associated communities with Great Kivas demonstrate the extent of the Chacoan system throughout the Southwest.

25. This was the Rito de los Frijoles that emptied into the Rio Grande.

in with their two sick boys. The first thing they noticed were the stacks of corn maize and ollas of beans left behind. The second thing they found were mice scurrying everywhere. They were so exhausted from their journey carrying pots and hides in the heat of the sun that they collapsed in this chamber. The boys were perspiring with their persistent fever and the grandmother began to cough as well.

After two days everyone became sick, except for the mason who desperately tried to comfort his family in their affliction. Within a week his entire family had succumbed to the coughing sickness and he was beside himself with grief. He realized he could not bury all five members of his family, so he made the difficult decision to entomb them within the storage chamber. Laying each of his loved ones sideways in the fetal position together with their possessions beside them, he then skilfully filled in the T-shaped door space with the same sandstone bricks found nearby using the same Chacoan masonry style. He neatly mortared all the cracks with clay, thereby burying his loved ones in a sandstone sepulchre. He spent the better part of a day completing this task, applying clay also to the adjacent walls. The result was a completely surfaced wall with no evidence that a door opening had ever existed; only a few of the mason's fingerprints remained on the mortar. In doing so he had unwittingly created a perfect time capsule in the desert.

The mason slept outside that night, weeping with anguish and despair over his tremendous loss, wondering why he had been spared. He had forgotten that a year earlier he had suffered a respiratory ailment while on a hunting trip that had laid him low for several days. He had recovered back then, not knowing that his immune system was now protecting him from acquiring the same ailment a second time. In the morning he slung his sack of food and tools over his shoulder and moved on towards the Rio Grande where he planned to rejoin many of his people and begin a new life. Others had done it, so he was not exceptional in his tragedy. He took comfort knowing that his family was safely entombed in a sandstone mausoleum that would protect them from predators or enemies who might desecrate the bodies. The rust-coloured sandstone wall bore the rigours of time, heat, and storms for the next eight centuries. Hundreds of explorers, soldiers, and pot hunters over the years passed by, unaware of the chamber of the dead hidden just behind the slate wall within the great house which the Spanish would later name the "Pueblo of Mice."

Chapter 28

Inhaling Water

Beware of the man who does not talk,
and the dog that does not bark.
~ Cheyenne Proverb

When a man moves away from nature
his heart becomes hard.
~ Lakota

After the Cessna had turned towards his RV, the driver noticed the plane banking east towards Albuquerque to escape the impending storm. He knew that the plane carried the university crew or at least some of them. Knowing they had left, the driver stopped his camper, sent a text message, and then popped two pills into his mouth. He quickly turned the vehicle around and headed back to the canyon as fast as he could, bouncing and banging the RV on the rough Navajo road. He could see the storm ahead as the fading sunlight slanted through dark ominous clouds laden with hundreds of tons of water.

I better move fast.

It began to rain. A soft patter at first. Then slowly increasing with sporadic drops, splattering loudly on the windshield. He could see dark sheets of rain blowing across the canyon. He turned on his windshield wipers which snicked back and forth, barely yielding visibility as the downpour increased. After a few minutes the rain began to strafe the glass and obscure his vision. Hail peppered the windshield, cracking and chipping it, creating a deafening noise. The driver knew every twist and turn in the road and kept moving. His rear wheels spun in the mud, fishtailing around corners, hitting potholes filled with water, and ripping over cattle guards. The worn-out shocks bottomed out whenever the camper drove over deeper potholes; only then did the driver slow down.

Determined to recover the pots that the archaeologists had stored in their Suburban, he increased his speed, driving furiously, hoping to outrun the *rain bands* — the curved bands of clouds that comprised the bulk of the storm front. Accelerating the truck, he created huge rooster tails of mud spewing in the air from the rear wheels. He knew no one else would be on this road in weather like this.

This is just nuts!

Arriving at a shallow depression through an arroyo he could see water rising up to the wheel wells of his truck. He was too late in outrunning the storm front. He swore.

Pulling the truck to the side of the road he stopped to consider his next move. The last thing he needed now was to get stuck here in the middle of an arroyo in the midst of a desert monsoon. A warning sign said, "Danger! Do not Cross if Wash is Flowing." He reluctantly backed up to higher ground at the edge of the wash which was now overflowing its banks. Rain continued to slash across the bleak desert landscape. It grew darker and colder.

Stepping out of the cab he waded through a foot of swirling water and retrieved his rifle in its hard plastic waterproof case from the back of the camper. Picking up a long pole for balance against the rushing stream, he decided to cross, leaving the truck on the bank of the arroyo. He had been sent to get the pots and he stood to lose a lot of money by leaving them sitting in the Suburban at Chaco Canyon. He knew he couldn't take them all, but he could carry at least three or four of them. They had been nicely packaged and he thought he could easily strap a few of them on his back.

That's gotta be an easy thirty or forty grand — like taking candy from a baby.

Having spent time living in the Chihuahuan Desert he had witnessed this type of flooding more than once. Nevertheless, he decided to chance it and began wading across the arroyo using the pole for balance, his rifle case strapped to his back. He was surprised at how much noise the flowing water made as it roared through the wash. The dry desert floor did not readily absorb rainfall and all the runoff converged abruptly and violently into the wash at once. The creek become a raging torrent; at first a low thunder, then a deep rumble before a tumbling wall of slurry knocked him off his feet. He was shocked to see two natives standing on the opposite side of the arroyo staring at him.

They wore robes draped over their shoulders and just stood there as ghostly sentinels.

Weird.

Before he could call out to them a four foot wave of water and debris caught him off guard as it came rushing through the wash, careening and cascading along the canyon floor. A large log struck him in the side.

Whoa! What the hell?

Swept off his feet, he immediately fell into the main flow of the turbulent stream even though it was only chin-deep. Grabbing the pole to anchor himself to the bottom of the stream, he lost his grip on the waterproof rifle case which quickly floated away and became snagged on a tree branch. The current was much stronger than he had anticipated. Sputtering and gasping, he was dragged under the water several times. If only he had something to hang on to he might just flow with the flood and slowly make his way to the other side of the arroyo. To make things worse, the muddy water was smelly and cold. Soon the arroyo was filled with six feet of water. He looked back towards the two natives but they had vanished from sight.

I wonder who those guys were. I could sure use their help right now.

His strength ebbed as his body temperature fell and he was no longer able to keep his head above the water. He had read somewhere that drowning was a peaceful way to die, but this was beyond frightening. He recalled the terrified look when he waterboarded prisoners in Iraq while serving with the military. It didn't bother him at the time, but now the shoe was on the other foot. He had always referred to it as an "enhanced interrogation technique" but in reality it was a euphemism for a very effective form of torture which yielded valuable information for the CIA.

"The only thing more unpleasant than running out of air is breathing in water," he recalled one of his CIA buddies saying.

"You lose all sense of time when you're drowning," he was told. Yet he had always been too afraid to try it on himself to see what it was like.

Now he was in full panic mode. He was moving rapidly with the flow, completely out of control. Several branches and logs caromed off his head. His arms and legs flailed and chopped furiously, but he solidified in the cold water like a statue. He coughed.

Gotta find something to hang onto.

Hyperventilating while he sank, each breath brought in more of the foul desert water into his lungs. He coughed one last time.

Well, damn. Now I finally know what they meant. I guess I should have . . .

And then complete darkness.

Chapter 29

Acoma— People of the White Rock

With thee, in the Desert –
With thee in the thirst –
With thee in the Tamarind wood –
Leopard breathes – at last!
~ Emily Dickinson

When you were born, you cried
and the world rejoiced. Live your life
so that when you die, the world cries
and you rejoice.
~ Cherokee

Following the week-long feast on passenger pigeons, the clan renewed their strength and continued south for four more days where they came to a large shapeless mesa rising 360 feet above the surrounding wasteland. A small group of Mimbres people from the Southwest had moved to this desert fortress fifty years earlier. Nestled atop a high sandstone mesa overlooking vast arroyos and valleys, the Acoma Pueblo would eventually become the oldest inhabited community in North America.

The Mimbres language was slightly different from that of Shadow Dancer's people, but they could still understand each other with the use of sign language. The Mimbres inhabitants of the mesa were overwhelmed by the addition of eight hundred people to their small habitation. Knowing they were outnumbered they had little choice but to welcome them. Within a generation, both groups had assimilated forming a strong community that has continued to thrive on the mesa top until present times.[26]

Shadow Dancer and Spotted Deer were relieved to be in a safe location after several weeks of travel from Chaco Canyon. They were able to move into a small adobe house vacated by its owners who had built a bigger one for their enlarging family. Shortly after arriving, they watched a flock of crows fly to the mesa top, one of them an albino, as white as the rocks that surrounded the mesa. It perched for a while and then flew off with the rest of the flock of black crows which seemed to keep their distance from the albino. The other birds avoided it when it came near, knowing that something was different about this white crow.

"Look at that white crow, Shadow Dancer. It knows it doesn't belong but it persists in being a member of the flock. It shows strength, don't you think?"

"Yes, it is a stranger among its own. Sort of like many of our own people, moving to this new home with different people who regard us as strangers."

Water was a precious commodity on the mesa top. The Acomans relied on two natural cisterns to capture rainwater which was enough to supply the needs of the burgeoning new community. In times of

---

26. The mesa community has since become a National Historic Landmark and the ancient Anasazi site is known appropriately today as Sky City. The isolation and elevation afforded by the mesa gave protection to the Acomans until the time of the Spanish Conquest four hundred years later.

drought, young men bearing large ollas strapped to their backs toted water they collected from distant springs. Climbing almost four hundred feet with these heavy burdens was no mean feat; frequent falls required the carving of steps into the cliff side to ensure safety. Living on top of the mesa offered little advantage to the people of Acoma other than defence. Yet the farmers soon became masters of dry land farming, growing crops with the meagre water available in the valley below the mesa.

Spotted Deer found it next to impossible to descend the steep steps to the base of the mesa as her pregnancy progressed. Instead, Shadow Dancer frequently went down to the nearby river where he found excellent clay for making pottery. He then hauled the clay up the steep cliffs in water-proof baskets made from yucca fibres and pine resin strapped to his back. Spotted Deer was thrilled to be able to resume making her pottery and with the help of the Mimbres people at Acoma she was able to improve her skills and add new colours. She began to incorporate parrots into her designs, colouring them with a rich rust-coloured ochre from the iron in the clay that her husband found for her. She made several multi-coloured ollas with this design.

Spotted Deer found that the clay at Acoma was easier to work with than the clay she used when they were living in the canyon. Instead of resisting, the clay that Shadow Dancer brought her released itself to the moulding process, becoming a thing of beauty within Spotted Deer's agile hands. Her pottery was whiter than that of other migrant groups. Although the clay was naturally grey, it took on a bright white as most Acoma pottery still does today because she layered it with kaolin, a type of soft white clay.

Eventually all of the displaced Anasazi separated into distinct Pueblo groups, each creating their own unique style of pottery, hundreds of miles away from each other.

Spotted Deer frequently spoke to the pottery as she crafted the ollas and jars as if her ceramics became as living beings. She expressed her grief for the loss of her homeland and many of her family and friends to the plague. She shared her fears of her own pregnancy to the pottery, and when she finished a piece she blew into it as if she were breathing life itself into her creation. Pottery became healing for Spotted Deer and as she progressed, her works seemed to take on a life of their own.

Her ollas, although thin-walled were durable enough to hold precious water and food. Many of her bowls and jars which were discovered centuries later inspired Southwestern natives to rejuvenate the ancient art of coiling pottery in the late 1800s. Spotted Deer began to incorporate animal motifs with geometric patterns featured in stark black and white called *migration symbols*. Swirls and rings represented their travels across the desert wastelands.

She added muted colours to special pieces used for ceremonial purposes, her pigments derived from minerals. Her work became prolific with bowls, seed jars, drinking pots, and large ollas on which she painted parrots with a yucca paint brush. The parrot design was influenced by Aztec traders from Mexico who brought parrots and macaws as trade items to the canyon.

"What will we call our baby, my love?" asked Shadow Dancer one day as his wife laid coils of white clay for the creation of another jar.

"I've been thinking of that ever since we arrived on this mesa."

"And?"

"What do you think of White Crow?"

"Sure. But what if it's a girl?"

"But I know it's a boy."

"Okay. You always seem to know more than I do. I just hope it doesn't have six toes," Shadow Dancer mumbled.

"I will be happy if he has six toes as long as he's healthy."

"I guess so."

A month later Spotted Deer gave birth to a healthy son, with six toes on each foot. "Well, at least we know who the father is, Shadow Dancer," Spotted Deer laughed.

The young parents embraced and Shadow Dancer held his newborn son for the first time. Overwhelmed by his beauty, he began to cry with joy and amazement at this little mewling creature that held him spellbound, its hands tightly coiled into tiny fists like pine knots. When White Crow finally opened his tiny black eyes, they glinted like a pair of obsidian beads. Shadow Dancer somehow knew that White Crow was destined for great things, but first he had to bring his newborn son with his six toes to Grey Elk for a blessing.

Chapter 30

Crown Point

My heart laughs with joy because I am in your presence.
~ Native American Proverb

Following the one-hour flight to Albuquerque, Rachel drove Isabella to the University of New Mexico Hospital. X-rays of her leg revealed a small radio-opaque object in her calf, approximately one centimetre under the skin. An ER physician froze the site and probed the tract that the stone created when it entered Isabella's leg. After several minutes he injected more local anaesthetic into the site and made a small incision to open the entry point. This enabled him to introduce long forceps into the tract and remove the stone. Isabella was sent for another set of X- rays to ensure the stone hadn't broken and left more material in the wound. After irrigating the wound and giving her a tetanus booster and antibiotics, the doctor discharged Isabella with instructions to change the dressings in a day or so. Rachel drove her home and then joined Boudreau for dinner at the El Patio restaurant once more.

"What a hectic day we've had, what with the shooter, Isabella's wounded leg, and getting out of the canyon in time before the storm came. I could sure use a drink right now, sweetheart. So, my hero rescues me once again. If it isn't a polar bear it's some deranged cowboy up on the top of the mesa with a sniper rifle. How did I ever manage before without you Roland Boudreau?"

"Aw shucks, ma'am, I just happened to be at the right place and at the right time, and you know that is entirely in the realm of luck, Rachel."

"Hey, I'm not so sure I believe in luck any more. There's gotta be more to it than that. I can't help but feel after today that I have some kind of guardian angel, Rolly. Last year I was almost attacked by a polar bear and then somehow survived smallpox. This week I tripped and almost fell head first off the steep part of the stairway behind Pueblo Bonito, and then today I barely missed getting shot. I think all of this is starting to flare up my PTSD. I need you around for a while, Rolly. Please don't tell me you're heading back home soon. This was supposed to be the honeymoon we had postponed, remember? I've hardly seen you in the past two weeks."

Rachel was clearly anxious and began fidgeting with a strand of her hair as she talked.

The waiter arrived with her gin and tonic.

"No, don't worry, love. I'm here for as long as you want me around. Things have slowed down back in Manitoba and besides, I miss you too much. Not to mention I rented the Cessna again for this Friday. I wonder whether you would like to fly over Chaco Canyon again with me as the forecast is for calm weather. It's really neat from the air and you can see a lot of outlier great houses, too. Plus I can show you a few things about topographic maps and aerial photographs. Remember how you wanted to learn more about those fields?"

"That sounds great, Rolly. But there is something else that is bothering me that you might help me with."

"What's that, sweetheart?"

"Well, I kept seeing this camper trailer around the site and then this afternoon it was driving awfully fast on that dirt road south of the canyon."

"You mean that old beater of an RV that you took pictures of?"

"Yes, I'm suspicious that maybe our shooter got away in that vehicle. But he could be anywhere, I suppose. Maybe I'm wrong but I can't help but feel there was someone in that camper who's up to no good. Call it woman's intuition if you want."

"Did you check to see if you got the licence number?"

"No, unfortunately the picture isn't as clear as I had hoped. The camper has been around for awhile so I really wonder whether the shooter used it as his base of operations. I mean, most tourists spend a day or so there and then leave so I'm more than a little curious about why this RV stuck around for the past few days."

"Well, he could have been a worker from the reservation or a repairman on some project at the centre. I phoned the state police earlier and they'll meet us at Crown Point in the morning. I told them everything about the shooting, but they already knew about it from the local Navajo police. It seems Dr. Nesbitt had notified them from the visitor centre yesterday. You can tell them about your mysterious RV then," Boudreau said.

"Yes, I can do that and I'll show them my pictures, too. Rolly, you have no idea how much I've missed you the past two weeks."

"I've missed you, too, sweetheart. Don't worry. We'll have lots of time together.

Tomorrow I'll fly you and Isabella over the canyon. It's pretty impressive from the air. You'll be amazed."

After finishing dinner they returned to their motel and made love for the first time in weeks. The next morning Boudreau, Rachel, and Isabella Sandoval flew back to Chaco Canyon to see what effect the storm had taken on the roads and the research area.

"Sure enough, look at those washed-out roads. Most of them are covered with debris. It would be next to impossible to land here now. We'll take a quick tour of the area and then land at Crown Point. They have a good asphalt runway there," Boudreau shouted.

The drone of the engine seemed louder in their ears as the Cessna cruised between the canyon cliffs. The effects of the flash flood in the canyon were everywhere; a confusion of dead corkscrew branches, mounds of sand and stones lined the wash, and a monstrous tangle of desert detritus stretched across the road. From the cliffs, water streamed down the sandstone face creating flickering patterns like icicles as the first gesture of morning sun reflected from them. Tourists were noticeably absent and only a few motorhomes remained in the campground. The visitor centre appeared closed except for Walter Etcitty who was standing on the parking lot waving a white cloth. He pointed to the Suburban and then south towards Crown Point across the muddy sheen of the old Navajo road.

"I think Walter is signalling us to fly to Crown Point. He'll probably pick us up later in the Suburban," Isabella advised.

Banking south, Boudreau followed the Navajo Road towards Crown Point for a landing. Behind him a red sandstone cliff wall four hundred feet high gleamed with a glossy desert varnish from the runnels of falling water. Below lay the Navajo Nation known as Diné Bikéyah, a 27,000-square mile-high altitude desert with steep canyons and red rock spires.

"Look, Rolly, there's that same motorhome just near the wash. It must have turned back after we flew over it last night, but it probably couldn't make it across with the flash flood. That water is still flowing pretty fast and I don't see the driver anywhere. I hope he's okay. We should let the police know as soon as we land." Rachel scanned the canyon for any sign of life.

"I dunno Rachel. Maybe the guy is just sleeping in the camper at the back. I hope Walter can make it across that stream with the Suburban. Boy, it's still flowing pretty fast," Boudreau said.

"Don't worry. He won't take any chances. we've driven through that wash many times before over the past two years on projects in the canyon. Walter has driven the Suburban through much deeper water. Besides, Jack says that truck has almost a foot of ground clearance," Isabella explained.

Upon landing the plane in Crown Point they discovered that members of the Navajo police and two FBI agents were waiting for them.

Chapter 31

Invaders from the North

The ground on which we stand is sacred ground.
It is the blood of our ancestors.
~ Chief Plenty Coups, Crow

Light snow had fallen during the night and blanketed the mesa top village like a glittering layer of crushed chalk. Shadow Dancer shivered and held his wife to keep warm. His infant son began to cry, and he knew his son was either cold or hungry, so he dragged himself from under the warm hides that covered them both and blew on the coals from last night's fire, hoping that the embers would reignite. Spotted Deer gently lifted White Crow to her side and nursed him under the soft hide. She noticed her breath appeared as soft puffs of smoke, floating ice crystals within the adobe and she knew it was going to be a cold day. She strapped her son to a cradle-board on her back and left to bring water from the cisterns back to their small adobe apartment.

The cradle-board was made of woven yucca fibres. It allowed Spotted Deer freedom to work, prepare meals, make pottery, and tan hides, while carrying her newborn son close by, swaddled and protected. The only problem was that baby White Crow would develop a flat head at the back just like his parents, something characteristic for all Southwestern native children who were nurtured with a cradle-board.

Meanwhile, stragglers arriving at the mesa described how more groups were leaving the canyon because of recurrences of the coughing sickness. With the diminished population of the canyon, invaders from the north had descended on several of the great houses, killing entire families, raping women, torturing and cannibalizing those who resisted.[27]

"I can't believe this happened! Who would do such a thing? There was enough food left behind for everyone to eat. The dried corn powder and beans would still be good for months. That's just terrible." Spotted Deer wept when she heard stories of the cruelty upon her people by the northern tribes.

"Grey Elk says they eat the flesh not because they are hungry, but to show their power over those whom they conquer. They are vicious animals and those who remain are powerless against them. Many have moved to dwellings in the cliffs and deeper canyons for safety. They've built their new homes on ledges almost invisible from the bottom, sort of like my own spirit ledge surrounded by stone walls. It's as if everyone has forsaken the canyon now because of the disease and the invasion by the man-eaters from the north. It's a good thing we left when we did," Shadow Dancer asserted.

"But what if they come here? I'm scared for our baby and our people. Shouldn't we move farther away?" Spotted Deer was

---

27. Centuries later the gruesome evidence found in skulls and bones at the great house of Pueblo Bonito and other Anasazi ruins left no doubt as to the savagery inflicted upon those unfortunate Chacoans who remained behind. In all, archaeologists found thirty-six communities in the Southwest where evidence of cannibalism was discovered.

trembling as she spoke and tears welled up in her deep brown eyes. She held White Crow close to her breast.

"Grey Elk feels we are safe here. Our cisterns are filled with enough water from the rains to withstand a siege of several months and we have enough food as well. We have thousands of rocks and stones to throw down on anyone who dares to attack us and we can lift up the ladders quickly. There is no way anyone can scale the cliffs to reach us, Spotted Deer. We also have hundreds of warriors who are prepared to defend our people here. Grey Elk says this place is perfectly safe so you mustn't be afraid. Just look down anywhere on the mesa and see for yourself."

Spotted Deer gave her baby to her husband to hold while she crept closer to the cliff edge behind the stone wall to see the preparations made for an assault on the mesa. Hundreds of men were hauling stones in baskets to the top. Others were busy reinforcing the stone wall and making arrows, while women were harvesting the remains of the crops in the fields. After a few minutes she seemed to relax. Taking her baby back to nurse she said to Shadow Dancer, "You may be right. This place looks safe. But how can you stop anyone from shooting arrows at us?"

Chapter 32

Interrogation at Crown Point

You can tell whether a man is clever by his answers.
You can tell whether a man is wise by his questions.
~ Naguib Mahfouz

Walter Etcitty arrived in Crown Point in the Suburban about an hour later with Nesbitt and Brown, just as the FBI agents were interviewing the two women regarding the shooting. Boudreau had finished giving them a statement regarding what he saw from the air.

"Just the man we want to see!" said the first agent with a name badge with blue lettering stating "Special Agent G. Pierce". He had been making notes in a black leather- bound journal; his partner, a svelte Afro-American woman in a crisp white blouse and black sports jacket holding a tablet, wore a similar badge around her neck with the name "Special Agent Spencer".

"I take it you are Mr. Etcitty?"

"Yes, but just call me Walter."

"Okay, Walter. We understand you were with the anthropologists yesterday in Chaco Canyon when the shooting took place?"

"Yes, I was but I think they prefer to be called archaeologists."

"Right, archaeologists. So who do you think this shooter was?"

"He was an *Oh-Behi*. In Navajo we call him a 'Pick-em-off', a professional sniper who likely served in the military," Walter replied, avoiding eye contact with the agent.

"How many shots did he take and what kind of firearm do you think he was using?"

"There were four shots and I think he could have been using a Heckler and Koch

PSG1 semi- automatic sniper rifle."

"Really? An HK? Those aren't very common Walter. So what makes you so certain he was using a sniper rifle?"

"He was shooting from the cliffs. He was very accurate aiming at our stuff and he was using a telescopic lens. I used a similar type of rifle in Fallujah, Iraq, in 2004."

"Okay. So you were with Delta Force then?"

"Is that information relevant to this discussion because I'd rather not talk about it if I don't have to. Brings back bad memories."

Walter had served two terms in Iraq and still fought with PTSD. Upon return to his homeland he had enrolled in a traditional Navajo ceremony for countering the harmful effects of *chindi* — the ghost left behind when the enemy dies. It has been performed for a number of returning military personnel as a form of spiritual cleansing for those involved in battle. As a sharp shooter, Walter had taken the lives of several enemy insurgents. He asked the elders to perform the ceremony known as *the Enemy Way* which took several days to perform. Following this ceremony, Walter found healing but he still fought lingering fears and occasional nightmares. He never discussed his experiences if he didn't have to.

"Uh, no. It's okay. We just want information on the shooter. We'll take your word for it, Walter. So how do you know he had a telescopic lens and why do you think he was shooting at you?"

"Well, I saw a flash of a bright light from the cliffs where he was shooting from. I don't know why he was shooting at us, but I wondered if the oil companies were trying to scare us away."

"Why do you say that, Walter? Do you have any hard evidence that the shooter worked for any of the oil companies?"

"No, just a hunch. You might want to check them out though. They stand to profit by keeping people away from the canyon."

"Well thank you for that information. We'll certainly look into it. Do you know anything about this mysterious motorhome that Dr. Thompson states she saw several times?"

"Yup. I just passed it on the way here. It's stuck near a wash not far from the canyon. It seems whoever owned it just left it there. I hope he didn't try to cross the wash on his own. The water must have been ripping through there last night from all the logs and branches on the road. There was still about a foot of water when I came through with the Suburban."

"Really? You saw it? Did you get a licence number?"

"I did. I also have the owner's registration here for you. The vehicle was left unlocked and I figured you might want it to find the owner. I checked it over with the two doctors on our way here." Walter handed the registration certificate to the agent named Spencer who copied the information into her tablet.

"So how can you be sure it's the same vehicle as Dr. Thompson saw?"

"Why don't you ask her? I took some pictures on my cell phone. Here."

After giving Agent Pierce his cell phone, Walter signalled for Rachel to join their discussion and look at her photographs.

"That sure looks like the same motorhome that's been there this past week. We saw it earlier this morning when we flew here from Albuquerque. It was parked on the edge of an arroyo. Here are pictures on my phone I took from the air yesterday when it was driving away. You can see it's the same one. Did you find the driver, Walter?"

Walter shook his head. Pierce compared the photos on the two cellphones and nodded. After questioning Nesbitt and Brown for another ten minutes the FBI agents headed to Chaco Canyon to see the abandoned motorhome for themselves. Two Navajo police officers followed in a separate SUV to find the driver since the arroyo traversed Navajo lands.

An hour later the university crew was in Thoreau, New Mexico, having lunch at the Bull Pen Cafe while discussing the events of the past twenty-four hours. Boudreau left the Cessna at Crown Point and all six of them piled into the Suburban.

"So when you found the motorhome, Walter, did you find anything suspicious?" Isabella asked.

"Just the registration, some fast food wrappers, and used Styrofoam drinking cups.

The back door was unlocked too. It was pretty messy inside. There were a few old issues of *Firearms News* and *American Outdoorsman* lying around."

"Hmm. Gun magazines. That sounds suspicious doesn't it?" Isabella asked.

"I don't know. A lot of people read that stuff. There wasn't much else to find," Nesbitt added.

"Okay. What was the name on the registration?"

"The FBI agent told me to keep that information to myself for the time being while their investigation is going on. Let me just say that he wasn't Navajo," Walter said with a smile.

"I think we should head back to the university soon and prepare for our next project at the outlier," Stan Brown advised. "You've all done a great job this week in spite of the shooter and the storm. Let me just say that this next dig should prove to be an interesting one."

The group drove Rolly back to Crown Point where he flew back to Albuquerque with Rachel and Walter in the Cessna; the rest drove back to the university in the Suburban. Walter had never seen the canyon from the air before. Rachel took several photographs of the great houses and the ancient roads using a high definition survey camera. Wanting to impress Walter Etcitty, Boudreau flew the Cessna as he had done the day before through Chaco Canyon and across the same spectacular terrain. Walter just stared dumbfounded from the passenger's seat as he drank in the rugged scenery of his people's ancient lands.

Boudreau continued to head south, past Mount Taylor towards Sky City on the Acoma Mesa. It soon appeared as a great table of sandstone projecting upwards like a colossal tree stump on the horizon.

Chapter 33

Place of Preparedness

If we must die, we die defending our rights.
~ Sitting Bull

After several months following the mesa resettlement at Acoma, news of raiders from the north once again came to the Chacoans. Guards were posted around the clock on all sides of the mesa and preparations for a possible siege were made. Serving as cisterns, two large natural depressions in the rock on the mesa top collected runoff rain, providing the inhabitants with water for months. Food had been harvested from the valley filling storage bins that could withstand a prolonged siege. All the corn, squash, and beans had been harvested and stored; nothing was left in the ground for their assailants. Thousands of rocks and stones were piled near the rims behind stone walls around the entire mesa. Bows were strung with animal gut. Arrows were fletched with turkey feathers and tipped with quartzite and chert arrowheads.

"If they come we will have everyone, including the women, throwing rocks down from behind the walls, Spotted Deer. The more rocks that fall on them the greater our chance for victory, my love," Shadow Dancer advised his wife.

"But where will our baby stay if there is a battle?"

"We have many large fortified adobe rooms in the middle of the village with young girls and older women taking care of the children if there is a battle. They will be safe in case any arrows should reach us. But Grey Elk doesn't think they can shoot their arrows this high. If they did the arrows would be slow enough that we could catch them in the air."

"Catch an arrow from the air without getting hurt? Bah! How can Grey Elk know these things? What kind of magic does he have that can do this, Shadow Dancer?" Spotted Deer scoffed at the notion shaking her head.

Spotted Deer remained skeptical about the preparations in spite of the shaman's calculations.

"Grey Elk ordered several men to descend to the base and try shooting over the mesa top, and the arrows flew very slowly by the time they reached the top. We will be able to shoot their own arrows back at them. I think Grey Elk is right, my love. We are in a good defensive position here. We will be prepared for them," Shadow Dancer reassured.[28]

Spotted Deer felt reassured with her husband's explanations and embraced him holding their infant son saying nothing.

A week later one of the scouts signalled that a large band of invaders was approaching from the north. These were the same Indians who had killed the remaining survivors of the coughing sickness who had stayed behind in the canyon. They also burned several of the timbered roofs and performed cannibalism on those who resisted as a final form of desecration on their enemies. By torturing survivors

---

28. The name of the main village, *'háák'u'* which meant "place of preparedness", the word from which *Acoma* was derived.

they learned that most of the community had left earlier, heading south of the holy mountain towards the mesa stronghold.

Arriving at the mesa in groups of fifties, four hundred warriors sought to destroy the peaceful Chacoans for no other reason than that there was food on the mesa and there were women for the taking. However they could not see the hive of activity on the mesa top. The defenders quietly took their positions, awaiting their leaders' instructions. Eight hundred Anasazi warriors including women, young adults, and old men lined up behind the stone walls, equipped with rocks and bows and arrows.

Grey Elk advised them not to waste precious arrows or spears on the enemy unless they began to scale the heights. He reasoned that a steady bombardment of rocks would probably discourage them from climbing and they could save their arrows. Ladders had been removed from the walls leaving only tenuous handholds carved in the rock to climb up to the mesa. Grey Elk felt confident that their fortress was ready for an all-out assault. Putting a peyote button in his mouth, he sat and waited.

Unknown to him the enemy brought ladders of their own and several enemy warriors began to climb the heights as soon as they approached the base of the citadel. Behind them hundreds of archers aimed their bows towards the top of the mesa and awaited the signal to shoot.

Chapter 34

Sky City

*A field of clay touched by the genius
of man becomes a castle.*
~ Og Mandino

The late afternoon sun lit the cliffs of Acoma Mesa a blazing topaz as seen from the air. The Cessna flew over the 367-foot-high mesa which overlooked an expansive grassy valley punctuated, with numerous rock formations, twisted trees, and gigantic knobs of wind-sculpted sandstone. It appeared as though a part of the earth's core had burst through its crust at the beginning of time.

On the mesa top the 380-year-old Spanish mission church of San Estevan del Rey arose majestically above the line of stone houses like a jewel in the crown of the Pueblo. The massive adobe walls supported twin bell towers which resembled a pair of giant salt and pepper shakers. The church stood squarely and solidly on the southern part of the flat-topped mountain as if it were a mystical cathedral transported from another world.

"That's Estevan del Rey Mission Church, built in 1642 by the Franciscans. I read that its walls are up to seven feet thick at the base," Boudreau shouted over the noise of the engine.

"I'd like to know how they managed to build an edifice like that on top of a four-hundred-foot mesa without cranes, trucks, or even roads. They carried hundreds of heavy timbers by hand from Mount Taylor thirty miles away for the ceiling beams. All they had was a hand-cut staircase carved into the sandstone. It defies belief," he added.

Walter Etcitty was silent. He had seen Sky City from the ground before but had never ventured up to the top, nor had he ever seen it from the air. He slowly shook his head, spellbound by the extraordinary site of Pueblo Indian and Spanish architecture in the nine-hundred-year old mesa community.

Below them a mesh-work of narrow dirt streets were lined by three hundred connected adobe homes, some three stories tall. Near the plaza a few cars and pick-up trucks were parked beside an amber-coloured school bus. From their altitude in the Cessna, tourists appeared as grasshoppers as they meandered along the streets and past the church.

"That yellow school bus takes tourists up to the mesa top from the interpretive centre at the base. They had to blast a road in the rock face back in the fifties to make it accessible to vehicles. Until then they just hauled stuff up steep narrow trails," Boudreau said. "It's amazing when you think about it."

"We Navajo don't go there because there are still some bad feelings between the Pueblos and our people. They're not friendly towards us because we attacked them long ago. But so did the Apache. They don't forget these things that easily," Etcitty said solemnly.

"I've heard about that before Walter. But look at the relation-ship now between the U.S. and Germany or Japan. Once mortal enemies, they're now allies and trading partners. Life has to go on. Look, I have an old friend who lives at Acoma and we've kept in touch over the years. His name is Victor Lewis. I met him back when I was in university trying to learn about other native peoples. I promised him I would pay him a visit while I'm down here and I'm planning to drive there tomorrow. I was wondering if you'd like to come with me?"

"I'll have to chew on that for a while. If I come with you I wouldn't want them to know I'm Navajo. But yes, it would be an experience to remember. Let me think about it."

As the plane turned east towards Albuquerque, another impressive sandstone citadel rose above the desert floor.

"That's Enchanted Mesa, once home to the Anasazi a thousand years ago. The cliffs are so steep it's almost impossible to get to the top. Victor told me that many Acoma people claim to have seen UFOs hovering over the butte every now and then."

Walter stared through the window at the desert grandeur below with a view of the pueblo of Sky City that he had never seen before from the air. He took several photos with his phone. Looking down he saw the black dart of the Cessna's shadow skimming over the desert landscape like a fish swimming on water.

When they finally landed in Albuquerque, Etcitty warmly embraced Boudreau on the tarmac and whispered softly, "Thank you brother. That plane ride was an experience I will never forget. Yes, I think I would like to go with you to Sky City tomorrow and meet your *Kiis'áanii* friend."

"But, Walter, they will know you are Navajo just by looking at you."

"I know. I was joking about that," he said dryly.

Turning to Rachel, Walter smiled and said, "A*sdzaa nizhoni,* you have a good man here.

Don't lose him."

Chapter 35

Battle for the Mesa

The weakness of our enemy makes our strength.
~ Cherokee

It is good that war is so horrible or we might grow to like it.
~ Robert E. Lee

The Anasazi on the heights waited until the very last moment for their enemy to surround the base of the mesa and begin their perilous climb. Numerous warriors shot arrows over the walls, but as expected, only half of them made it much higher than the mesa rim. Dozens more bounced harmlessly onto the plateau behind the stone wall.

Several of the younger men behind the walls attempted to pluck the slow-falling arrows from the air. A few were successful.

At the signal from Grey Elk, the Anasazi began throwing rocks and stones as fast and as quietly as they could. A shower of thousands of rocks per minute followed; dozens of enemy warriors were killed within the first few minutes. A quick retreat followed immediately; many of the invaders stumbled over the rough ground as they tried to dodge the shower of falling rocks. Several of the defenders managed to dislodge a three-hundred-pound boulder with the use of pine poles as levers. The ground shook when it stuck the bottom and tumbled mercilessly into the valley below, taking out a swath of the northern invaders and crushing them instantly.

Many of the surviving invaders were injured and maimed from a deadly shower of smaller rocks and stones. After several minutes the enemy managed to withdraw from the base of the cliffs. Scrambling for their lives, they dragged a few of their wounded to safety, leaving behind over one hundred dead and wounded warriors at the cliff base.

The lofty and isolated table mountain proved to be impregnable to its assailants.

The attackers soon realized the futility of their position. It was impossible for any of them to climb very far when confronted with the constant barrage of rocks, many weighing upwards of thirty and forty pounds. One determined and courageous invader stood on a ladder, vainly attempting to scale the cliffs; within a second his head was split open and his remains were sprawled on the ground. The assault of falling rocks proved to be relentless and severe with the sound of clattering and scraping, as rocks caromed off the cliffs. The leaders of the invading force were stunned by the sudden realization that they would have to either retreat or be buried. They stood screaming and cursing, shaking their fists at the mesa top, angered that they could not even see their enemy. A few warriors vainly shot arrows, many of them clipping the mesa walls. Grey Elk observed the enemy in silence before raising his arm for his next signal.

The assailants retreated from the base of the mesa and gathered in a column on the north side, trying to figure out what to do next, when a massive volley of arrows gracefully soared towards them from a hundred archers behind the walls. Although the invaders were safe from falling rocks, they did not anticipate arrows could reach them. Another forty warriors collapsed and the invaders had to retreat even further. Again, silence from the mesa top.

Grey Elk could see the hopelessness of his enemy's situation. He had envisioned this. He knew they could withstand a siege for months if necessary; if any of the enemy came close to the mesa they would be met with more rocks and arrows.

He was right. After a short-lived siege of three days the northern invaders left, licking their wounds and burying the few dead they could reach without being killed themselves. The rest were already beginning to stink in the desert sun and hundreds of ravens, vultures, and other scavengers feasted on them. That night the Anasazi celebrated their victory around bonfires with dancing and singing. From the base of the mesa the sound of their singing was as a distant soughing of wind through a forest of piñon pines. Yet no one was left to hear the celebrations except for a few dying enemy warriors scattered broken among the rocks. To recognize their great victory the Acomans hung turquoise pendants from their noses and ears.

The Anasazi at Acoma were secure for now.[29]

---

29. For the next four hundred years the Acoma people remained safe on the mesa until the time of the Spanish Conquest. In 1541 some six thousand of their descendants lived at the Acoma Pueblo before the conquistadors arrived with Coronado. Following the arrival of the Spanish and the diseases they carried, fewer than six hundred descendants remained.

Chapter 36

Pottery Preserved

But we have this treasure in earthen vessels.
~ 2 Corinthians 4:7

The archaeologists met the following Tuesday morning in a conference room at the university after unloading the Anasazi pottery from Chaco Canyon. Several professors, PhD students, and researchers assisted in the work, each one marvelling at the remarkable state of preservation of the relics. The entire display room was abuzz with talk of the discovery. A professional photographer recorded each artifact, handling each one carefully as if it were a newborn baby. Others took pictures of the pottery on their cellphones. They were soon stored on shelves behind secure Plexiglas panels for public viewing with their neatly typed labels.

"So we head out tomorrow to an outlier of Chaco Canyon where we have reason to believe a walled-in room exists that has yet to be explored. The outlier is called Pueblo Pintado. It is technically on Navajo land. We have known about this room for some time and have finally received permission from the Navajo tribal council to explore it. If you will follow me into the next room we can see the mapped coordinates on the computer," Stan Brown announced.

FREDERICK ROSS

The group gathered around the computer.

"As you can see, we've used GPS-fixed tripod positioning to give us an accurate perspective of the ruins. Keep this to yourselves as there are still a lot of pot hunters out there who would be all over this site if they knew anything of value could be discovered. Since the 1870s they have stolen thousands of artifacts from Chaco Canyon and many other prehistoric sites in the Southwest. And they're still out there today, so remember 'loose lips sink ships,'" Nesbitt pronounced.

Rachel smiled at Nesbitt's antiquated expression which he likely learned from his father during the Second World War. She made a gesture by sealing her lips together and pulling an imaginary zipper across them. She proceeded to pull out several photos of the area taken the day before with her survey camera to show to Jack Nesbitt.

"These are great photos, Rachel, and you have captured the very site that we will be exploring tomorrow. Show them to Stan; he'll be impressed. This gives us an idea of just how bad the roads have been damaged from the storm in case we need to make any detours."

Rachel was thankful for Boudreau's instructions in aerial photography. "Where's Walter? Shouldn't he be here with us?" Isabella asked.

"He's spending the day with Rolly. The two of them are driving up to Acoma Pueblo. Rolly has an old friend there that he met when he was in university and they have kept in touch all these years," Rachel replied.

"Boy, that sounds like an interesting meeting. A Navajo, a Pueblo, and a Canadian Metis of Cree descent meeting at the ancient pueblo of Sky City. Wouldn't you love to know what they're talking about?" Isabella exclaimed.

"Well, I overheard Rolly talking to Walter on the phone this morning, and they were talking about which pick-up trucks are the best. It seems they are both fans of the Ford F-150. Does that help you understand how native groups of different backgrounds bond?"

"Hah! Men are the same everywhere," Isabella exulted.

"By the way, I got a call from FBI Agent Pierce this morning," Nesbitt announced. "They found the driver's body a couple of miles down the wash quite mangled. The ravens were already picking it apart by the time they found it covered in branches and mud. He had his wallet in his pocket so they know who he is but they won't reveal any information on him right now other than he is ex-military. They also found his sniper's rifle still in its protective plastic case at the edge of the arroyo not too far from the RV. Of course, Walter knows the guys name from the registration he took from the truck. He just said his initials were T.J. So it's highly likely this guy is our shooter. It seems he got caught in a flash flood and drowned."

"Wow, I feel safer already. But why was he shooting at us?" Isabella asked.

"They won't say anything until their investigation is complete. He said that other FBI agents are questioning the oil company executives about this but they are doubtful that any oil companies were involved. The FBI are bringing a metal detector to our site to try and recover any spent bullets for ballistics to see if they match the rifle," Nesbitt explained.

"There should be a couple of bullets in the sand near the rincon where we worked. One of them hit the sand right behind Walter. He was lucky he didn't get killed," Isabella added.

Stan Brown, the team director who had been silent to this point, interjected and said, "Well I'm sure they'll find whatever they are looking for. In the meantime we have to get back to work. So let me brief you on the project at the outlier. First we drive out to the trailers at Chaco after lunch and get our equipment set up. Then we head out to begin the dig. We'll take a pair of Jeeps to get us to the site as it will be too rough for the Suburban over sixteen miles of old Navajo roads. We'll have to pack everything on the roof and make two trips to get everything on site. Any questions?"

"What about Walter? Should I give him a call to meet us at the usual place?" Isabella asked.

"Yes, that would be great because it seems I left my cellphone somewhere. This is embarrassing, but has anyone seen it? I must have left it in the trailer after the night of the storm. That was a pretty hectic night," Brown said awkwardly.

Chapter 37

First Contact

The first white man we saw was a black man.
~ Joe Sando, Pueblo historian

Whispering Dove was fascinated by her grandfather's stories of the past. Green Feather was an elder in the small community at the great mesa of the Acoma and he enjoyed telling his inquisitive granddaughter about their ancestors and the history of her people. He knew of things going back generations from stories that his own grandparents had told him. It was through these stories passed down from one generation to the next that Whispering Dove learned about her people's history. Unlike many of her friends on the mesa, she was intrigued by the stories of her ancestors. She hung on every word once her grandfather started talking about the past. She was still grieving the tragic loss of both her parents who had succumbed to a mysterious ailment; her grandfather was raising her as his own daughter. His many stories helped feed her natural inquisitiveness. She kept busy grinding maize with the other young women of the mesa and coiling clay into pottery, painting her work with simple black-on-white designs.

Whispering Dove had lived all of her seventeen years on the mesa, seldom venturing more than a few miles from her home. She wore a deerskin dress with a woven cotton blouse decorated with small turquoise stones. Small leather straps plaited her long black hair which glistened in the sun. When listening intently to her grandfather's stories, her deep penetrating eyes had a tendency to stare straight ahead, betraying a natural curiosity and intelligence beyond her years. Always eager to learn, she wondered what life was like elsewhere, and she longed to visit the place where her people had once lived in the great canyon to the north. She wondered what people from other pueblos were like and she questioned what kind of disease could had driven them from their ancestral homelands.

Young women of the mesa however, were not permitted to leave the mesa or travel to the north, especially to the great canyon which was off limits to everyone because of its dark history from so long ago. Her grandfather tried to answer her questions but there were so many things he didn't know either.

One morning Whispering Dove was awoken by the sound of a great tumult in the village. Four strange men had just arrived at Acoma and her neighbours were going wild with excitement. She asked her grandfather who these men were and where they came from.

"We don't know, my child. They are very strange indeed. They are not from any tribes that we know, for their skin colour is different. Three of them are white and one is a very dark colour," Green Feather answered.

"But what are they doing here, Grandfather?"

"We don't know that either. They speak a different language and we can't understand them, but they do not seem dangerous."

"Can I go and see them? Please?" Whispering Dove begged her grandfather.

"Yes my child, but you must stay with me to be safe."

After walking across the mesa top, she encountered a crowd that had formed around the strangers. Whispering Dove was amazed to see that one of the men was black and the three others were white just as her grandfather had said. She noticed that their clothing was in tatters and they spoke a strange language. Their lips were dry and cracked and they were emaciated. They were animated using hand gestures to communicate and the black stranger drew pictures in the sand. Many of the men of the mesa touched them and kissed their hands and feet, marvelling and believing that they had come from the sky. Several squatted at their feet and stroked their legs as if to see that they were made of flesh and bones. Later, several of the women likewise sat around the men, touching their hair and clothes, while others began laughing at their strange appearance. Two giggling women brought them warm corn meal in ceramic bowls. Sitting on rough-hewn log benches, the four strangers ate heartily as people danced and sang, "the men from the sky have arrived."

White Dove joined the throng of gawkers and was immediately taken with these strange looking men. She soon found herself laughing, too.

Would they tell us stories of the outside world? Where did they come from? Why are they different in colour?

That night, dancing and singing went on for hours on the mesa. Whispering Dove couldn't fall asleep as she pondered this extraordinary visitation.

"Grandfather, do you really think these men are from the sky?" she asked.

"No, my child, they look too poor and they have no meat on their bones. I think they have travelled far, but not from the sky. They are not gods; they are just different people."

"Will they stay with us on the mesa?"

"Yes, I think so. They are too weak to travel for awhile and they will need to restore their strength. In the meantime, we can try to learn their language. Perhaps you can help understand what they are trying to say and teach them our language. Just be careful not to be alone with them," he admonished.

Whispering Dove was thrilled with the arrival of these foreigners to the mesa and for the first time in years, like a fog lifting, she forgot the pain of her grief.

Chapter 38

Pueblo Pintado ~ Village of the Mice

Nothing beside remains. Round the decay
Of that colossal wreck, boundless and bare
The lone and level sands stretch far away.
~ Percy Bysshe Shelley

After setting up their equipment the next day, the group met in the conference room of the visitor centre at Chaco Canyon with Special Agent Pierce of the FBI.

"So it appears your shooter was an ex-military sniper and served in Iraq for a couple of tours. His initials on the case matched his name and the fingerprints on the stock were his. We found two bullets at the dig site; one had smashed against a rock but the other was buried in the sand. We found a ballistics match for the sniper's rifle based on this bullet. We just aren't sure why he was shooting at those of you who were working there. Presumably he was trying to frighten you away from the site. We also don't know who he may have been working for. We believe that the theory that he was working for one of the oil companies in the area has been ruled out," said Agent Pierce.

"What about the shooter's cell phone? Would you be able to obtain information from that?" asked Isabella.

"Good question but no, it seems his cell phone must have been washed away in the flash flood. It was likely ruined by the water even if we did find it," Pierce explained.

"Do we know his name?" Isabella asked.

"The name on the registration is Thaddeus Jackson but we suspect that could be an alias. We have his true identity from military records, but we are keeping it from the public for now; I think you will understand why. It appears he was living in that beat-up motorhome. The keys which we found in his pocket fit the lock in the vehicle. The Navajo Tribal Office in Window Rock has no record of him either. He seems to be a rather elusive character likely from out of state and we suspect he is a 'for hire' hit man operating alone," Pierce added.

"What about the gun? Can you trace it to the owner?" Nesbitt asked.

"We're checking his military records as we speak but there's very little known about him. At this point we suspect he may have been a sniper for the military. By the way, the rifle is a Heckler and Koch PSG-1 precision rifle, just as Mr. Etcitty suggested. It has no serial number on it which is not unexpected but at least it survived the flash flood thanks to its waterproof case. By the way where is Mr. Etcitty? I wanted to congratulate him on his knowledge of firearms."

"He's with my husband on a trip to the Acoma mesa." Rachel said.

"Okay. Are there any questions?" Agent Pierce asked.

Everyone in the room remained silent. Stan Brown stood up to make an announcement.

"Well, in that case we should get to work, ladies and gentlemen. I'm sure the FBI will sort this fellow out soon enough. Thank you, Special Agent Pierce, for taking the time to discuss your investigations to us. Since the shooter is dead and we are moving to a new location twelve miles upstream from the main Chaco area, we should be safe."

Later that afternoon the group drove to the outlier great house of Pueblo Pintado and walked around the site looking for what had earlier been identified as a sealed storage room. Their boots crunched in the dry rocky soil of the ancient Anasazi site. They soon found what they were looking for. The red sandstone bricks in the mortared wall fit almost perfectly, creating a seal over the door from the rest of the world for over eight hundred years.

"So this is the great house of Pueblo Pintado," pronounced Jack Nesbitt in his usual professorial style. "As you can see it's another massive sandstone stronghold built in the Chacoan style and also mysteriously abandoned around the end of the twelfth century. It was first discovered by Americans in 1849 when the Washington Expedition came through here under Lieutenant James Simpson. They were surveying Navajo lands at the time and found this amazing place. They called it the *painted village* or Pueblo Pintado in Spanish. It was also known as *Pueblo do los Ratones*, or *village of the mice*. Not sure how it got that name but there must have been a lot of mice around at the time."

"Archaeologists call Pueblo Pintado a Chacoan great house which served as a civic and ceremonial centre for surrounding communities. You will notice it is an L-shaped building open to the southeast. It contains ninety ground-floor rooms, forty second-storey rooms, and five third-storey rooms," Stan Brown added.

"Over here we have recently discovered a room that has never been excavated; the outer wall has been sealed with clay mortar, sort of like an adobe plug. Over time the mortar has disintegrated and you will notice the faint outlines of a T-shaped door that has been filled in. It was likely a small storage room that has eluded archaeologists and pot hunters until now because it was built within the main wall which surrounds the complex."

"Boy, whoever added this room did a good job. Imagine all the explorers and archaeologists like us who walked past this secret room. Even the US cavalry rode past it in the 1870s without noticing anything," Nesbitt added.

"So are we to dismantle the sandstone bricks to this door and survey the contents of the room?" Rachel asked as she ran her finger over the crumbling clay mortar between the bricks and noticed dried fingerprints which the Anasazi mason had imprinted eight hundred years earlier.

"Not so fast, Rachel. I don't know how you do things in Canada but first we're going to drill a hole and insert a flexible scope just like they do when you have a gastroscopy. In fact, we will actually use a veterinary endoscope to see what's inside before we decide to dismantle the wall. No point taking it apart if there's nothing inside," Nesbitt explained.

"And if you see anything with the scope? Then do we dismantle the wall?" Rachel asked.

"Yep. Brick by brick. We'll number each one so we can put them all back as precisely as we found them. We will lay them on a tarp in the same order as we remove them, too. By tomorrow we should be inside if Jack sees anything worth investigating in the next ten minutes," Brown advised.

After drilling a half-inch hole between two bricks with a cordless DeWalt drill using a concrete bit, Nesbitt carefully blew the dust away through the hole and inserted the fibre optic scope.

"Why not just use a GoPro camera and scope Jack?"

"Good question. Try telling the university that we need funding for a piece of technology like that for the Department of Anthropology. Of course they said no, but I was able to borrow a gastroscope from an old veterinarian friend who retired in Phoenix a few years ago. After they saw what we were using they relented and gave us a GoPro unit. By that time I got used to this one. But a good endoscope has become a bit of a must have tool for plumbers these days. Once an expensive tool used solely in the medical profession, now we have scopes which are easy to use, effective, and very affordable. It certainly comes in handy in situations like this for people in our profession. This one is six feet long and comes with an LCD monitor so you can all see if you gather round me. It will also record whatever we see on an eight gig SD card. We'll see a video image of the scene in real time on the screen in a moment."

"Rachel, as you can appreciate, Jack is a bit of a geek," Isabella said smiling.

After turning on the battery-operated fibre optic light, Nesbitt pushed the long flexible tube through the opening. Rachel smiled at Nesbitt's knowledge of technology as he reminded her of Gordon Dowling, her own mentor who also loved gadgets.

"Say ahh!" Nesbitt quipped while the other team members gathered around him in suspense. Isabella rolled her eyes at his attempt at medical humour.

"Hmm. Hard to believe this room has been closed to the public for almost a millennium. Let's see now — Oh, wow! I can see several white flakes on the ground. Might be bone. Wait — now I see four skeletons in what appears to be a burial chamber of sorts. I think we've hit the jackpot on this one, Stan. Jeepers — Pottery, sandals, and skeletal remains. There's lots of archaeology in there, boys and girls. Here, Isabella, have a look," Nesbitt said.

Isabella looked at the LCD monitor and gasped as several alabaster bones appeared on the screen. "I'm just glad that Walter isn't here for this dig. He doesn't mind digging pots but bodies give him the creeps. He would have to go for a cleansing ceremony after working here. It's just as well he is with Rolly today."

After each member of the team had a look through the endoscope they began the tedious job of labelling the bricks. They gently removed the crumbling mortar from between each one of the bricks. By the end of the day, seventy-eight shale bricks had been removed and placed on the tarp for re-assembly later. Peering inside the three-foot-diameter hole thus created, they saw spider webs hanging heavily with pendants of crumbled clay and mice droppings. A strong musty smell which emanated from the hole remained long after the opening was enlarged. Isabella was small enough to climb inside and take several photographs. Stan Brown being lean, also crawled inside the chamber to inspect the skeletons and the relics.

"It looks like two kids and two adult females lying side by side in the fetal position.

These people had to be Anasazi likely from the late twelfth century. Dozens of mice skeletons, too. Unbelievable," Brown said.

"And surrounding them are several Red Mesa black-on-white jars and pots decorated with the classic geometrical patterns of the Anasazi. This is a fantastic find!" Isabella shouted from within the chamber.

After spending several minutes inside the tomb the two researchers clambered out covered in dust, covering their mouths with bandanas.

"What an incredible find but I feel this place is holy ground and we should probably have one of the Navajo elders here," Isabella pronounced.

"Whoa! Whatever for? We already have tribal permission to do this project. In fact it took months of paperwork just to get this wall opened. Besides these people aren't even remotely related to the Navajo," Stan Brown exclaimed as he inhaled through his pursed lips.

"Well, shouldn't we at least ask Walter when he gets back tomorrow? I mean, he would know what prayers or ceremonies should be performed before we inadvertently desecrate this site with our project?" Isabella asked.

Rachel quietly nodded in agreement. She was aware that modern-day archaeologists commonly acknowledge their moral responsibilities to the descendants of the subjects whose remains they disturb. She knew this case was no exception as she caught Isabella's concerned eye.

After several minutes of heated discussion, Jack Nesbitt intervened.

"Heck, if we've waited this long, Stan, what's another day or two? I think Isabella's right. We are on Navajo lands and we need to show respect for the dead even if these people are genetically unrelated to them. If word gets out that we didn't follow the Navajo rituals when discovering a tomb of the *ancient ones* we might never get permission for any other projects. We sure don't want to piss them off, is all I'm saying."

After considerable argument, Brown finally conceded. Being an outsider Rachel kept silent on the matter, but she could see the consternation on Isabella's face. She couldn't understand why the team leader should oppose such a reasonable request.

After taking photographs and bone samples, they covered the defect in the wall with tarps and a make-shift stone wall, the team left a "No Trespassing" sign before returning to the Chaco visitor centre for clean-up and dinner. The pottery was carefully package in bubble wrap, labelled, and placed in cardboard boxes for transport.

None of the group was in good spirits following the earlier wrangling over having a Navajo healing ceremony for the dead. Yet it was a significant discovery and they managed to quietly celebrate around a mesquite campfire drinking beer. Nesbitt took over the barbeque and dished up a plate of overdone hamburgers. Stan Brown was nowhere to be seen.

"When Walter's with us we never argue," Isabella whispered to Rachel. "I don't understand why Stan is in such a hurry all the time to get things done. Walter wouldn't put up with this, that's for sure."

Rachel nodded quietly and sipped her beer.

Shortly after the team left the burial site a large bull snake slithered inside the vault-like chamber at Pueblo Pintado. Writhing slowly in the darkness near the skeletons, it coiled itself around a desert wood rat with a powerful embrace. Holding its head in its expanding unhinged jaws, it swallowed the rodent in its entirety over several minutes.

Chapter 39

Estebanico's Journey

If a man is to do something more than human,
he must have more than human powers.
~ Tribe Unknown

Following their joyous and momentous arrival, the four men lived among the Acoma people for several months. The elders were curious to know from where they had come. More maps and numerous sketches were drawn in the sand. The black member of the quartet was adept at languages and after four months on the mesa he was able to communicate with several of the elders in their own language. He said his name was Estebanico and it was time for him to tell them his story. Whispering Dove sat with her grandfather and listened intently.

"I was born in 1501 in Azemmour, Morocco, a small town seventy miles south of Dar al-Beïda on the Atlantic coast of Africa. My journey has been a long and terrifying one across the ocean. My friends and I have been travelling for many years and we have been enslaved by natives who lived near the great water during most of that time."

But the elders had no idea what he was talking about and they puzzled over the maps that showed a great expanse of water. Few of them had ever travelled more than sixty miles from the mesa; the only water they had seen was in the runoffs of the local arroyos.

Estebanico explained that a famine enabled slave traders to sell him to a Spanish aristocrat named Andres Dorantes de Carranza who had a grandiose plan to explore and colonize Florida and the Gulf Coast. After all, it was barely thirty years since Columbus made his famous discovery and Dorantes believed there was opportunity in the New World to discover gold. But none of the elders at the Acoma mesa had heard of the Gulf Coast or the Spanish or Columbus for that matter. Regardless, Estebanico again tried to explain how they had arrived in their country. He described the horror of watching so many men from the ships die of malaria while wandering along the coastline.

But in spite of his stories and sand maps, none of the elders could visualize what a ship was or what malaria was. As for horses, the concept of a large four-legged animal that could carry men over great distances was totally foreign to them as well. They did understand what gold was, but even so, several of the elders walked away shaking their heads at the nonsense this strange black man was telling them. Eventually all of them left except Whispering Dove and her grandfather. She felt this man and his white friends, having travelled so far, had no reason to lie to them so she believed them and wanted to hear more. Intrigued, she asked many questions.

"What is a horse? How can it carry you on its back? Wouldn't it be very large to do that?" she inquired.

One of the Spaniards drew a picture of a horse in the sand for her. Estebanico went further and made a clay model of a small horse for her. Whispering Dove took it gently in her hands and carefully placed it in a fire, covering it with large shards of broken pottery and baked it until it was hardened into a piece of pottery. After several hours she could stand the little horse on the four legs that Estebanico had cleverly crafted. Her grandfather finally began to let her visit the four men by herself.

Each day Whispering Dove visited the strangers, asking questions, enthralled with their stories. She learned about ships and slavery, cannons and swords, kings and queens, and faraway lands. Captivated by his fascinating tale, Whispering Dove soon became attracted to this handsome and charismatic black man. She wanted to know if there were many other people that were also black and whether she could go and see them in Africa. When she asked Estebanico if he would take her there, he burst out laughing at her request for there were millions of Africans living at that time. He kindly explained to her that it would be impossible to get there.

Whispering Dove was hurt by his reaction to what she thought was a reasonable question.

"Why do you laugh at me? How can your home be so far away that we can't go and see it?" she asked.

Estebanico realized Whispering Dove was an inquisitive but sensitive girl and he tried to comfort her; he drew more maps in the sand to explain the vast distances that he had travelled.[30] He described to her how after the shipwreck the survivors managed to build five shallow draft boats out of horsehide.

"We drifted for days, many dying of thirst. Then carried by a strong wind we crashed onto the rocky shores of a large island and we lost our boats along with all of our equipment. Many of the men

---

30. By this time Estebanico and his Spanish companions had travelled farther by foot than anyone in recorded history. Over his lifetime, a conservative estimate of the number of miles Estebanico walked was likely around 21,525 miles, almost the equivalent of walking around the entire world.

were weakened and emaciated. For days many bodies washed up on the shores."

"We struggled scavenging for food along the shore for weeks until only eighty men out of six hundred were left. Those of us who survived this ordeal were soon enslaved by local Indians."

To demonstrate his point, Estebanico collected hundreds of small stones and removed eighty of them into a separate pile. He then removed four and applied soot to one of the pebbles to demonstrate to Whispering Dove his plight. He even carved a model ship out of a piece of firewood that one of the workers had carried to the mesa top. He attached a few pieces of cloth as sails.

"What was it like to be a slave?" Whispering Dove asked.

"It was a terrible experience. We were beaten and forced to work and serve our masters all day in the heat of the sun for years. And you never knew when they were gong to beat you for no reason," he explained. "There were times we wanted to die but we encouraged each other every day to be strong as we planned our escape together."

"Why did you make this terrible journey in the first place? What were you searching for?"

"Ah. Good question. We were searching for gold in the new world."

"The new world? Why do you call it that and why was gold so important for your masters?"

"Because your country and all the vast lands beyond are all new to those of us who came from Spain and Africa. And gold makes us rich. But let me finish my story, dear girl."

After hearing the rest of the story, a tear trickled down Whispering Dove's cheek. Estebanico gently reached out and stroked her long black hair before carrying on with his narrative.

"After a year on the island, four of us managed to escape, the rest simply disappeared or died of starvation." Estebanico shared how he and his three friends were taken to the mainland only to be once again enslaved by Indians.

"We lived naked for the next five years serving our Indian masters, until one day we managed to escape. We then followed the sun for the next year until we finally arrived here at your mesa village. And here we are now with you. And we are free!" he exclaimed.

A few moments later one of the women brought the four new-comers a meal of maize and beans in small clay bowls. Whispering Dove watched in fascination as the three white men bowed their heads to pray while Estebanico bowed to the ground. She listened intently to what the three white men were saying.

"Why do the others touch themselves after they pray, Esteban? What does it mean and why don't you do it? Why do you bow down?"

"Because we worship different gods. They touch themselves to make a cross that protects them and shows respect to their god. I am a Moor and my god is Allah and we do not do this," he tried to explain.

"My people bow down to worship our god; these men make a sign of the cross." Whispering Dove couldn't comprehend this con-tradiction and she avoided further questions about their religious beliefs for the time being. Yet she tried to memorize the prayers the white men uttered each day and asked one of the Spaniards to teach her the words to one of their prayers. He willingly obliged and taught her how to make the sign of the cross.

Surely these are interesting but strange people.

She watched the men eat together. They seemed to be such close friends in spite of their differences. She grabbed Estebanico's arm and held it close to examine its unusual colouration.

"What is the matter, young girl?"

"Why is your skin so different from the others?"

"Because we come from different countries. There are many people in Africa who have even darker coloured skin than mine. Your skin is closer to mine than the Spaniards don't you think?"

"Yes, but I have never seen either colour before. You are very different from my people," she said without thinking.

"Really? And what about your six toes? I haven't seen any of your people with six toes since we've been here?"

Whispering Dove blushed and turned away for a moment.

"My toes are a special gift. You shouldn't make fun of them. Many of my ancestors who had six toes on each foot were shamans and leaders of our people."

"My dear child, I am not making fun of you. I am just pointing out that we are all born differently. I was born with black skin and you were born with six toes. Yes, we are all special." Estebanico smiled. His travelling companions of the past eight years nodded in agreement as they finished eating.

"But tell me why so many of your people wear the blue stone in their nose and ears?

What does it mean?"

Whispering Dove touched both her ears and said, "This is turquoise and it celebrates a great victory over our enemies long ago." She described the assault on the mesa that took place hundreds of years ago. Estebanico glanced over the cliff edge and slowly shook his head.[31]

"I can't imagine anyone trying to scale these cliffs against weapons."

"Our elders tell us our weapons were stones and rocks. Even women and children helped to defeat our enemies from this height. Ever since that time we feel safe here."

"Yes, I can see that. We had great difficulty climbing up here. If it weren't for the ladders the young men lowered to us, we could not have made it here. But tell me, what do you do here?"

"I live with my grandfather who is an elder and I make pottery. I am still learning how to make large pieces." She brought out several pieces of pottery she had designed. One olla featured a simple parrot design that caught the attention of the Moor who had seen similar birds during his enslavement and afterwards in his travels. He was intrigued that this young woman would draw these birds on her pottery without having ever seen one.

"Do you have these birds here?"

"No, I have never seen one, but our ancestors owned them. Traders from the south once brought them here. My people have continued this design from copying older pieces of pottery from our ancestors."

After several months the four visitors decided it was time to leave the mesa; they graciously thanked the elders and bid farewell to their new friends. Whispering Dove was devastated for she found herself attracted to Estebanico and his wonderful stories about

31. The first mention of Acoma was in 1539 when Estebanico was the first non-Indian to visit Acoma and reported it to the viceroy of New Spain after the end of his expedition. Acoma was called the independent Kingdom of Hacus. He called the Acoma people *encaconados*, which meant that they had turquoise hanging from their ears and noses.

faraway lands. Her grandfather was not unaware of her fondness for this stranger but he was pleased when they finally left the mesa. Whispering Dove cried herself to sleep for several nights. She kept her clay horse and the little boat that Estebanico carved for her in a leather pouch by her bedside.

Chapter 40

Ancient Enemies

We are related to all things;
the earth and the stars. Everything.
~ Black Elk

Whether we walk among our people or alone
among the hills, happiness in life's walking depends
on how we feel about others in our hearts.
~ Anasazi Foundation

While the archaeology team was excavating the hidden storage chamber at Pueblo Pintado, Walter Etcitty and Rolly Boudreau drove in a rented Ford F-150 pick-up truck to Acoma, sixty miles west of Albuquerque and twenty miles south of the I-40. It had been years since either of them had seen the mesa and Etcitty had never been to the top. The men stopped at the Sky City Cultural Centre and the adjacent Haak'u Museum where they admired ancient artifacts and pottery dating back to the pre-Columbian era.

"This style is sure different from Navajo pottery. The Acoma people like the parrot and they put it in a lot of their designs," Etcitty observed.

"Yeah, it says here that the parrot design goes back centuries when the Anasazi traded with people from Central America because there are no parrots or macaws within hundreds of miles from here," Boudreau read from the comments inside the glass case.

Just then a voice from behind said, "Welcome to the Pueblo of Acoma! The oldest continuously inhabited community in the United States."

Turning around, Boudreau found himself face to face with a friend he hadn't seen in over twenty years. A warm embrace was followed by laughter and a long handshake.

"Man. It's been a long time. Let me introduce you to my new friend, Walter Etcitty. Walter meet Victor Lewis of Acoma Pueblo." Boudreau beamed with joy at seeing the two men together. Lewis and Etcitty shook hands and smiled warmly at each other.

"Walter, it's a pleasure to welcome a Navajo to our pueblo. Rolly told me all about you. Our people fought in the past but we have 'buried the hatchet' to use a white man's expression." All three chuckled at the twist Lewis put on the hackneyed phrase.

"Thank you for inviting me. I've always wanted to visit this sacred place, but it finally took a Canadian Indian to convince me to come here. He's quite the pilot and we flew over the mesa yesterday. It was very impressive to see Sky City from the air," Etcitty said.

"Well, why don't you finish checking out our new museum here and afterwards I'll take you guys up to see the pueblo and the church. We have a pottery-making demonstration and after that my wife has prepared lunch on the mesa. How does that sound?"

"Wonderful, Victor. We can't thank you enough for your hospitality," Boudreau said with Etcitty nodding in agreement.

"Aw, I'd do the same for a white man," Lewis quipped. More laughter and high fives followed.

The rest of the day was spent on the mesa top where Victor acted as a tour guide, reviewing the thousand-year history of the pueblo and its ancestors whom he referred to as *Ancestral Puebloans.*

"When we Acomans visit Chaco Canyon, we feel a connectedness with the place, to a primal time when our ancestors lived there. We too, are amazed that such construction took place without modern equipment by a people whom you refer to as the *Anasazi.* No offence Walter, but you know we still don't like the name your people gave to our ancestors. We don't refer to ourselves as *Anasazi.* Sounds too much like *Nazis* if you ask me. We have never considered our ancestors as *ancient enemies* which is what *Anasazi* means, but of course, over the years the term has entered all the archaeology textbooks. We just wish that someone had asked us what we wanted our ancestors to be called," Lewis explained.

"I know how you feel. In Canada we don't like the term *Indians* and we're finally getting white people to refer to us as *First Nations.* But these things take time to change and I think we have to be tolerant," Boudreau replied.

"Yeah, you're right, Rolly and things are slowly changing here too. Tour guides everywhere in the Southwest now use the term *Ancestral Pueblos* which is more politically correct. But changing the subject, Sky City is not just another tourist destination. For us Acomans, it is our ancestral home after we left Chaco Canyon. It's also part of New Mexico's heritage, and as I said before, it's America's oldest continuously inhabited community. Of course, the Hopi in Arizona and the Tewa at Taos Pueblo will argue with that, but we have more archaeological proof to support our claim. Generations of Indians have been living here for two thousand years," Lewis proudly asserted.

Looking at the vast hardscrabble landscape from the mesa top under the vast sweep of cerulean sky with soft bulbous clouds, Etcitty and Boudreau took several photos. Across the plain a

towering sandstone monolith known as Enchanted Mesa stood, surrounded by a surreal landscape of soaring buttes and piles of gigantic
boulders. Etcitty also used a small digital camera to capture this
wondrous scene.

"Can you imagine defending this place from attack? You'd need
guards posted all around the mesa night and day," Boudreau said.

"Yes, and it's happened on more than a few occasions in the
past against the Spanish, the Apache, and against the Navajos, your
own people, Walter. And yet here we are 'still holding the fort' so
to speak."

"I can see how it might be easy to defend this mesa in an attack.
But from what I've read it sounds like the Spanish conquistadors
were really a bunch of ruthless thugs," Boudreau said.

"Well, that's certainly one way of putting it. There's no question
the Spanish were cruel to all the native tribes of the Southwest and
they came close to wiping out our people with Oñate. Over there
you can see a row of houses on the mesa that still retain the scars
from the cannon fire which occurred during the infamous Acoma
Massacre of 1599." Lewis pointed to a series of ancient adobes.

"A massacre? Wow, that's like, over four hundred years ago. What
happened then?"

"Well it's a long story, but basically Oñate ordered an attack on
the mesa in retaliation for a battle that caused some of his men to
die. Somehow they managed to make it up the cliffs with a cannon
to the pueblo here. Once inside, the Spanish set fire to the pueblo
and then rooted out the warriors who were hiding in the various
rooms and kivas of the pueblo. Several warriors, realizing their fate
was sealed, jumped off the cliffs rather than surrender to Oñate's
men who went on a rampage slaughtering five hundred men and
three hundred women and children."

"Whoa! That's brutal," Boudreau exclaimed.

"Yes, very brutal. By the time it was over the Spanish had killed eight hundred people which decimated a good portion of the population of six thousand at the time. we've never recovered our numbers since then. They also imprisoned approximately 500 others. By noon the next day the pueblo finally surrendered. The Spanish lost only one of their men. The Acomans were simply no match with their flint-tipped wooden arrows against gunpowder, cannon, swords, and armour. It's a sad story that still resonates within our community. You can see how it has made us wary of outsiders. In fact, the intense privacy of our people can be traced back to our horrific ordeal at the hands of Oñate four hundred years ago," Lewis said.

"Yes, I certainly can see that. What a tragedy. But how is it that Oñate is such a hero in New Mexico?" Boudreau asked.

"Good question. The irony of this sad tale is the overblown glorification that history has reserved for Juan de Oñate. Many streets, schools, and fiestas have been named after him in New Mexico. His legacy has likewise been rewarded with numerous statues in El Paso, New Mexico, and Spain in spite of the fact that he is one of the lesser-known conquistadors."[32]

---

32. In 1998 at the four-hundred-year anniversary of Oñate's first Spanish settlement in the American west, an imposing twelve-foot statue of the conquistador riding on a horse was erected a few miles north of Española, New Mexico. This was in conjunction with numerous *Cuarto Centenario* celebrations all over the state recognizing the great man as the "founding father of New Mexico".

On a moonless night in early January, 1998 a group of anonymous "foot thieves" calling themselves the "Brothers of Acoma" according to the *Albuquerque Journal* surreptitiously "stole" the right foot of Oñate from the new statue. They claimed that, "We see no glory in celebrating Oñate's fourth centennial, and we do not want our faces rubbed in it. We took the liberty of removing Oñate's right foot on behalf of our brothers and sisters at Acoma Pueblo. We will be melting this foot down and casting small medallions to be sold to those who are historically ignorant."

"Did the Acomans ever recover from this massacre?" Boudreau asked. "Well, it was a very slow, painful recovery."

"How so Victor?"

"Following the massacre the Spanish proceeded to amputate the right foot of every man over the age of twenty-five. Oñate then forced them into slavery for twenty years. The Spanish also captured males between the ages of twelve to twenty-five and females over the age of twelve taking them away from their parents, forcing most of them into slavery for the next twenty years. Many enslaved Acomans were distributed to various government officials and missions where they lived. Most of them died forgotten. It changed things forever for Acoma."

"Unbelievable," Boudreau said.

"But over the centuries many Puebloans have adopted Catholicism as their religion.

Many of them still speak Spanish and several have Hispanic names. Yet many still continue to cling to their traditional ways and it often presents as a conflict among our people. But let me show you around some more. We still have four homes here that existed at the time of Coronado in 1541. How's that for history?"

"That's amazing, Victor. By the way, what's with all the ladders?" Boudreau asked. "You'll notice that there are no stairways inside the homes, so these ladders are the only way to reach the next level. Many pueblos in the Southwest have these kiva ladders. They also serve as a cultural symbol. The wooden ladder connects its users to their ancestors, the universe, their spiritual beliefs, and to one another," Lewis explained.

"Makes sense," Boudreau replied as he took pictures of the buildings with the ladders.

"Say, Rolly, did you know that the first non-native to visit Acoma was an African guy and not a European?"

"No kidding. How did that happen?"

Lewis related the story of Estebanico from Morocco who, with three Spaniards first visited the Acoma pueblo around 1539.[33]

"That's just crazy," Boudreau exclaimed. "Who would believe that an African came here first."

"Yes, it is perhaps a little disquieting to many Americans to realize that the original 'discovery' of the Southwest belongs to an African. And yet he was the first non-native to visit the Acoma Pueblo in its protracted thousand-year history since the time of the Anasazi migration. He and his friends basically walked across what is now the southern United States when Henry the Eighth was still ruling England." Lewis then directed his guests around the corner where two Acoma women were making pottery.

"And here we have a couple of descendants of Lucy Lewis, one of the first potters at Acoma in the modern age. With the arrival of the railroad to the Southwest in the 1880s came a renewed interest in Indian pottery. Tourists from the east were fascinated by the pottery here although there wasn't much of it at the time. Several of our women began making pottery again using the traditional method of coiling clay. They sold their products to tourists arriving by rail, and since that time pottery has become almost synonymous with Acoma.

---

33. Comparing the exploits of Estebanico and Oñate in the Southwest and the accolades that history has given them leads one to cynically respond that perhaps much of history is already in a "revisionist" state. The contrast between Oñate and Estebanico is stark, one a brutal and violent tyrant who murdered thousands, the other a gentle long-suffering African who travelled more than any non-native in the New World. One is recognized as a founding "father" of New Mexico, whereas the other barely receives a footnote in the history of the Southwest. Such are the vagaries of history.

We're making some of the finest pottery in the Southwest. Of course we see pottery as being the link that connects us to our ancestors," Lewis explained. He smiled at the women who were working over a wooden bench and said something to them in the Keresan language.

After watching the potters for an hour, the men moved on to explore the great church of San Esteban del Rey.

"So this is the church that you saw from the air yesterday. By the way, I saw you fly over and tip your wings. The church was built in 1629 and named for the patron saint of the Acomas since the 1600s when the first missionaries arrived. Actually, it took twelve years from start to finish. If you look up you'll see forty-foot ponderosa pine logs that our ancestors carried by hand from Mount Taylor, a distance of over thirty miles away. The priests would not allow the beams to touch the ground. How they managed to do that I have no idea. They must have worked in teams," Lewis said craning his neck to admire the four-hundred-year-old ceiling beams.

"Well, gentlemen, one brief look at our cemetery out front and we'll go for lunch. I'm sorry, but pictures aren't permitted here. This is sacred ground for Acomans. Anyways, I hope you're hungry," Lewis announced.

Victor's wife had prepared a traditional Acoman lunch for the visitors on a long table with a red checkered tablecloth. Red chili soup, Pueblo tacos, butternut squash and black bean enchiladas, fry bread with ground beef, beans, lettuce, tomato, and green chili sauce reminded Boudreau of the Hispanic influence on Pueblo cuisine.

"Holy cow, what a spread!" Boudreau exclaimed. "What a kind and gracious hostess we have here."

Victor's wife smiled and nodded and shook hands with the two guests. Walter removed his hat and bowed to show his respect towards Victor's wife. He then presented her with a turquoise pendant on a silver chain that he had made himself. Boudreau was moved to see his two friends act so kindly towards each other when he realized that their ancestors had been ancient enemies.

Following lunch, the three men drove back down the mesa road to the museum where they bid each other farewell. Lewis gave each of the men a small bowl with Acoman designs as a souvenir of their visit. Walter Etcitty pulled a package out of the back of the truck and gave it to Lewis.

"This is my way of saying thank you and to remember the peace between our people, Victor. It was a great day and Sky City is a wonderful place. *Yéigo ahéhee.*[34] "

"You are most welcome, Walter. Please come and visit us again," Lewis replied, opening the gift-wrapped box which contained a Navajo domed silver concho belt. "Wow! This is fantastic. Did you make this, too?" Lewis asked, knowing how expensive this belt was.

Etcitty smiled and nodded.

"You know, Rolly, the native peoples of the American Southwest called turquoise the *sky stone*. It has spiritual significance and also has sacred healing properties," Lewis said.

"Well, I have something here for you that has healing properties, too," Boudreau reached into his backpack and gave Lewis a bottle of Crown Royal in its distinctive blue bag.

"Victor, this has been a most enlightening day. Thank you very much for the tour, the lunch, and for your friendship," Boudreau said as he pointed out the "Made in Gimli, Manitoba" on the label with its distinctive gold lettering. With handshakes all around, Boudreau and Etcitty left Acoma driving down the 117 in their pick-up truck. On their way back to the I-40, Walter was beaming.

---

34. Thank you from the bottom of my heart.

"I should be thanking you for this, Rolly. I had a great day. I've always wanted to visit Sky City but the relationship between our people as you know has always been strained. It's been a good day, but I'm afraid you'll have to drive me up to Chaco Canyon to meet with the team. They're working on a new project and I should be there to help them."

"No problem. This truck should handle that Navajo road and I can see Rachel there this evening. In fact, I can even sleep in the truck if I have to." After driving a few miles he decided to breach a touchy subject.

"So how does the team treat you, Walter? Do you ever sense any racism from any of the members?" Boudreau asked.

"Nope. They treat me well and make me feel as one of their own even though I do mainly field work. I couldn't stand working for weeks on end in the confines of the university like they do, writing reports and scientific papers. I enjoy the outdoors too much. I sometimes don't feel comfortable around Dr. Brown though," Etcitty replied.

"Really? Why do you think that is?"

"Don't know. He's too quiet. Just a gut feeling. It's an Indian thing, I guess. You know what I'm talking about?"

Boudreau nodded, although he wasn't exactly sure what Etcitty meant.

Turning at Thoreau on Highway 371 north, the two men stopped at Crown Point to pick up a case of beer for the archaeologists. The late afternoon sun cast an amber sidelight over the barren landscape as the pick-up bounced and jostled over the rough washboard trail, leaving a wake of rust-coloured billows as it headed north towards the canyon. Several high wispy cirrus clouds shone pale yellow in the western sky as a lifelong friendship was sealed over the bumpy road.

Chapter 41

Caballo

*"Do you give the horse its strength or clothe its neck
with a flowing mane? Do you make it leap like a locust,
striking terror with its proud snorting? It paws fiercely,
rejoicing in its strength, and charges into the fray. It laughs
at fear, afraid of nothing; it does not shy away from the sword."*
~ Job 39:19-26

A few years later on a warm summer afternoon, Whispering Dove
was seated near a fire as she watched her ollas and clay jars being
heated. Later she would sand them off and add a glaze after they
had cooled. A ghostly veil of cirrus clouds spread across the western
skies as a curtain. Whispering Dove looked and saw in the distance
a strange shimmering of the air. She had witnessed desert mirages in
the past on very hot days but this day was barely warm. She held her
hands above her eyes to shield her vision from the brightness of the
overhead sun. After several minutes of focusing, something caught
her eye; from the western plains a star flashed; a few seconds later
another flash followed with numerous bright sparkles. Whispering
Dove became mesmerized by the blinking and flickering in the distance. Soon a dense cloud of dust arose between the mesas. Through
the dim obscurity within the dust cloud, the continuous barrage

of flashes grew brighter, alerting her to the possibility that enemies could be approaching.

Frightened, she called her grandfather and several neighbours to see this unusual desert spectacle.

"What do you think those lights are, Grandfather? And look at those dust clouds. I think they're growing larger by the moment."

Her grandfather just stared. "I don't know, my child. I have never seen anything like this before. Maybe your friend the black man has returned with more of his friends. We need to warn the rest of the families on the mesa so they can draw up our ladders and prepare to defend themselves."

"Do you think they will hurt us?"

"I don't know, but we must be ready in case they mean harm. It frightens me to see how many there are." her grandfather said, ruefully shaking his head.[35]

After the dust clouds settled, Whispering Dove could see a strange procession of fair-skinned men in shiny armour astride fearsome beasts bearing down on the mesa. It didn't take long for the mesa inhabitants to prepare a defence; men pulled up the many ladders that led to the desert floor, and women and boys piled rocks near the cliff edge. Several warriors armed themselves with bows and arrows.

As the army approached their village citadel, Whispering Dove saw that it was the bright desert sun reflecting from the hundreds of metal helmets which created the sparkling lights she had seen earlier.

---

35. This massive army contained around 250 armed horsemen, 70 foot soldiers and some 1300 Indian allies gathered from central Mexico. Herds of livestock with 1000 horses, 500 pack animals and large herds of sheep, oxen and cattle raised much of the dust. This was the enormous expeditionary force known as the Coronado Expedition of 1540 to 1542, the largest undertaking of its kind anywhere in the New World.

Soldiers were mounted on great beasts that she knew must be what her friend Estebanico had called *caballos*. They were much larger than she had imagined from his stories and there were so many of them. Behind the horses were other strange animals that no one had ever seen. They made all sorts of strange noises and sent a foul odour that she could sense even from the mesa top. Soon the huge contingent gathered around the base of the mesa, completely encircling it. She was overwhelmed by the noise and the smells and the sheer magnitude of people. Yet she was fascinated by the revelation of this extraordinary world that had first been described to her by the black slave two years ago. In her excitement she began laughing and crying at the same time.

Several of the men on horses looked up and cheered, some waving white flags while others brandished red-and-yellow striped flags. Several men waved banners with red crosses while men on foot wearing dark clothing held spears with crosses on the top.

Hundreds of native people unloaded bundles of supplies from the oxen and pack animals. Whispering Dove recalled Estebanico's description of the cross that his friends made before meals, and she tried to remember the prayer that they had taught her.

What does all this mean? What are they doing here?

Several of the elders and some of the young men descended to meet these strangers and the peculiar but fearsome creatures that carried them. Attempts to communicate were met with failure in spite of using sign language and drawing pictures in the sand. After many attempts the visitors became angry and belligerent.

Green Feather called his granddaughter. "You need to come down to the base to talk to these men as you are the only one who might be able to understand them. They seem to be looking for something but we don't know what they want. Don't worry, I will go with you."

Never before had the elders consulted with women on the mesa and Whispering Dove was anxious. She obediently followed him down the steep pathway, trying to remember some of the words that her Moorish friend had taught her. As she descended, she clutched a leather pouch holding cornmeal and her small clay horse.

After slowly climbing down the various ladders, she arrived on the desert floor and was immediately overcome by the stench of the horses and cattle. She had no idea that the horses would be so huge or that they made such frightening blowing sounds. The bleating of sheep, the lowing of cattle, and the cacophony of shouting men were all strange sounds to her. Never had she witnessed such a large gathering of people and animals. Dust swirled everywhere and she caught herself sneezing.

A scowling priest in robes holding a cross brusquely approached her. She smiled and clumsily made a sign of the cross that she had learned from the three other visitors who had come with Estebanico two years ago. The priest stopped dead in his tracks. He stared open-mouthed and then broke into a smile. He spoke to her in his own language but Whispering Dove had no idea what he was saying. She was able to answer only with a few random phrases that she had learned from the visitors.

"Padre nuestro que estás en los cielos, Santificado sea tu — tu — Nombre.[36]*"*

She hesitated, hoping the priest wouldn't take offence at her halting Spanish. His face lit up at once and he warmly embraced her. Calling one of his men, he pointed to the mounted soldiers wearing a suit of metal that glinted in the late afternoon sun. Bearded and surrounded by an entourage of mounted guards holding the red-and-yellow flags, the soldier carried himself with a regal bearing. Wearing

---

36. "Our Father who art in heaven, Hallowed be thy name."

a shiny metal helmet with a large red feather at the back which projected vertically, he appeared to be the leader of this great horde.

This must be one of their elders. I wish I knew more of their words.

After several minutes three men on foot approached the soldier on the horse and told him something as they pointed towards Whispering Dove. She suddenly felt very uncomfortable in the presence of so many strange men and animals. Looking downwards and blushing she clutched her clay horse as the dignified-looking soldier whirled his horse around, dismounted, and walked over to her. Pointing to her hands he asked what she was clutching. Uncertain of what he said she showed him the little clay horse that she had fired and painted, a few years ago.

"Caballo," she whispered softly. She held it in her outstretched hand for this impressive man who at this time was surrounded by several armoured subordinates.

"Ah! Si, es un pequeño caballo de cerámica!"[37] He held the figurine in the air for the others to see. Several of the men gasped at this unexpected sight and cheered.

After a few more awkward words of exchange the bearded Spaniard introduced himself to Whispering Dove, *"Me nombre es Francisco Vázquez de Coronado. Ahora donde podemos encontrar oro?"*[38]

She knew what *oro* meant and shook her head saying, *"Oro? no tenemos oro aquí."*[39]

---

37. "it's a small ceramic horse."

38. "My name is Francisco Vazquez de Coronado. Where can we find gold?"

39. "We have no gold here."

Looking up to the mesa top, Coronado saw the numerous piles of stones and boulders along the cliff edge. Numerous villagers peered above the rock piles. Frowning he uttered, "*Es imposible!*"[40]

Whispering Dove realized that these men could not climb the cliff walls to her village with their heavy armour and horses and she knew that her people were safe. Coronado extended his hand towards Whispering Dove and returned the small clay horse to her open hand. "*No hay oro?*"

"*Gracias. No hay oro,*" she softly repeated, smiling at the imposing man. She knew that they were searching for gold because Estebanico told her that his men had also been searching for gold. Whispering Dove was intrigued by the Spanish obsession with gold.

Why was it so important if you can't eat it or drink it? It is too soft a metal to be used for weapons. They are indeed strange people to have travelled so far for this gold.

Twenty minutes later the same priest walked over and gave Whispering Dove a small wooden cross attached to a metallic chain and placed it around her neck, making the sign of the cross over her.

The priest then pronounced a blessing over her in Spanish.

Whispering Dove pointed to one of the horses and asked a nearby soldier if she could sit on it. Without hesitation, the tall armoured conquistador lifted her in the air, placing her in the well-worn leather saddle. He then bowed before her ceremoniously with a flourish of his gauntlet-covered hand and smiled. Many of the other men laughed aloud and also bowed like chivalrous knights before Whispering Dove atop the steed. It didn't matter that her feet didn't

---

40. History records that Coronado was the first European to encounter Acoma since Estebanico, a native Moroccan who was never given any official recognition for his accomplishments. Yet there was uncertainty as to whether Coronado actually even made it to the mesa.

reach the stirrups. Beaming, she held her clay horse in the air and yelled "*Caballo!*" She was immediately answered with the enthusiastic cheers from a hundred armoured men while the horse beneath her nickered with joy. She would remember this moment for the rest of her life.

Whispering Dove spent the rest of the afternoon examining the other horses and animals in the company of one of the priests and her grandfather. She quietly wondered what kind of lives her people would lead if they were to own horses. She knew that they could travel far which would make hunting much easier. She could envision that what previously would have taken weeks to hunt food for their families would now take only days with the horse. She smiled and gently stroked one of the large beasts whose dark intelligent eyes mesmerized her with its almond-shaped pupils. She spoke quietly to the large chestnut gelding in her own language as if it could understand her. She giggled when it gently nuzzled her neck with its soft velvety nose. Reaching into her pouch she removed a handful of cornmeal and held it out to the towering creature and said, "How much you could change our lives. We would treat you so well."

The horse ate from her hand and then sighed for more.

After several days of feeding their animals and drinking from the small stream that flowed south of the mesa, the great expedition moved on. Mounted soldiers led in the front, foot soldiers behind, and then the Indians and priests followed with their great herds of animals. Remaining behind were numerous piles of bones from the animals used in feeding the horde, mixed with corn cobs and other debris. The Spaniards without permission had helped themselves to the Indians' fields of maize and beans, but gave them the hides of the animals they slaughtered as well as a few sheep as payment. The elders stood in awe at the devastation to their crops in such a short period of time. Those crops that had not been taken as food were trampled by the horses and cattle.

"These people have taken much of our food and broken the rest. We are fortunate to have kept much of it in storage on the mesa top, but I am afraid they have not left us very much down here. I hope they don't return or we will starve this winter," Green Feather said to his granddaughter.

Ignoring her grandfather, Whispering Dove stood spellbound as she watched the great expedition engulfed by huge clouds of russet-coloured dust slowly wind its way around the mesa to the east in its relentless search for gold.[41]

---

41. When the natives asked Hernán Cortés as to why the Spaniards had such a passion for gold, the conquistador answered, "Because I and my companions suffer from a disease of the heart which can only be cured with gold." Coronado's men eventually made it to the middle of Kansas before they gave up searching for gold and turned back.

Chapter 42

Purification Ceremony

Hataałii Hózhóni

In beauty I walk
With beauty before me I walk
With beauty behind me I walk
With beauty above me I walk
With beauty around me I walk
It has become beauty again
~Navajo prayer from the Blessing Way ceremony

After a week's work at Pueblo Pintado the team returned to the university to bring back several of the ancient relics and pottery discovered at the work site. Hundreds of on-site photographs and measurements of the remains of the four Anasazi skeletons were taken and documented. A Navajo elder had been called, – a *Hataałii Hózhóni*, the medicine man or chanter to conduct an elaborate purification and cleansing ceremony which lasted two hours. The private ceremony involved chanting, prayer, and smudging.

Removing corn pollen from a medicine bag, the healer touched his tongue, his head, and gestured to each of the four directions. Keeping his distance from the entombed remains, Walter Etcitty turned to Rachel and explained the significance of the ceremony to her.

"What he's doing is intended to dissipate negative past experiences and influence a positive beginning. You never know if spirits continue to linger in the room even after eight hundred years. These people likely suffered before they died so their spirits need to be released. Do you see how the elders will lift the smudge bowl to each of the four directions in turn? They use sage, cedar, sweet-grass, and tobacco as the Four Sacred Herbs. Each one is significant for purification to make this place beautiful again or as we say *hozho naasha'*. The balance and harmony of this place must be restored." Etcitty quietly explained.

Rachel found this ceremony fascinating and asked Walter if it was done for other reasons.

"It's done for military personnel returning from battle who suffer from PTSD. It can last as long as a week and everyone is invited to participate but it's much more complex than this. We call it *the Enemy Way Ceremony*."

"What's he saying now?" Rachel asked.

"He's reciting a prayer which translated means, 'In beauty I will rest my heart. In beauty all will be in balance. In beauty all will be restored.'"

Walter had carried a Navajo medicine bag with him to the ceremony. Pinching some corn pollen from the bag, he touched his tongue, his head, and gestured to the east, south, west, and north just as the healer had done, then tucked the bag into the inner pocket of his jacket.

All members of the team were invited to watch the ceremony and were advised to remain silent and not to take photographs. Local native stonemasons repaired the opening which had been made by the archaeologists. They used the same sandstone blocks which had been numbered and placed on a nearby tarp when the door opening was made the previous week. The masons covered the cracks with a mortar made from the same coloured clay, filling in much of the wall to remove any evidence that might tempt pot hunters to break into the storage chamber.

As elated as he was, Jack Nesbitt was confused with their discovery of the burial chamber at Pueblo Pintado. Following the healing ceremony, he addressed the team with his concerns.

"There's something missing here that doesn't make sense. This chamber held no turquoise beads, parrot feathers, or seashells. Often you will find cardium shells or fragments of abalone shells imported from California. There are also no ceremonial baskets or carved sticks, all things you might expect in a well-protected funerary chamber with this many people. It's almost as if these people were buried here at the last moment with very little preparation. The pottery could have been already stored there prior to their internment. After all, it is a typical storage room built in a masonry style with fully coursed and chinked walls. No, there's a story that we're missing here," Nesbitt explained. No one had anything to suggest that might shed light on the four Anasazi skeletons or the reason they were buried in this room.

Following the solemn ceremony, they returned to Albuquerque to write up their reports. After taking one more flight over the canyon with Rachel, Boudreau returned the Cessna to the Albuquerque airport where he had rented it several times during his stay in Albuquerque with his wife. After a thorough inspection, he found a cellphone under the front passenger seat. He took it to the desk and was told that no one had claimed a missing cellphone. He decided to keep it in case it belonged to one of the team members that had flown with him over the past two weeks. The battery was dead, so he put it in his jacket pocket for the time being.

It was time for Boudreau to head back to Canada where he had work to do for his private airplane charter company. He had enjoyed the beauty and history of New Mexico immensely and looked forward to seeing more of the state in the next few months before Rachel's contract came to an end. In the meantime she remained to complete her work with the team at the Office of Contract Archaeology in the Maxwell Museum.

Rachel booked their favourite restaurant for a farewell dinner for the next day before Boudreau was to fly back home and she invited the rest of the team. She knew Rolly had come to appreciate them and enjoyed their company. She received a text message later that afternoon from Isabella.

"Rachel, I'm so sorry to have to bow out from dinner this evening. I've been feeling terrible for the past two days with a cough and fever. I hope I don't have bronchitis or something. I have an appointment to see my doctor tomorrow. Tell Rolly I'm sorry I won't be there to say goodbye. Please give him my warm regards and tell him I look forward to seeing him soon."

Rachel was disappointed. That evening Stan Brown also failed to show up at the El Patio restaurant.

"Does anyone know where Dr. Brown is?" Rachel asked. Both Nesbitt and Etcitty shrugged.

"I haven't been able to get hold of Stan since he lost his cellphone," Nesbitt replied. "I hope Isabella is okay. She sounded pretty sick when I spoke to her earlier today. She must have a bad cold. I hope it's nothing more serious," he added.

"I wonder if this could be his cellphone. I found it under the seat of the Cessna when I returned it today. Maybe Rachel can give it to him when she sees him next, since I'm leaving tomorrow morning," Boudreau said.

"He's been looking for it all week. I'll bet he lost it in the plane at the same time he lost his lunch when you did that barrel roll in the canyon," Nesbitt grinned.

"Yeah, maybe that wasn't such a great idea. I don't think he's ever forgiven me for it," Boudreau said:

Rachel recalled Stan Brown's opposition to seeking the Navajo elders to bless the site when they closed it up and his negative reactions towards the healing ceremony. She said nothing.

"Perhaps you could pay him a visit tomorrow at his office at the university and give his phone back to him, Rachel. That'll sure take a burden off my mind. As you know, this last site has presented a ton of paper work, cataloguing relics, collating photographs, making reports, et cetera. As head of our team I suspect this has been stressful for Stan also."

"No problem, Jack. I'll see him right after Rolly leaves," Rachel replied.

After leaving the restaurant Rachel and Rolly returned to their apartment. Rolly told his wife about the interesting day he had experienced at the Acoma mesa with Walter Etcitty. He also mentioned Etcitty's intuitive feelings regarding Stan Brown.

"He said he didn't feel comfortable around him, whatever that means. He said it was nothing specific, just an 'Indian thing.' Anyways, why don't you charge his phone and see if you can get into it sweetheart?"

"Oh, Rolly, Shame on you! Don't you know that's an invasion of privacy? Besides, I wouldn't have a clue how to do that. You're so bad," Rachel teased, shaking her head.

Boudreau smiled and embraced his wife. They ended the evening by retiring earlier than usual.

Chapter 43

Oñate, the Last Conquistador

A city that is set on a hill cannot be hid.
~ Matthew 5:14

Whispering Dove was an old woman of almost eighty, having lived her entire life on the mesa. She had married not long after meeting Coronado, the great conquistador. Her hair was long and grey and she wore a rust-coloured manta held together by a woven sash over her stooped shoulders. Years of exposure to the sun and dry desert winds had turned her once beautiful soft face into a fissured leathery texture, resembling a piece of clay pottery that had been broken and glued back together several times. Her great-grandchildren often asked her about her extraordinary encounter with so many people and animals visiting the mesa.

"Show us your clay horse, Grandma. Please?" they asked.

And so Whispering Dove would share her memories about the famous Spanish expedition that travelled through their country so long ago.

"The great Coronado did not come up to the mesa, but instead he sent one of his men to see how we lived. They wanted to learn our ways but mostly to see if we had any gold."

"What did he look for when he came up here?" one of the children asked.

"They were interested in examining our clothes, our deer hides, our woven cotton, and our food. They tasted our bread and ate pine nuts and maize while they were here. They were very interested in our jewellery, especially the turquoise."

"Will they ever come back Grandma? Will they be friendly?"

"I don't know. We were very afraid of them at the time, but they didn't hurt us. My grandfather told us not to trust them. He had bad feelings about them and warned us about them. Before he died he had many bad dreams that they would come back and hurt us," she said hesitatingly. She did not wish to frighten the children, but her grandfather's premonitions were strong and she often had similar dreams herself about the white soldiers.

"Yet that was so long ago and we have been safe here since then."

"But, Grandma, where did they come from?" one of the boys asked.

"They came from far away across a great water. They called their home *Reino de España*. But many live to the south now in our lands and they are still looking for gold."

"What's gold?" her great-granddaughter asked. "What was it like to sit on a horse, Grandma?"

Whispering Dove described the joy of sitting on one of the conquistador's horses when the expedition passed through her people's land. Very few Spanish had visited since then, but her people knew about these animals since the Spanish never travelled without them.

A few months later the days were getting shorter and cooler. Whispering Dove again had one of her dreams about the Spanish.

Is this what Grandfather dreamt about?

The next day at noon, several of the children were yelling and pointing to the southwest where a great cloud of dust was sweeping upward from the plains. It looked familiar to Whispering Dove as she recalled the Coronado expedition sixty years ago. Soon she could see the familiar procession of mounted soldiers wearing shiny armour and helmets that glinted in the sun. She smiled to see so many horses once again. With mixed feelings about this visitation, she gathered her grandchildren to the safety of a thick-walled home in the pueblo.

Zutacapan was the leader of the Acoma people at this time; he descended with several warriors to greet the soldiers. He knew that resistance to these men would be futile for he believed the Spanish to be immortal. The Spanish leader refused to get off his horse to meet Zutacapan.

"My name is Juan de Oñate. I am the governor of New Mexico and I demand your immediate surrender and obeisance to the King of Spain," he announced.

To demonstrate his power, he ordered one of his men to fire a cannon they had brought from Mexico city. The sound of the explosion dropped Zutacapan and his men to their knees while holding their ears. They had never experienced the harsh retort from a Spanish cannon. Several of the younger men trembled at the sound of the explosion.

"We need food for my men. You have maize and beans that you must give us or we will aim our cannon at your men," he warned.

After much scurrying to the nearby fields, the Spanish pack animals were loaded with sacks of maize, beans, and squash.

Zutacapan realized that the sooner he gave them what they wanted, the sooner they would leave. The next day the entourage left much to the relief of Zutacapan and the Acomans. Watching the encounter from the mesa top, Whispering Dove was fearful that there would be violence. She had no idea that the white men were able to create thunder. She was relieved to see the long train of horses and men trailing off toward the east. She questioned her premonitions and those of her grandfather, for there was no bloodshed and no one was harmed.

Perhaps another time.

Chapter 44

Dr. Stan Brown

There is nothing as eloquent as a rattlesnake's tail.
~ Navajo Proverb

Stan Brown had been feeling unwell for several days. He stayed in bed shivering with severe chills one minute followed by profuse sweats the next. He was so weak he could barely get up to go to the washroom. His muscles ached all over with back pain and neck pain; he had a terrible headache and felt like throwing up. He slowly dragged himself out of bed and drove to a nearby walk-in clinic around eight o'clock in the morning shortly after it opened. The light hurt his eyes and he began to cough.

"I think I have the flu, doc. I feel like I've been hit by a truck," he managed to say between coughing bouts.

"The flu? In the summer time? Have you been around anybody else with these symptoms?"

"Can't recall." Brown shook his head slowly.

Dr. Bradley Carlson was intrigued with Brown's symptoms, knowing it likely wasn't influenza with no other cases around. He had recently read an article citing the extended range of Valley Fever into New Mexico and that it had been under-diagnosed in the state. A dust-borne fungal infection, common in the San Joaquin Valley of California and parts of Arizona, the disease had been moving northward in recent years, affecting large population centres, such as Albuquerque and Santa Fe as heat and drought made soils more welcoming to the fungus. Carlson asked a series of questions about where Brown had been and what kind of work he was doing, since many of his symptoms were consistent with Valley Fever.

"I'm an archaeologist and I've been working in the desert up at Chaco Canyon the past few weeks. No one else is sick to my knowledge," Brown moaned.

After listening to his chest, Dr. Carlson became concerned and gave Brown a complete physical examination. He sat down beside him applying an oximeter to his index finger. The pulse oximeter readings enabled him to determine the amount of oxygenation in his patient's blood. Dr. Carlson explained that a normal reading was between 95 to 100 per cent and that a reading less than that indicated hypoxia or low oxygenation. Moderate to severe hypoxia was represented by a reading of 80 to 90 per cent. Stan Brown's reading was 81 per cent. and his cough was productive of rusty-brown sputum.

Carlson now became more concerned that his patient might have another type of pneumonia. Although Carlson had considered the possibility of Valley Fever earlier, the telltale fine crackles on both sides he heard in Stan Brown's lungs were more consistent with fluid build-up in the lungs. Valley Fever seldom presented these severe symptoms.

Something else is going on here.

"So, Stan, whatever infection you have is preventing your lungs from exchanging carbon dioxide for oxygen. There is very little air moving into the base of your lungs which explains your shortness of breath and your cough. Your oxygen level is low and so is your blood pressure. You have a fever and I think you almost certainly have a pneumonia of some kind. We should get you to the Presbyterian Hospital as soon as possible. By the way, how did you get to our clinic this morning?"

"I drove here myself, doc, but I don't think I can make it to the ER alone," Brown whispered.

"Of course not. I'm calling an ambulance to take you there and I'll let them know you're coming."

Later that morning, after a short time in the ER Brown was seen by a respirologist. His temperature was 39.4 °C, his heart rate was 118 beats per minute, his blood pressure was 107/74 mm Hg, and his respiratory rate was 30 breaths per minute. His chest Xray revealed diffuse interstitial and alveolar infiltrates in both lungs, and his white blood cell count was up to 15,000. He was admitted to the intensive care unit with a diagnosis of acute, unexplained respiratory distress syndrome, likely pneumonia. He was started on intravenous vancomycin, ceftriaxone, doxycycline, and methylprednisolone with oxygen at six litres per minute delivered by nasal cannula. Blood gases confirmed a mild hypoxia. His physician, a thirty-five year old Navajo internist named Sarah Chee introduced herself to him.

"Dr. Brown, I'll be your physician as long as you're in the intensive care unit. You have a pneumonia which is quite severe and we're trying to figure out what's causing it. Dr. Carlson notified us regarding your condition and he's concerned that you may have contracted Valley Fever since I gather you have been working in the desert for some time. However, we think your illness is too sudden and severe to explain that diagnosis. we've also checked your sputum for the presence of coccidioides organisms and they're just not there and your test for coronavirus is also negative. Nasopharyngeal swabs for influenza A and B as well as respiratory syncytial virus are likewise negative. We're giving you three different antibiotics intravenously while we wait for cultures in the event that it is bacterial. However, we think your symptoms could be consistent with hantavirus pulmonary syndrome or HPS. Are you certain that no one else on your team is sick?"

"Can't think of anyone else. I lost my cell phone over a week ago so I haven't been keeping in touch with most of them, but you can call Jack Nesbitt, one of my associates and ask him. He's one of the researchers on our team. I'll give you his number. He'll know."

"Certainly, I'll do that, but I want to interview all members of your team and get titres on each of them for hantavirus also."

Stan Brown nodded, exhaling through his pursed lips.

Dr. Chee ordered specific lab tests for hantavirus, serology using immunohistochemistry. The CDC used an enzyme-linked immunodeficient assay (ELISA) to detect IgM antibodies in order to diagnose acute infections with hantaviruses. Due to the virus being prevalent in New Mexico the test was also available at the New Mexico Scientific Laboratory. Dr. Chee figured she would have a definitive answer within twenty-four hours. In any event, there was no treatment for HPS other than supportive measures, which her patient was currently receiving in the ICU.

The next morning Brown's blood gases deteriorated revealing severe hypoxia.

Computed tomography (CT) of the chest revealed ground-glass opacities in both lungs and interlobular septal thickening. Small bilateral pleural effusions were also present. Chee decided to intubate him because of these poor results and because his breathing was becoming too laboured. He was subsequently sedated, paralyzed, and hooked up to a ventilator. Shortly afterwards his oxygenation improved slightly as he lay unconscious in the ICU.

Jack Nesbitt showed up with Rachel after he received a phone call from Dr. Chee and the two stood by Brown's side, astonished to find him in such a critical state. Rachel immediately thought of Isabella and called her from the bedside. Reaching into her pocket she pulled out Stan Brown's cellphone by mistake. She had charged it last night but was unable to open the phone as it had fingerprint recognition access. Pondering what to do next, she asked Nesbitt if he wouldn't mind getting her a coffee from a vending machine they had passed earlier down the hall. Nesbitt mumbled that he could use a coffee, too, and sauntered off leaving Rachel alone by the bedside with the unconscious Stan Brown.

She then took the phone to Brown's bedside and placed his right index finger on the face to see if it would unlock. Fortunately the oximeter was attached to his left index finger. She knew from her own hospital experience that she would trigger alarms if she took it off. After a few attempts at pressing his finger into the phone it lit up, showing the screen and the app icons. Tapping the screen to keep it from collapsing, she opened his email and read his contacts. Every member of the team was included in recent contacts. Then Rachel noticed that over a week earlier several calls were made to a "T. Jackson".

Boy, that name is familiar. Where have I heard that before?

Soon Nesbitt arrived with two Styrofoam cups of coffee. "Did you get hold of Isabella yet?"

"Um, I'll try again."

Caught off guard, Rachel phoned Isabella using Stan Brown's phone. After a few rings a weak voice answered.

"Yes, Stan, what is it? You found your phone at last. Listen I'm sorry I can't make it to work today as I feel just awful. I guess —"

"Isabella. It's Rachel. Where are you and how are you feeling? Stan's in the ICU at Presbyterian Hospital. He's very sick and I'm worried about you."

"That's strange. I'm just downstairs from you. I'm in the ER at the Presbyterian and I feel terrible. I'm waiting to see a Dr. Chee from the ICU. Why are you using Stan's phone and where is he now?"

Chapter 45

Return of the Conquistadors

*For the thing which I greatly feared is come upon me,
and that which I was afraid of is come unto me.*
~ Job 3:25

Like her grandfather before her, Whispering Dove suffered from recurrent dreams of impending doom regarding her people on the mesa. It didn't comfort her to know that many of the elders held to an ancient prophecy that predicted that an army from the south would arrive and conquer all the lands thereabouts. While some scoffed, Whispering Dove knew that the prophecy was true. Yet Oñate and his men had come and gone and no one had been injured, although several of the warriors who met the Spaniard were afraid of him. While she was coiling pottery a day later, the leader of her people, Zutacapan, walked by her adobe. She decided to warn him about her dreams.

"If they return you must not provoke these people nor allow them to provoke you. My grandfather had visions of these people coming to harm us when I was still a young woman. Now I have dreams that do not bode well for our people. If you wish to be a great leader, you must listen to the visions of the elders," she exhorted.

"I am listening, Grandmother. I do not have your insights. Tell me what it is that you are seeing in these dreams," Zutacapan asked attentively.

"I cannot say for certain, but the dreams tell of great violence to our people. We must not allow them to climb the mesa to our village. I am not the only one who feels this way." Whispering Dove wiped the wet clay from her hands on an old cotton cloth.

"Thank you for telling me this, Grandmother. They have not returned yet, but if they do we will be careful with them. I believe they are immortal for their weapons are sharp and their horses are fierce."

"Please promise me you will not provoke them."

"I promise you, Grandmother," Zutacapan said solemnly.

Six weeks later Juan de Zaldívar, Oñate's nephew, reached Acoma with thirty men and traded peacefully with them. They placed an order for ground corn for their troops but had to wait several days for the Acomans to prepare it. Whispering Dove and all the other women worked frantically to grind the large amounts demanded by Zaldívar for his men. She was concerned as she knew the Acomans themselves needed their own food to survive the coming winter.

A few days later, Zaldívar rode back with sixteen armoured men to Acoma to find out why it was taking so long to get their corn. Zutacapan met them and directed them to the homes where the corn was being held. Whispering Dove was shocked to see these foreign Spanish soldiers in their village on the mesa top.

This should never happen. Why are they here?

Whispering Dove watched Zaldívar's people divide into groups to collect the corn. Suddenly she heard screaming coming from one of the adobes. Several women rushed out with two soldiers running after them. A child who got in the way was struck by one of the Spaniards and fell unconscious. Soon several Acoma warriors stepped in to protect the women and children. The Spaniards were totally unprepared for a struggle from these docile people and in the melee twelve of them were killed including Zaldívar himself who fell off the cliff to the rocks below. Whispering Dove was horrified and feared there would be severe retribution.

"What have you done?" she screamed at Zutacapan and his men.

"We can't just let them abuse our wives and daughters. They came for the maize but they wanted more than that. They wanted our women, too," Zutacapan answered.

"But I warned you about them. They should never have been allowed to go into those homes alone. And you have killed their leader as well. Where are the others?"

"I'm afraid five of them escaped," Zutacapan said sheepishly.

"They will find the others and return. This is not good. They will bring war and destruction. I have seen it," Whispering Dove pronounced solemnly.

"Then we will just have to defend ourselves. Yes, we will need to prepare for war if Oñate returns with the rest of his men. I will ask if men from the other villages will help us," Zutacapan said, shaking his head.

Whispering Dove buried her wrinkled face in her cupped hands and wept.

Chapter 46

Cytokine Storm

Humankind has not woven the web of life. We are but one thread within it. Whatever we do to the web, we do to ourselves. All things are bound together. All things connect.
~ Chief Seattle, Duwamish

Rachel and Jack Nesbitt stood by Isabella's bedside as she lay coughing on a hospital gurney in the emergency ward. She wore an oxygen mask and was hooked up to an EKG. They had just left the ICU where Stan Brown was now listed in critical condition, intubated, sedated, and breathing 100 per cent oxygen. Rachel held Isabella's hand and sat down beside her. She had grown to love this young woman over the past month and admired her intelligence and kindness. She was worried sick over what was happening to her two colleagues after their exciting and interesting three weeks in the field. She was relieved to see that everyone in the ER still wore masks for fear of coronavirus.

"Omigosh, Jack, what's happening here? You're a doctor. How did they both get so sick so fast? Do you think they could have coronavirus?"

"Beats me. Hopefully the doctor can explain this to us because between you and me I'm worried that we might be next. After all, we've been working together every day for weeks. Whatever it is they have could be contagious," Nesbitt speculated.

Rachel shuddered and thought of her own illness a year earlier when she almost died of smallpox. The nurses in the ER, the beeps and alarms from the various monitors, and the background sounds of sirens and doctors barking orders brought back memories of her own frightful experience in the ER. Just then a nurse asked them to leave the department while Dr. Chee examined Isabella. They decided to grab a quick lunch in the cafeteria.

"I'm supposed to take Rolly to the airport this afternoon as he's flying home to Winnipeg for a few days, but right now I don't want him to leave," Rachel said.

"Call him now, Rachel. Tell him to postpone his trip. He should stay here with you and besides, he might also be susceptible to whatever this bug is. Which reminds me, I should call Walter and let him know about Stan and Isabella," Nesbitt replied.

For the next ten minutes both archaeologists were on their phones. Etcitty told Nesbitt he was fine and at home in Window Rock. Boudreau was just packing to leave and he agreed to cancel his flight to Winnipeg.

"Rachel, of course I'll stay here in Albuquerque with you. Boy, this story is eerie and kind of reminiscent of what we went through a year ago. Do you think they may have picked up some kind of bacteria from the dig?"

"Gosh, Rolly, I don't know, but it does sound suspicious now that you mention it. Jack and I are hoping to speak to Dr. Chee, who is taking care of both Stan and Isabella. I mean what are the chances of that?"

"Unreal. Make sure and tell him where you've been working and what kind of work you've been doing. It might help him in making a diagnosis," Boudreau advised.

"I certainly will. The doctor is a woman by the way. Her name is Sarah Chee and she works in the ICU. I'll let you know what she says after we meet her. Could you meet me here at the hospital, Rolly? I'm really scared."

"Of course, sweetheart. Hang in there. I'll just call the airlines to cancel my trip, unpack, and be there in an hour," Boudreau reassured.

Dr. Chee found both the archaeologists in the cafeteria and sat down beside them.

Following an introduction she questioned the scientists about their work, how they were feeling, and whether they had any medical problems that might put either of them at risk. Chee referred frequently to her tablet during the conversation.

"What do you think it is, doctor? Could it be coronavirus?" Rachel asked.

"No, it's definitely not coronavirus, but we're concerned that they might have contracted hantavirus even though we haven't got the tests back yet. If so, you may have also been exposed. I want to do blood tests and chest X-rays on both of you if you don't mind, even though you're feeling well," Chee advised.

"Of course, but hantavirus? Interesting. May I ask what makes you come to that conclusion doctor?" Nesbitt questioned.

"Well, for starters, you were all working in an area that has been highly endemic to hantavirus. The first outbreak recognized in America was back in 1993 near the Four Corners area not far from Chaco Canyon. Your worksite is located only ninety miles from the Four Corners so that raises our suspicions. Secondly, the presenting symptoms of both your colleagues are consistent with hantavirus. Of course, as I said we won't know for sure until their serological tests come back. In the meantime, I would suggest you keep in touch with me on a daily basis and let me know if you have any symptoms at all. I suggest you all stay in Albuquerque for a while," Chee advised.

"Like what kind of symptoms, doctor?"

"Fever, chills, headaches, muscle aches, vomiting, diarrhea or abdominal pain in the early stages."

"And the late stages?" Rachel asked.

"A cough that produces secretions, shortness of breath, and fluid accumulating within the lungs. Having a low blood pressure is usually an ominous sign in hantavirus pulmonary syndrome or HPS," Chee explained.

"I've read about hantavirus before. It's spread from mouse droppings, isn't it?" Nesbitt asked.

"Indeed. Hantavirus is carried by rodents, particularly deer mice. The virus is found in their urine and feces, but it doesn't make them sick. It's believed that humans can get sick with this virus if they inhale contaminated dust from mice nests or droppings.

Approximately thirty percent of the deer mice tested in the Four Corners area have shown evidence of infection with hantavirus. So you see, they are carriers of the disease.

The only reason we don't see more of it in that area is because of the low population density. But every year there are half a dozen cases in New Mexico that show up."

"Jeepers, Rachel. That storage chamber at Pueblo Pintado was full of mouse droppings. And Jack said there were desiccated mice skeletons all over the place," Nesbitt exclaimed.

"But those mice have been in there for centuries. How long can the virus stay viable in the dryness of that room?" Rachel asked Dr. Chee.

"Not for more than a few days according to the studies. But if there were infected mice there in the past, there could still be live, infected ones running around now. They could be transmitting the virus within their colony from one generation to the next. And those old ruins are a great habitat for deer mice. It's best to err on the side of caution and treat all wild rodent waste areas as if they are infectious. You see, hantaviruses are what they call enzootic viruses, which means they maintain persistent infections in their rodent hosts without having any apparent disease symptoms. So yes, the virus could have been carried and transmitted to generations of mice for centuries in the area where you were working," Chee explained.

"So I need to know exactly who went into that room and who stayed out?"

"I never went in. It was just Isabella and Stan come to think of it. Did you, Rachel?" Nesbitt asked.

"I did stick my head in for a minute or two just to look around, but I never actually went in. I tend to be a little claustrophobic," Rachel replied.

"How long ago was this project?"

"We started about ten days ago and just closed it a few days ago," Nesbitt answered. "That would be about right, although it often can take longer for symptoms to develop.

In fact, it can take as long as four weeks after exposure for patients to get sick. So that's why I want you to stay in touch with me and stick around. Please don't leave town, okay?"

"Of course, but this is kind of scary don't you think?" Rachel asked.

"Yes, it is. I don't mean to frighten you, but neither of you are sick right now and neither of you entered that room. There was probably an aerosol of mouse droppings and urine in there, but your exposure may have been limited, unlike your friends who actually went inside that room. Anyways, we just have to wait and see. Fortunately it's not contagious from human to human," Chee advised.

"So, you really think this is hantavirus, Dr. Chee?"

"Well, as we say in medicine, 'If it walks like a duck —'"

"So how does it make people sick?"

"Once a virus infiltrates a host it attaches itself onto a cell and burrows its way into the cytoplasm where it takes over the molecular machinery to replicate itself, creating more viruses to infect others. Basically, a virus is a parasite that can kill with elegant simplicity. In a way it would act similar to coronavirus," Chee explained.

Rachel recalled how her own physicians had explained to her how smallpox replicated within the human host when she was ill with that virus a year earlier. Dr. Chee went on to describe Stan's current condition.

"Frankly, he has me worried as his lungs are very inflamed with this illness. We think he has what's called a cytokine storm syndrome. We're throwing everything we have at him including high-dose steroids and antibiotics but he's not responding. He also has excellent ICU nurses with lots of experience dealing with COVID-19 patients. But we are concerned as it's getting more difficult to ventilate him and his carbon dioxide levels keep increasing. It's like fighting a forest fire with a garden hose."

At this point Jack Nesbitt spoke up, "Dr. Chee, as a physician myself, I'm intrigued from a medical point of view about the mechanism of the cytokine storm that causes this pulmonary failure. You see I haven't been in medical practice for some time and never had to deal with this problem. Perhaps you could explain it to me,"

"Well, it's basically a form of pulmonary edema in which the protein-rich fluid builds up in the airways of HPS patients. We believe a capillary-leak syndrome is responsible for pulmonary edema in this disease. We see similar capillary-leak syndromes in other viral infections, particularly dengue hemorrhagic fever. Studies suggest that the development of plasma leakage in these conditions relates to activation of T lymphocytes and monocytes, with systemic production of vasoactive cytokines, including tumour necrosis factor alpha, interleukin -2, and interferon gamma."

"I don't have a clue what the two of you are talking about. Can you both speak English, please?" Rachel said.

Just then Dr. Chee's phone buzzed. Checking it she said, "I have to go to the ICU now. It looks like your friend Stanley Brown is not doing well. Code blue. Sorry, I gotta go."

Dr. Chee ran through the cafeteria, grasping her stethoscope, her white lab coat fluttering behind her as she left, her heels clicking across the cafeteria floor. Both Nesbitt and Rachel looked at each other with incredulous looks.

"Did you understand all that stuff, Jack?"

"Not really. Not my area of medicine. It's all Navajo to me. I'm almost sorry I asked. Stan is obviously in good hands but all I can say is it doesn't sound good. But Dr. Chee certainly knows her stuff."

"What's a code blue?" Rachel asked

"It's a medical emergency. Boy, this brings back memories from my days as a physician. I'm glad I'm not working in a hospital anymore. Maybe we should head up to ICU to see what's happening," Nesbitt said.

"You go there Jack. I'm going back to Emergency to see how Isabella is doing. She doesn't look well."

Sarah Chee was astounded at how quickly her patient had deteriorated in the ICU in just the past few hours. Even with one hundred percent oxygen flowing, Stan Brown's colour had taken on a dusky appearance. His skin had become cool, clammy, and mottled. His eyes were half open with a vacuous stare. Serosanguinous fluid was bubbling up through his endotracheal tube which the nurses were frenetically suctioning. Each time they removed the oxygen to insert the suction tube, a gurgling sound burbled from his chest and a crimson froth filled the tube. Both nurses perspired under their full body protection with face shields that were fogging up as they alternated suctioning Brown's lungs.

"What have you given him since I left?" Chee asked as she quickly read the chart. "After we gave him the dexamethasone you ordered he went into ventricular fibrillation so we shocked him and gave him some intravenous Lidocaine. He's in pulmonary edema so we just gave him a bolus of Lasix before you got here. He reverted to ventricular tachycardia a few minutes ago. I'm afraid there's not a lot of air moving in his lungs, Dr. Chee," one of the nurses said ruefully.

"We haven't had time to chart the meds yet. Everything happened so fast," said the other nurse.

"What's his blood pressure doing?" Chee asked.

"Seventy systolic. We thought his intra-arterial line was blocked so we flushed it twice," the nurse answered.

Sara Chee just nodded as she scanned the monitors. She fidgeted with the turquoise beads on her stethoscope, wondering what to do next.

The EKG monitor showed a tachycardia of 160 beats per minute and Brown's heart was throwing several PVC's. Sarah Chee ordered a bolus of Amiodarone and more Lasix, but she realized there was little else she could do. Stan Brown was drowning in his own pulmonary fluids as his body was covered with strings of tubes and wires connected to the various monitors and intravenous solutions. Several minutes later Brown's ventricular fibrillation returned and in spite of several attempts at cardio-version he expired.

An hour later Boudreau arrived at the hospital and met Rachel in the ICU waiting room.

"What! You can't be serious, Rachel. He was fine just a few days ago and now he's dead?" Boudreau exclaimed. Rachel had been crying.

"Dr. Chee said she's certain that Stan had hantavirus because of the rapid onset of his illness. I just googled it on Stan's phone and it says 'HPS is characterized by a brief prodromal illness followed by rapidly progressive, non-cardiogenic pulmonary edema' whatever that means. I'm so afraid for Isabella as she seems to have the same illness.

Rolly, we have to pray for her."

They both bowed their heads in the privacy of the small waiting area and said a short prayer for Isabella. Rachel felt stunned and once again was overwhelmed with fear at the recollection of her own stint in the ICU a year ago. She wanted to call Jack Nesbitt who was somewhere in the hospital. Once again, she inadvertently pulled Stan Brown's cellphone from her pocket.

"Rolly I have a confession to make. I did what you said and unlocked Stan's cell phone."

"Wow! Smart girl. How did you do that? I mean he must have had password protection, right?"

"No, he had a fingerprint scanner on his smartphone. I used his fingerprint to unlock it. I thought I should contact his family but he doesn't have a lot of contacts outside the university so I checked his emails to find out who we should notify."

"Okay, but why would he let you do that?"

"He didn't. He was unconscious in the ICU. I saw his email contacts, Rolly. He was in touch with someone named T. Jackson. That name sounds familiar but I can't recall where I've heard it before. I've met so many new people down here since we arrived in New Mexico. Anyways, I forwarded several of his emails to myself as I didn't think I should go back to the ICU to open his phone again."

"Hmm. I don't know what to say. I suggest you call Dr. Nesbitt for advice on this one, luv."

"I just left a message for him. He's with Isabella now and we need to go there. She's been transferred to a regular hospital room with isolation. I don't think she knows about Stan yet. What do we tell her if she asks about him? Omigosh, Rolly, this is terrible. I'm worried sick," Rachel replied, holding back tears.

Chapter 47

Acoma Massacre

They shall lay hold on bow and spear; they are cruel, and have no mercy; their voice roareth like the sea; and they ride upon horses, set in array as men for war against thee,
~ Jeremiah 6:23

Whispering Dove watched it all. She climbed two flights of ladders to a third story adobe room where she lived. She had several ollas of water and a small fire pit where she cooked corn meal and beans. She slept on the clay floor on a deerskin over a mat of woven grasses.

Once Oñate learned of Juan de Zaldívar's death he was furious. It took six weeks for him to obtain permission from the friars to put down this insurrection and prepare his men for revenge. He ordered Juan's brother, Vicente de Zaldívar, to lead an expedition to punish the Acoma and set an example for other Pueblo people. Zaldívar willingly complied in order to avenge the murder of his brother. He finally arrived at the mesa with seventy armed soldiers and several pack animals carrying food, ropes, weapons, and a small cannon.

"By crushing these rebellious Indians we will send out a warning to other pueblos in the event others decided to revolt," he told his subaltern. Oñate had instructed Vicente de Zaldívar that this was

278

not merely a localized conflict against the Acoma Pueblo but a battle for all of New Mexico. Meanwhile Zutacapan and the Acomans enlisted support from several other tribes to defend against the enraged conquistador and waited for them.

Whispering Dove saw the invaders arrive at the base of the mesa. Several soldiers tried to climb the steep treacherous hand-and-toe trail but they were met with a barrage of rocks, stones, and arrows from the rocky stronghold above. From her higher vantage point she could hear the clanging of the stones against the metal armour. Men were shouting and swearing as they ran for cover. That night the invaders had to sit and wait in the valley below while listening to drums and insults from the defenders. Zaldívar fumed.

The citadel seemed impregnable. The only way up was by a single, treacherous hand-and-toe trail.

"We need to distract them or we will never conquer these people," Zaldívar said to his subaltern.

"What we need to do is send a larger force to one side of the mesa while we attack from another side. Tomorrow evening I will take sixty men to the north side as if we are prepared to attack. That will keep their attention. Then you will take ten of the younger men and climb the heights of the south side during the night. Using ropes you will hoist up the cannon and once established you will begin the attack on them from the rear.

When we hear the cannon from the top of the mesa then we will know that it is time to advance. Do you understand, lieutenant?"

"*Si gobernador.* From the rear." The subaltern made a sign of the cross as he considered this formidable undertaking.

The next day Whispering Dove watched Zutacapan take his warriors to the north side of the mesa. In the evening the Spanish feigned their attack while the subaltern scaled the heights on the south side with his small squad of men with ropes. Using stealth, they successfully climbed to the top hauling their cannon up with ropes. Once they set it up in the dark they began blasting the walls from point-blank range. This enabled them to breach the walls and drive the defending Acomans back. For the next two days a fierce battle involving hand-to-hand combat ensued. The cannon proved too powerful for the Acomans. After just a few blasts, a large fire engulfed many Acoma homes. The conquistadors then stormed the settlement and wreaked havoc on its inhabitants.

Whispering Dove watched in horror as the Spaniards carved their way through hundreds of villagers with sword and pike, slicing and piercing men, women, and children, young and old, and without mercy; such was the fury with which Zaldivar sought revenge for his brother's death. These were people she had known all of their lives; most of the Acomans were related to each other. She had watched many of them grow up from infancy and now they lay dying or dead in the streets. She watched in horror as several of her people ran to the edge of the mesa, leaping to their deaths rather than be captured by the Spanish.

After a while the roar of the cannon, the screams of women, the shouting of men, and the crying of children became intolerable. Whispering Dove covered her ears with her hands. She knew that sooner or later the Spanish would come up to her room looking for anyone they could capture. She crawled into a depression on the ground by the corner of her room, pulled a deerskin over herself, and wept. Her own children and grandchildren and great-grandchildren were on the mesa facing this slaughter and she shuddered to think what was happening to them. Clearly, the Acoma warriors were no match against crossbows, halberds, and artillery.

The screaming, the shouting, and the cannon fire continued into the night. After several hours Whispering Dove heard soldiers climbing the ladder to her room. She lay perfectly still under the deerskin and recited the prayer in Spanish that she had learned years ago.

Padre nuestro, que estas en cielo, santificado sea tu nombre —

The voices grew louder. Her heart pounded in her frail chest and she began to perspire under the deerskin. One of the soldiers peered into the room and saw only the flattened deerskin on the floor beside some pottery. Banging his sword against the door frame he yelled, "*Nadie aqui!*" and they moved on to the next house.

Whispering Dove breathed a sigh of relief. Afraid to move, she stayed in her room under the deerskin all night.

The next morning the devastation was frightening. The pueblo lay in ruins; dozens of homes were destroyed by the fires. Dead bodies lay everywhere. Whispering Dove descended the ladder to the sounds of moans and weeping. Two small children ran to her and clung to her as they buried themselves in her arms and wept.

She recognized them as the children of her young neighbours who were nowhere to be seen. The children were at least four or five years old and had managed to escape the sword of the Spaniards by hiding. At age eighty, Whispering Dove's frail body could barely carry one child at a time. She could not leave them alone so she walked hand in hand with them across the mesa in search of water. She ran into one of the elders who told her that the Spanish had killed many of the women and children.[42] He had not seen the children's parents. Whispering Dove continued searching.

More bodies lay strewn in the streets. Hundreds more of her people were being led to the base of the mesa in shackles for the trip to the San Juan pueblo where Oñate held his headquarters. Two soldiers saw her with the children but did nothing, more out of fatigue than compassion. Most of them had not slept during the two-day battle and they were too tired to pursue the carnage any further.

Whispering Dove found a broken bowl which she was still able to use to scoop up water from one of the great cisterns for the children. Later she returned to her home and made them a bean soup which they heartily ate. They both fell asleep in her arms.

How will I ever take care of these little ones? Please help me, God.

She crossed herself as the Spanish explorers had taught her to do so many years ago.

Exhausted, she slept soundly with the eerie quietness of the village and the two little ones at her side. Only the dark echoes of her mind resonated following this horrible day. A few fires still burned on the far side of the mesa. The next day the era of reconstruction of the Acoma mesa began. At last Whispering Dove found the children's parents safe and sound. Having been separated from their children in the battle they had managed to climb down to the bottom of the mesa during the battle with several other Acomans who hid behind rocks. She was greatly relieved to see the family reunited for she knew

---

42. An estimated five hundred men were killed in the battle, along with about three hundred women and children. Some five hundred prisoners were taken. Following a trial at San Juan Pueblo, Oñate sentenced every male above the age of twenty-five to have his right foot amputated and to be enslaved for a period of twenty years. Twenty-four men suffered this brutal fate. Males between the age of twelve and twenty-five were also enslaved for twenty years along with all of the females over the age of twelve.

she could not take care of the little ones. A week later Whispering Dove was found in her room, having slipped away during the night in her sleep. The Acoma massacre was too much, even for her great heart. She was buried in a shallow grave on the mesa with her little clay horse and the cross that she carried with her for the past forty-eight years.

Chapter 48

Ghost Sickness

Keep thy heart with all diligence;
for out of it are the issues of life.
~ Proverbs 4:23

The rainbow is a sign from
Him who is in all things.
~ Hopi

After several days of languishing in the Presbyterian Hospital in Albuquerque, Isabella began to make a slow recovery. She felt weak and continued to cough. Her eyes were still red from the hantavirus infection, but she was able to get up and walk around for short periods of time and began eating again. Her room overlooked the greenery of Highland Park across Oak Street, a refreshing view compared to what she was used to seeing in the dryness of the western desert around Chaco Canyon. She slowly tidied her hospital room and straightened several vases of flowers from various well-wishers and read the cards again. She was especially touched by one from Rachel and Rolly which had a Bible verse written as encouragement. It said,

For I know the plans I have for you, declares the LORD,
plans to prosper you and not to harm you, plans to give
you hope and a future.
~ Jeremiah 29:11

Isabella had plenty of time to think about her new Canadian friends and appreciated them now more than ever. They both visited her daily over the next few days. Rachel brought a box of Magnum dark chocolate bars in a freezer bag every day and they sat around reminiscing about the events of the preceding weeks as they ate them. After several visits like this, Rachel decided to share with Isabella the story of her own narrow escape with death the year before when she was smitten with smallpox. She had never told any of the team regarding this traumatic episode in her life. Isabella was fascinated with her friend's story and felt encouraged, knowing that Rachel could identify with her own suffering. For Rachel it was therapeutic as well by divulging a secret that had weighed heavily upon her to someone she could trust.

"I had to laugh when you warned me that I might lose my mani-cured nails when we first met, knowing that I had almost died with smallpox. It left me with some pretty bad scars which are nearly invisible now thanks to laser therapy. Fingernails were the least of my concerns coming down here," Rachel laughed.

"Why didn't you tell me this before Rachel?"

"Um, well you know, it was pretty traumatic for me at the time and I'm still processing it now. I also lost a good friend and colleague and I felt responsible for his death. Rolly got sick too but ironi-cally smallpox brought us together. Illness has a way of doing that," she said.

"Yeah, I guess so." Isabella reached out to hold Rachel's hand.

"By the way. I've been doing more research on my converso ancestors. Guess what, Rachel?"

"I don't know. What?"

"I am descended from Juan de Oñate, the Spanish conquistador."

"Really? He was a converso?"

"Well, he was a descendant of them. Apparently in the 1300s his ancestors were the Ha-Levi family, a Jewish family that converted. But back then so many Jews who converted intermarried through the generations to such an extent that you would be hard pressed to find a Spanish or Portuguese noble family without Sephardic ancestry. I just read that up to a quarter of all Latin American people according to DNA studies have converso roots."[43]

"That's amazing, Isabella. But wasn't Oñate responsible for the Acoma massacre?"

"Yes, he was. So I'm not sure whether to be proud or ashamed of this news of my ancestry. I'd like to think descending from a converso family, Oñate was a good person but he was eventually banished from New Mexico by the King of Spain once his atrocities against the Acomans came to light."

"This is so interesting Isabella. I really want to learn more about this, but I promised I would meet Rolly at the El Patio for dinner."

Ignoring hospital rules, the women hugged each other farewell and Rachel left to meet her husband.

---

43. Oñate's mother, Doña Catalina Salazar y de la Cadena had among her ancestors Christians of Jewish origin who served in the royal court of Spanish monarchs from the late 1300s to the mid-1500s. Although she was of Spanish ancestry, she descended from conversos. Many conversos were persecuted well before the Spanish Inquisition through pogroms in the late fourteenth century.

The next day Rachel and Rolly brought Walter Etcitty with them. As a precaution everyone had to wear masks, gowns, and gloves when entering Isabella's room. In spite of this regulation, they all untied the bottom of their masks in order to eat the Magnum bars.

"How are you feeling these days Walter?" Isabella asked.

"I'm fine. Never felt better. I'm sorry about you and Dr. Brown. Back in 1993 there was an outbreak of this same virus that affected several of my people. Twelve people died back then and twice as many were sick. But our leaders have reported similar outbreaks in the past that occurred in 1918 and 1934. Dineh tribal stories tell of mice as sources of bad luck and illness going back over a hundred years ago. We used to call it *Sin Nombre* virus but the name was changed to hantavirus after they learned more about it. But the first people to die of it were Navajo," Etcitty explained.

"Dr. Chee said the only reason they don't see more of this disease is because of the low population density in the Four Corners area. But what if there were thirty or forty thousand people living in that area as there were in the twelfth century? I mean, just because it was first recognized in 1993 doesn't mean it didn't exist before," Rachel said.

"Good point. So if it doesn't kill mice but just people, then the Anasazi could have had an epidemic on their hands. There must have been lots of mice back then for that to happen," Isabella speculated.

"Walter's point regarding the virus being recognized by Navajo people long before the medical community knew about it makes you wonder if it was the cause of the Anasazi migration from Chaco Canyon in the twelfth century. Dr. Chee referred to this species of hantavirus as a 'New World virus' and so it could have been around long before Columbus's time, don't you think?" Rachel asked.

"But how do the mice spread the virus?" Isabella asked.

Pulling out her cell phone Rachel read from the notes she had made during her discussion with Dr. Chee. "She said that hanta-viruses are most likely aerosol-transmitted, and infection occurs when closed, non-aerated, unused buildings such as barns and cabins to which rodents have had access are reopened and cleaned. Stores of corn, beans, squash, and drinking water would readily become infected by the saliva from the mice and from aerosolized particles from urine and feces. The desert wood rat, *Neotoma lepida*, has also tested positive to the disease, and routinely builds its nests in dwellings."

"Boy, you're getting to be an expert on this infection, Rachel. But that does make a lot of sense. Stan and I likely caught the virus from mice droppings in the Pueblo Pintado burial chamber that was sealed for eight centuries. There were still lots of mice running around the place, which means they probably got in there through small cracks and burrows," Isabella mused.

"Hey, I just thought of something. We could write this up as part of our study, don't you think?" Rachel asked.

"Absolutely!" interrupted Jack Nesbitt who at that moment strode into the room wearing a mask, gown, and his Tilley hat. The latex gloves were too small for him so he just carried them in his hands. As a physician, Nesbitt wasn't worried that he could contract hantavirus in a hospital setting; he considered the reverse isolation measures as totally unnecessary.

"Yes ladies, I overheard your discussion as I was getting gowned and I agree. And you are just the one to do it, Rachel. I also want Isabella to help you as a co-author when she's feeling better. It will give you something to do while you're recovering. It shouldn't be too stressful. After Stan's untimely death the university has appointed me as team leader so I get to boss both of you around now. How does *'Hantavirus as an explanation for the Anasazi migration from*

Chaco Canyon and its Outliers in the Twelfth Century' sound as a working title?"

"It sounds great as long as Isabella feels up to it," Rachel replied.

"I think that would be a fascinating paper, Jack. Congratulations on your new appointment by the way. Why don't you sit down and celebrate with a Magnum bar? Rachel has a freezer bag full," Isabella said.

"Why thank you, Isabella, I will. But I have some more bad news for you regarding Stan. I hate to tell you this. Rachel told me about the emails on his cell phone. She wisely saved many of them by forwarding them to herself. Special Agent Pierce recognized that Stan knew Mr. Jackson. It appears from Stan's bank account and from several of his emails that he had hired Jackson to scare you away from the worksite near the rincon. It was Jackson who was your sniper. The FBI eventually found his body downstream in a pile of debris from the flash flood. His prints matched those on both the rifle and the motorhome," Nesbitt explained.

"Of course! T. Jackson was the shooter that Agent Pierce talked about. The guy that owned the beat-up motorhome. How stupid of me," Rachel exclaimed immediately seeing the connection.

"Oh dear, why on earth would Stan do that? Why would he sabotage his own research project and put us in danger? It was such a great site and we got some wonderful Anasazi pottery from that dig. That just doesn't make sense, Jack," Isabella said bewildered.

"Well, it does if you know how much money he was getting for some of those pots.

That's right, around thirty grand apiece. We found several pots, ladles, and jars in a private storage locker at the university. All of them black-on-white Anasazi circa 1200 CE. It seems Dr. Brown had been secretly collecting them for some time."

"How on earth would they know about that?" Boudreau asked.

"It seems the FBI were able to unlock his phone without using his fingerprint. They have apparently invented a hacking device that can break into most phones. Anyway, they discovered he was selling pottery to some very wealthy pot hunters from out east on the sly."

"That's unbelievable. You mean we were working with a pot thief all along?"

"I believe Stan Brown was a top-notch archaeologist. He loved his work and he was a good guy to work with. But at some point, he crossed the line by surreptitiously selling his discoveries and not reporting them to the university. It probably started with one small piece to a wealthy collector. Fortunately, he kept a record of his buyers and what he sold to each of them. The FBI are already onto a few of them and they will eventually repatriate most of the stolen relics to museums. Of course, the Maxwell Museum is checking its inventory for anything missing which could take months. All I can say is he sure fooled me," Nesbitt said, biting his lip as if to keep it from quivering.

"But, Jack, if Stan had survived his illness he would be doing jail time. They take the Antiquities Act very seriously down here. Boy, it almost makes you wonder if there really is some kind of curse on pot thieves. Both Stan and this Jackson guy died terrible deaths after stealing pots. You can certainly see why the Navajo believe in this curse on looters," Isabella said ruefully.

Walter Etcitty nodded in approval and whispered, "It's called the *ghost sickness*. We call it *chindi* in Navajo because the spirits were stuck in that burial room. That's why you needed that purification ceremony. To restore the balance," he stated matter-of-factly.[44]

Rachel was reminded of her discussion with the Bandelier Park guide who told her about the tragic endings that many looters suffered and the superstitions surrounding them. She found Walter's Navajo natural spiritual beliefs intriguing — a connection to the cosmos that took the problem of evil seriously.

No one spoke for several minutes as the group pondered Walter's sombre pronouncement. Isabella finally broke the awkward silence.

"By the way, my doctor told me I will likely be discharged in the next day or so. She says I'll be in recovery at home for a few weeks though."

"That's wonderful, Isabella. I'll stay with you until you get back on your feet. I'm sure Rolly won't mind as he needs to head back north soon. We can start the preliminary article on the hantavirus and the Chaco Canyon Anasazi together while you're still recovering," Rachel said.

After another fifteen minutes of lively discussion the group dispersed. It had been raining outside during their visit but just as they left the hospital the sun came out.

Isabella watched her colleagues dodging puddles on the street below from her hospital window. She was thankful for their friendship.

---

44. With Navajo religious belief, *chindi* is the ghost left behind after a person dies, believed to leave the body with the last breath of the deceased. It is everything that was bad about the person left behind.

Traditional Navajo believe that contact with a *chindi* can cause illness which they call the ghost sickness and death. Since the *chindi* are believed to linger around the deceased's bones or possessions, they are often destroyed after death and contact with bodies is avoided.

Passing cumulus clouds expanded slowly into great pink billows like candy floss. Shortly a magnificent rainbow appeared, splitting the sky, its arc forming a bridge between earth and heaven. It immediately gave Isabella joy and she knew in her heart that she would recover from this illness. Nevertheless, she felt a little nervous regarding Walter's comments about the supernatural and the *ghost sickness* and its relation to the grisly deaths of Stan and the shooter. Reaching into the drawer of her night table she found a Gideon Bible. Opening the Bible randomly, her eyes fell on a few verses from Psalm 91:

Surely he will save you from the fowler's snare and from the deadly pestilence.

You will not fear the terror of night, nor the arrow that flies by day, nor the pestilence that stalks in the darkness, nor the plague that destroys at midday.

This immediately gave her comfort, and after reading the rest of the chapter she fell asleep, the Bible open on her lap.

Meanwhile, Rachel and Rolly returned to their hotel after picking up stir-fry from a local restaurant. Boudreau opened a bottle of California Cabernet Sauvignon and they enjoyed dinner together while discussing their future and deciding when Boudreau should head back to Winnipeg. He had several contracts waiting for him and had already transferred three of them over to other pilots.

"What a week it's been. I'm so thankful that Isabella has made such a remarkable recovery. Rolly, did you know that Dr. Chee told me that hantavirus has a thirty percent mortality rate? That's just crazy," Rachel exclaimed.

"Yep, that's almost as bad as smallpox. You are two tough women to survive these diseases. I'm beginning to think that field archaeology is a dangerous occupation. Do you want to watch the local news and see if there's any mention of Stan's death?

"You know, I think I'm going to turn in early. I hope you don't mind but I feel really tired, Rolly."

Boudreau kissed his wife goodnight, put away the dishes, and watched the news in the next room before going to bed himself.

The next morning Rachel awoke feeling terrible. She threw up several times and felt dizzy and light-headed. She lay down in the bed looking rather pale. Boudreau called the hospital immediately and drove her to the Presbyterian Hospital ER where she was met by Dr. Chee who ordered a battery of tests. After two hours the internist came back to the ER and sat down beside Rachel with her tablet in hand, reviewing her lab results. By this time Rachel was feeling better but she remained slightly pale from throwing up.

Boudreau had a pained look on his face expecting the worst.

"Well, Rachel, I have a diagnosis for you and it's not Valley Fever. Nor is it hantavirus.

And you certainly don't have coronavirus."

"Then what's wrong with me, Dr. Chee?"

"Rachel, you're pregnant!"

Acknowledgements for
Desert Enigma: Plague in Chaco Canyon

Arnold, David L., "Pueblo Pottery: 2000 years of Artistry." *National Geographic* 162, No. 5. Washington D.C: National Geographic Society, November 1982.

Boerger, Paul, *The Ghosts in the Stones: An Anasazi Saga.* College Station, Texas VBW Publishing, 2010.

Cadieux, Charles L., *The New Mexico Guide.* Golden, Colorado: Fulcrum Publishing, 1992.

Canby, Thomas Y., "The Anasazi: Riddles in the Ruins" *National Geographic* 162, No.5 Washington D.C. : National Geographic Society, November, 1982.

Childs, Craig, *Finders Keepers: A Tale of Archaeological Plunder and Obsession.* New York, New York: Little, Brown and Company, 2010.

Childs, Craig, *House of Rain: Tracking a Vanished Civilization Across the American Southwest.* New York, New York: Little, Brown and Company, 2006.

Chee, Chester, *Code Talker: The First and only Memoir of the original Navajo Code Talkers of WWII*. New York, New York: Penguin Books, 2011.

Creamer, Winifred and Jonathan Haas, "Pueblo: Search for the Ancient Ones" *National Geographic* 180, No. 4. Washington D.C.: National Geographic Society, October, 1991.

Davis, Carolyn O'Bagy, *Hopi Summer*. Tucson Arizona: Rio Nuevo Publishers, 2007.

Diamond, Jared, *Collapse: How Societies Choose to Fail or Succeed*. New York, New York: Penguin Books, 2005.

Fishbein, Seymour L. *Grand Canyon Country — Its Majesty and Its Love*. Washington D.C.: National Geographic Society, 1991.

Gear, Kathleen O'Neal and W. Michael Gear, *People of the Silence*. Tom Doherty Associates, Inc.: New York, New York, 1996.

Hayes, Allan and John Blom, *Southwestern Pottery Anasazi to Zuni*. Flagstaff, Arizona: Northland Publishing Company, 1996.

Hillerman, Anne, *Tony Hillerman's Landscapes*. New York, New York: Harper Collins Publishers, 2009.

Hillerman, Tony, *The Hunt for the Lost American*, New York, New York: Harper Collins Publishers, 2001.

Hillerman, Tony *Dance Hall of the Dead.* New York, New York: Harper and Row Publishers,1970.

Hillerman, Tony, *Listening Woman.* New York, New York: Harper and Row Publishers, 1970.

Hillerman, Tony, *The Blessing Way.* New York, New York: Harper and Row Publishers, 1970.

Hillerman, Tony, *The Best of the West: Anthology of Classic Writings from the American West.* New York, New York: Harper and Row Publishers, 1991.

Hindley, Geoffrey, *A Brief History of The Crusades.* London, England: Constable and Robinson Ltd. London, 2003.

Jacka, Jerry, *Pottery Treasures: The Splendor of Southwest Indian Art.* Portland, Oregon: Graphic Arts Center Publishing Co., 2000

Lekson, Stephen H, *A Study of Southwest Archaeology.* Salt Lake City: The University of Utah Press, 2018.

Lekson, Stephen H. *The Archaeology of Chaco Canyon: An Eleventh Century Pueblo Regional Center.* Santa Fe, New Mexico: School for Advanced Research Press, 2006.

Lister, Robert H. and Florence C. Lister, *Those Who Came Before.* Tucson, Arizona: The University of Arizona Press, 1983.

Lister, Florence C. *Trowelling through Time: The First Century of Mesa Verdan Archaeology.* Albuquerque, The University of New Mexico Press, 2004.

López de Gómara, Francisco, *Historia de la Conquista de Mexico, vol I, ed.* Mexico City: D. Joaqon Pamirez Cabanes, 1933.

Noble, David Grant, *In Search of Chaco: New Approaches to an Archaeological Enigma.* Santa Fe, New Mexico: School of American Research Press, 2004.

Oldstone, Michael B.A., *Viruses, Plagues, and History,* New York, New York: Oxford University Press, Inc.,1998

Paul, Sherry, *Ancient Skyscrapers: The Native American Pueblos,.* New York, New York: Contemporary Perspectives, Inc. 1978

Preston, Douglas, *Cities of Gold.* New York, New York: Touchstone Books, Simon and Schuster, 1992.

Radetsky, Peter, *The Invisible Invaders: Viruses and the Scientists Who Pursue Them.* Toronto, Ontario: Little, Brown, and Company, 1994.

Roberts, David, *In Search of the Old Ones: Exploring the Anasazi World of the Southwest.* New York, New York: Simon & Schuster, 1996.

Roberts, David. The Old Ones of the Southwest *National Geographic* 189, No.4. Washington, D.C.: National Geographic Society April, 1996.

Roberts, David, *The Pueblo Revolt: The Secret Rebellion that drove the Spaniards out of the Southwest.* New York, New York: Simon and Schuster Paperbacks, 2004.

Rohn, Arthur H. And William Ferguson, *Puebloan Ruins of the Southwest.* Albuquerque, New Mexico: University of New Mexico Press, 2006.

Rose, Joshua, *Turquoise, The Sky Stone, Native American Art: The Turquoise Issue,* Scottsdale, Arizona, 2020.

Sagstetter, William and Beth. *The Cliff Dwellings Speak: Exploring the Ancient Ruins of the Greater American Southwest.* Santa Fe, New Mexico: Benchmark Publishing of Regional Center, School of American Research Press, 2011.

Sherman, Irwin, *The Power of Plagues.* ASM Press, Washington, D.C.: ASM Press, 2006.

Stuart, David E, *The Ancient Southwest: Chaco Canyon, Bandelier, and Mesa Verde.* Albuquerque, New Mexico: University of New Mexico Press, 2009.

Tuska, Jon, *The American West: The greatest Tales from the Masters of Fiction*, Portland, Oregon: Bristol Park Books, 1982

Vivian, R. Gwinn and Bruce Helpert, *The Chaco Handbook, An Encyclopedic Guide.* Salt Lake City: The University of Utah Press, 2012.

Wilson, James C, *Hiking New Mexico's Chaco Canyon, The Trails, the Ruins, the History.* Santa Fe, New Mexico: Sunstone Press, 2019.